Final Surrender

Final Surrender

Surrender Series

Book 2

By

Deanna Jewel

Published by
Swallowtail Productions, LLC
Lewiston ID 83501

Copyright © 2018 Deanna Jewel

Cover by Fiona Jayde Media
Edited by Donna Clifford

ISBN: 978-0-692-08856-2
Printed in the United States of America

Dedications

This book is dedicated to each one of my readers who have waited for the release of *Final Surrender*, the continuation of Kate and Brandon's story. Thank you for your patience. Without each of you reading my work, there would be no reason to continue telling stories. I appreciate you!

I'd like to thank my editor, *Donna Clifford*, and my proof-reader, *Tami Goodell*, for the time they put into this work to help me make it a better book. Your ideas and eye for detail were of more help than I can express. I'm blessed that you love to read! My beta readers have also helped. Your eyes have been invaluable to me. Thank you to my team of *Tami and Tammy*!

1.

Kate covered her face with the comforter and moaned as she turned away from the morning sun shining in the window. Her temples throbbed with yet another headache. The surrounding warmth of the blankets begged her to stay while the fresh scent of sagebrush drifted in on the warm breeze, tugging at her senses. She loved the smell of sagebrush and took in a deep breath as she stretched beneath the covers.

A nearby radio softly played country music.

Cuddling deeper into the soft down of the comforter, pillow feathers poked her cheek as she moved. The pain in her head persisted and she fluffed the pillow. Kate raked her fingers through her hair to try and release the pressure that felt like a steel band wrapped around her head. A bump with a crusty cut on her head made Kate wince when she touched it, instantly awakening her.

How and when did I hit my head?

Memories swirled through her mind and realization struck hard.

Wait a minute!

Snapping her eyes open, Kate sat up and glanced around. A clock-radio sat on the dresser playing the country music she had heard earlier. A white feather comforter covered the bed. What had happened to the lean-to and buffalo hides?

And what of Taima?

Damnit, her mind was a blur.

The massive lodge pole bed was an exact replica of the one she'd admired at The Grizzly Moon Gallery. A lodgepole chair, bedside table, and five-drawer dresser matched the bed. Deep blue curtains matched the plush carpeting. The walls were constructed of huge pine logs and the room was large enough for two beds. Where the hell was she now? Kate wondered at the home beyond her door and how she came to be here.

Swinging her legs over the edge of

the bed, Kate noticed the over-sized green denim shirt she wore. The sleeves nearly covered her hands, the tails would surely reach her knees. She didn't remember putting it on, so someone else must have dressed her.

Kate sniffed the air. A familiar scent of men's cologne hung in the room. Where was she and how did she get here? She couldn't remember a thing. Taima had last taken her to see the ancient petroglyphs and now she sat in a beautiful home.

Her breath lodged in her throat as memories flooded her mind.

She must have somehow returned to the future, but…how? Thinking sharpened the pain in her head. Then she glanced at her hand, turning it over, checking her nails.

No blood…yet she knew Taima's blood had completely covered her hand, as he lay dying when she'd cut her tethered ring from around his neck and gave it to his son, Kelee. She'd been unable to help Taima at all and now her heart ached again with the pain of her losing the man she'd come to love so much.

This couldn't be happening.

Closing her eyes, she massaged her temples. *She couldn't handle much more confusion.*

An animal growled behind her and she nearly bolted off the bed. When she turned toward the door, she came face to face with a wolf. Distant boot steps sounded beyond the door of her room and the wolf disappeared down the hall. A man's deep, velvety voice filled the quiet air and recognition gave way to hope that Taima would appear in the doorway. Her heart pounded as too many explanations mingled in her mind. *How could Taima be here in the present?*

Taima conversed with someone in the hall.

Kate was certain.

Holding onto the log bed frame at the foot of the bed, she padded toward the door and turned into the hall. She gasped as she bumped into a broad, unfamiliar, naked chest. His musky, yet familiar, scent assailed her senses. The man grasped her upper arms as she tried to back away. When she persisted in her struggle, he gently released her and she stepped back to hold onto the foot of the bed. A snarling gray wolf reappeared in the doorway but stayed behind the legs of the stranger. He spoke to the wolf, his voice obviously calming the animal.

Holding tight to the bed for support, her breath lodged deep in her lungs and she felt the blood drain from her face as her world careened precariously. She stared at the handsome half-breed who stood before her wearing an unbuttoned blue denim shirt, his muscled chest broad and chiseled. He could easily be the warrior of her dreams.

God, he was beautiful.

Taima?

A new sense of foreboding surrounded her, like whenever she awoke from dreaming of the warrior back home. The familiar blue eyes that met hers immediately weakened her knees.

Long dark hair accented his bronze

features…the same eyes, the same cheekbones…that jawline.

Even the same tiny scar high on his cheek like Taima's.

Kate touched her forehead and blinked, unable to believe the resemblance. The sensations of her dream enveloped her. Her heart raced; her breath still caught in her lungs. Struggling to breathe, she gripped her chest. If she didn't sit down soon, it would be too late. Kate continued to stare at the man, so much like the warrior from her dream.

Then she saw it…the emeralds sparkling back at her in the ring that hung at his throat.

Goosebumps covered her body.

"Oh my god," she whispered, feeling her knees begin to buckle.

The man lunged forward to catch her before she hit the floor. Kate gratefully accepted his help, but when he lifted her in his arms, she tried to object.

"Please…" His arms were strong

and his hand warm against her bare thigh.

Ignoring her plea, he held her tight. "You aren't in any shape to be out of bed just yet.

Smoke heard you moving, so I came to check." He looked at her and smiled. "I'm Brandon Wakiza. Do you remember me?"

Recognition came in bits and pieces. The same man she'd seen in the Mercantile Store in Dubois. The same man who'd shown her the petroglyphs in Whiskey Basin. Mesmerized by the voice that sounded too much like Taima's, Kate placed her arm around his shoulder for support and stared at the stranger. No words came from her throat, though many questions went through her mind. She could only listen to his soothing words as he carried her to the other side of the bed where he placed her near the center.

After pulling the feather comforter over her legs, he sat on the bed, leaned over her legs, and placed a hand on the mattress.

Nearly lost in the blue of his eyes, she missed the question he had asked. "I'm sorry, what?"

His warm smile spoke of a gentle nature. "You've been here for three days. I've had a doctor look you over, but didn't know who else to call for you regarding friends or relatives."

Tucking the comforter beneath her arms, she avoided his gaze and looked at the white shadow-stripped pattern of the comforter. "I'm out here alone on vacation from Pennsylvania. My name is Kate Bradach."

"Do you remember going to the petroglyphs in Whiskey Basin?"

Surprised, she met his gaze. "Yes, I do, but…"

"You hit your head on a huge boulder. It must have been quite a bump to keep you out for so long."

She touched the bump on her head, but the ring at his throat held her attention. As she stared at it, she remembered Taima's dying words to Kelee, echoing in her mind…Pass this down to your sons, and they, to their sons until Kate reclaims it.

Kate shivered and shook her head. "It just can't be…"

Brandon continued to watch her and tipped his head. "Is something wrong? What do you mean…it can't be?"

Kate could hardly get the words out, but she had to know. "Where did you get that ring?"

Brandon's long fingers touched the ring at his throat and searched her eyes for a long time. For a moment, it seemed he might recognize her, though that was impossible. They had never met before showing her the petroglyphs.

Then suddenly his eyes widened and he whispered, "It can't be."

Kate drew her eyebrows together. "What can't be?" she asked, becoming more confused.

He looked at her hair, her face, her mouth. "This ring has been passed through my family for several generations." Brandon paused. He narrowed his eyes, his gaze holding fast to hers.

"Why do you ask about this ring?"

A sense of loss tugged at Kate's heart. She contemplated an answer. Not wanting to sound foolish, she changed her mind and glanced out the window at the snow-peaked mountains.

"Never mind. It can't possibly be."

Warm fingers beneath her chin slowly turned her face back to his, but she kept her lashes lowered. His touch affected her more than she wanted him to know, and if she met his gaze, he would surely see.

"Kate, look at me."

She pulled in her lower lip. How many times had Taima said those exact words to her? Desperately missing him, a tear spilled down her cheek, like a satin caress. She reluctantly met Brandon's gaze as more tears pooled in her eyes and he became a blur.

"What can't possibly be? You must tell me," he insisted, desperation edging his voice.

When he touched her chin, and

gazed deep into her eyes, Kate could have sworn Taima sat before her. Brandon's mannerisms were too similar, and her heart ached for a future with him that could never be.

He tenderly wiped away a tear with his thumb, again, the way Taima would have, making it even harder for her to speak. The memories were too painful. She inhaled deeply, holding his gaze. "I used to have a ring exactly like that. What I'm going to say sounds ridiculous, yet I know in my heart it wasn't a dream. I gave that ring to my husband, Taima, to wear around his neck."

Her heartbeat thudded in the silence following her admission. Kate waited, almost afraid of Brandon's pending reaction.

A muscle twitched in his jaw.

To her surprise, he reached up and untied the leather strip that held the ring. The same way Taima had worn it.

He pulled the ring from the leather and scrutinized it, then looked at her. "There's an inscription inside."

Kate's anticipation took her breath. She knew her parents had inscribed the inside of her ring. She couldn't possibly hope the ring was the same one Taima had told Kelee to pass down a century ago. This man was a stranger to her, although too familiar, yet he held the key to unlock her confusion.

Unable to grasp that the ring could be the exact same one, she had to know. "The inscription says…Always with you."

Brandon took her hand to place the ring on her palm and the heated touch of his fingers sent a tremor up her arm. "How could you possibly know what it says inside?"

"Because it's the same ring I gave to Taima, passed on by Kelee to his son…and somehow you have it now. I don't understand how three days could encompass a hundred years back. How can this be explained?" She tried to pull away, but he held tight to her hand and he still held onto the ring. Kate met his wide-eyed gaze. He'd felt it, too. The slight shrug of his shoulder proved it.

The pressure on her hand increased as he continued to hold on and stare at her. "It *is* you, isn't it? I *have* found you at last," he said, his voice almost a whisper.

"What do you mean?" Kate tried to calm the excitement fluttering in her stomach like butterflies. To hope *he* could be Taima reincarnated was impossible, yet here he was.

He hesitated, as though in thought as he turned the ring over in his fingers. "For many years, I've had a vision of a woman who looks exactly like you. This vision is like a dream. I've had it once a month, once a week, sometimes once or twice in the same week." Brandon folded her fingers on the ring and caressed her cheek with the back of his fingers. "Your face has become so much a part of my life. My grandfather is an elder in our tribe. He told me that his grandfather spoke of a story many times, of Taima giving this ring to his son to pass on, until you came to claim it. When I recognized you in town that day, I knew I had to bring you here, to find out who you are and *why* you're here."

Kate only shook her head in disbelief, yet somehow knew Brandon spoke the truth of his ancestors. Dare she tell him *what* had happened? She hardly believed it herself. Time travel thus far was a myth, nothing more.

Reaching up, she tenderly touched the scar high on his cheek. "Taima had a scar in the same spot. You are so much like him…it scares me."

"I promise, I won't hurt you…or scare you."

She drew back her hand, but hesitated before continuing. "I have also had a dream that's haunted me for many years, of a warrior mounted on his horse before snow-peaked mountains. I had to come out west in search of those mountains…in search of answers. There was a lake nearby. Whenever I'd awaken from this dream, it was as though I sensed the warrior had stood in my room, disappearing just before I woke up." Kate toyed with the edge of the comforter. "It all sounds so silly, but with you this close, I feel that same nearness, almost like *you* were in my dream."

With a knuckle beneath her chin, Brandon raised her face again. "Perhaps it was. I prayed that I'd find you each time I had my vision. I'd go into town with the hope that one of the tourists would be you."

Her pulse nearly raced out of control at his warm touch. "I did see you in the Mercantile Store. If I've been here for three days, then I saw you three days ago. I sensed something about you, but you never turned around."

"You mean when I picked up the package from the store counter? I did sense something. I should have paid more attention to it and turned around." Brandon opened her fingers to display the ring. "This matches your eyes, you know."

She smiled. "Taima used to tell me that."

He lifted her hand and easily slipped the ring onto her finger. Kate held out her hand and admired it. *Her ring.* It had to be hers. Quickly removing it, she peered at the inside and read the inscription her parents had put there. Shocked and elated at the same time, she looked at Brandon.

He gazed at her for a long moment. Leaning closer, he brushed a strand of hair from her cheek. "I think we have both lived before, though many would think us crazy…so we'll keep that between us for now. But I *do* believe in fate…we were meant to be together. Our meeting is no accident."

Chills crept up her spine. As if on cue, the radio played an appropriate song by Tracy Byrd. She listened to the familiar words, which made more sense now than she ever thought they could.

"The Great Spirit *does* take care of the stars…and our fate in finding each other. I have searched for you too long, Kate." Their lips were mere inches apart as he searched her soul.

His musky scent filled the close space between them and for a moment, she was frozen in time. "If you are the one I have searched for, I have so many questions."

Brandon laced his fingers through her hair and leaned in. "I think in due time, we will both find the answers we seek." Then he drew her in for a kiss with the passion of lost love, a kiss that held all the familiar passion she thought she'd lost forever. Closing her eyes, it was Taima who kissed her now and she got lost in the moment. To kiss a stranger so soon shouldn't happen, but was he a stranger, really? His warmth and tenderness embraced her soul and she knew she had finally found the man of her dreams.

Every nerve in her body sparked as his tongue swept her mouth and then he released her to meet her gaze. "I'll not apologize for that. Somehow we are connected and I *will* find the answers."

His thumb grazed her lower lip with a tenderness Kate needed right now and the heat from his hand on her cheek comforted her. She searched Brandon's blue eyes, looking from one to the other and their souls connected on a level she couldn't explain.

They were strangers, yet not.

He'd been waiting for her as long as she'd been trying to find him and now their journey of discovery could begin. She had so many questions. "I'm not sure where we need to begin. All of this feels so real, but we don't know anything about each other."

Kate leaned into the palm of his hand and placed hers over his. As she let her fingers trail down to his forearm, the corded muscles spoke of his strength. So much like Taima, whom her heart ached for right now. Another tear slipped from her eye, making a warm trail down her cheek. "You are so much like *him*. I want to go back but…god, the dream was so real, Brandon."

A sob tore from her throat and he pulled her against his chest and scooted closer. When his hand caressed her back, she fisted her fingers in his open shirt; his strong arms embraced her and held her tight. Spicy cologne filled her senses with images of Taima…his blue eyes beckoning to her from a distance and she could have sworn she saw a smile.

Brandon rocked her on the bed until her body stopped trembling. "Your dream is a way for the spirits to show us what's happened in the past that we need to pay attention to. They made you feel everything from our past." He caressed her back again. "I think you need to eat something. I have fresh coffee, let's start with that. What do you say?" He lifted her face and through her blur of tears, nodded to him.

Knots in her stomach might go away with food. Brandon said she'd been asleep for three days. *How was that even possible?* She glanced at the bathroom. "Let me get cleaned up and then I'd love a cup of coffee."

He stood, helped her stand and then stepped aside. "We'll get some food into you and then you'll be ready for a shower."

Three days and no shower! Food and coffee first. Kate stepped toward the bathroom in her room. "I'll be right out." She turned toward Brandon, his broad shoulders towering over her.

"Thank you for all you've done."

Closing the bathroom door, she heard his boots walk into the hall and toward the kitchen as he talked with Smoke. After finally relieving herself, Kate stared into the mirror. Sunken, dark eyes stared back, her hair a mess. She raked her fingers through it, straightening as best she could and turned to find her jeans.

When she'd buttoned and zipped, Smoke stood in her doorway with his head tipped to the side as he watched her. Something about his eyes was familiar but she couldn't place why. *Was Smoke a shapeshifter, too?* "Who are you, Smoke, really? Should I know you?" A paw waved in the air. His tail wagged as she walked barefoot toward him and soft fur met her fingers as she patted his head. "Have you come to escort me to the kitchen? Come on then, show me the way if you won't tell me who you are."

Kate followed him down the hall

that opened into a spacious living room and kitchen with log furniture and dining table. A yellow log interior towered above her, a wall of glass showed her the snow-capped mountains in the distance. The view made her gasp as she stepped closer to the windows. A warm pine-scented breeze came in through the open patio doors that led to a deck bigger than her living room at home.

"Kate, how do you take your coffee?"

She turned when he spoke her name. His eyes portrayed of his silent concern. "Lots of cream, please. Thank you." Brandon set her stone mug on the counter and she smiled at the pine cone decoration on it.

"Are you up to bacon and eggs with hash browns? I'm a pretty good cook." His smile only reminded her of Taima and the last three days she'd spent in the past.

"I'm starving. That sounds great." She took a seat at the counter at the center island where he set out pans on the stove. Watching him cook would be fun. She could admire him, get to know his moves…again, so much like Taima that Kate had to shake her head. Taking a drink of coffee, she savored the flavor as well as the company.

Placing her fork on her empty plate, Kate leaned back in her chair and gazed at Brandon. His relaxed nature kept her from wanting to bolt, although she probably should start making plans to drive back home. Realizing how silly that thought was, driving very far in her weakened condition wouldn't be a good idea.

"You'll need a few good meals today to make up for not eating for three days. I've got a few steaks and potatoes for supper later. Thought we might throw them on the grill." Brandon stood, collected their dishes and loaded them into the dishwasher. "More coffee? We can relax on the couch and enjoy the mountains. I'd like to get to know you better." He refilled her cup and set the half and half on the counter.

"Thank you." Pouring in enough

creamer to turn her coffee a light caramel, she put the carton back in the fridge, grabbed her mug and headed toward the leather couch where she'd have a full view of the snow-capped mountains. Tucking one leg beneath her, Kate sank into the supple leather and cuddled into the corner. "The view is beautiful from here. I bet you spend a lot of time looking out this window."

Brandon got comfortable in the chair and watched her. "I do and then my mind wanders to other things, dreams I've had and then I wish for what might be. I enjoy my peace and quiet and being alone, but lately, I've been rethinking that…like since I started having visions of *you* more often."

Kate dared to turn her head and look into his blue eyes, bright against his tanned features. Wisdom beyond his years gazed back at her as she felt a tug on her heartstrings. She wondered if he could feel their connection or was it all in her head? If she didn't know better, she'd swear Taima sat across from her.

Graceful calmness is how she'd describe Brandon. He moved with the grace of a cougar and she was sure a powerful strength lay coiled just beneath the surface of his broad chest and shoulders. "Tell me more about your visions of me. I'm curious, since we both seem to have had the same type of dreams…if that's what you could call them."

2.

Kate could sit and watch Brandon all day. This handsome stranger had saved her life, yet was he actually a stranger?

He sipped his coffee and his gaze never left hers. "I feel like I know you, yet we've not met until this week. I'm still amazed at the almost identical likeness between my visions and the real you. Nobody understands how it works. My great-grandfather and I have talked in depth about you and what I would do if I ever found you."

Brandon stared at her and she couldn't look away, as though their minds connected and held a conversation of their own. She clenched her inner muscles as the sensual spark passed between them and traveled along every nerve in her body, making her want to be closer to pursue their unspoken connection.

"I still have no idea how to proceed now that I *have* found you. Where do we go from here? We aren't total strangers, considering the past life that you just experienced, yet we know nothing about the other."

"Your grandfathers must be very wise men."

"My great-grandfather has lived a long time and has seen our people go through many transitions and their stories have become reality. Too many of his visions have come true, which is why our people look up to him. He's knowledgeable on a different level."

"Yet now, *you* seem to have the ability to see the future."

He continued to stare at her as though he were drawing information telepathically. "I wish I had that ability. I want to know more where *you're* concerned." Brandon smiled and shook his head. "I don't understand any of this, but I'm glad I found you. What happens from here, who's to say? You could go back to Pittsburgh and I might never see you again." He paused, took another drink of his coffee and searched her face.

The tenderness and caring she saw in his eyes tugged at her heart. His manners were impeccable, of what she'd seen so far, and she'd hate to think that she'd never see him again. "At least we have a few days before I need to get back. No one knows I'm here. Oh my god. My cell phone…it must be dead by now!"

"It's on the kitchen counter. I turned the ringer off so it wouldn't wake you and I forgot about it. Luckily, it takes the same charger cord as mine. After I brought you back here, I went to your motel room. I know the owners, told them what happened and they gave me your belongings. Your suitcases are at the back door. Let me grab your phone."

Kate's heart knotted as she realized how many days had passed since she'd talked with her best friend Monica. Brandon handed her the phone and went to refill their coffees. Several messages from Monica were the only ones she'd received and she laughed out loud. Taking her mug from Brandon, she set it on the end table and called her friend immediately.

Brandon stood in front of the sofa. "I can leave you alone if you'd like."

"Oh, no, sit down with me." She listened and waited for Monica to answer.

"Oh my god, woman! Where the *hell* have you been? Do you have any idea how worried I've been about you? This better be some good shit. I was about ready to book a flight out there. Of course, only God knows where the hell I'd start looking for you! Damn you, Kate!"

"Hey, hey! I'm so sorry that I worried you, but yes, something has happened. I'm fine now and don't know where to begin. Brandon says I've been out of it for three days and I just woke up." Kate proceeded to tell her what she knew…or was it what she'd dreamed? "I feel like I need to wait a few days before I leave. Brandon said I've not eaten in those three days."

"Who's Brandon? Put him on the phone, right now!"

Brandon hadn't taken his gaze off of her since she'd made the call. "She wants to talk to you, but I don't want to put you on the spot. She can be worse than a detective."

"I'll talk to her." He leaned over to take the phone and listened. After a brief pause, Brandon smiled and shook his head as he basically repeated what Kate had told Monica about her care. "I'll make sure she eats and that she's fine to drive back." He handed the phone back to Kate.

"You call before you leave and call me every night when you stop on the way. I want to hear more about this dream guy you've met."

Kate laughed. Leave it to Monica to get straight to the point. "He's the perfect gentleman. You'll like him, too."

"You do understand the meaning behind the three-day dream, right?"

"What do you mean?"

"Being worried sick about you brought your spirit guides to mine along with bits of visions that you've been dreaming. They're from a past life you both shared over one hundred years ago, if you can believe that. Does Brandon have any idea of your past life together?"

Kate glanced at Brandon. "Yes…he does. I wish you were here. You could help us understand all of this."

"Put me on speaker so he can hear, too." Kate hit the speaker button. "Okay, both of you already know of your past connection. I *feel* that clear back here now that I have you on the phone. Right now, don't stress that you don't understand it. This happens more often than people think. Soul mates *do* exist and for this exact reason. Take your time with the relationship, keep an open mind and let things work themselves out. I sense a lurking danger for both of you. I can't put my finger on it, but looking over your shoulder isn't a bad thing."

"You're scaring me, Monica. What kind of danger do you mean?"

"I don't know. Just be alert to your surroundings and people you meet. I'll let you go. You two have a lot to talk about. I love you, Kate! Take care." Kate ended the call and looked at Brandon.

His smile gave her comfort. "She's a smart woman."

"We've been friends for a long time. She's the one who told me I needed to come out west to find the answers to the dreams that tormented my nights. I'd wake up in a sweat and swear I could smell that someone was in my room…the scent of a man…*your* scent. I can't explain it and now, sitting here with you…but it's like *you* stood in the dark corner of my room." Blood rushed through her veins as she thought back on her dreams.

Then she remembered the times Taima had made love to her as she stared into Brandon's eyes…deep blue seas of emotion that could so easily pull her in. She took in a ragged breath as something passed between them and she looked away toward the pine trees on the distant mountains that reminded her of the treacherous traveling she'd done with Taima. *Had Brandon read her thoughts? Would they have the same type of connection between their souls?* They were strangers, yet not. A connection had sparked between them. Kate felt the snap of energy, the same she'd felt with Taima.

"I feel the connection between us. I want to know more, Kate. I want to know everything that passed between us in your dreams, the frustrations, and the struggle to follow your heart so many years ago."

Kate pulled in her lower lip and ran her tongue along the soft flesh, thinking of Taima and the sexual heat he'd made her feel. Their turbulent emotions had kept them apart and wasted so much time that they could have used loving one another. She'd finally surrendered to him in the end, only to lose the love of her life too soon. She'd wasted so much precious time arguing and resisting him. Kate looked back at Brandon. "If you *are* Taima, I don't want to waste time fighting what I know I feel for you. As Taima, you and I lost many months arguing, resisting what our hearts kept telling us. I was stubborn back then. I hope I've learned from this."

"I want to piece together the images I've seen in my thoughts and dreams. I was afraid you'd try to go back to the motel right away. We wouldn't be able to talk things out if you do that. You're welcome to stay until you're ready to go back east."

She searched his face…familiar brows, the cut on his cheek, the look of love she'd seen in Taima's eyes each time he saw her. *Could they have the same kind of love they felt so long ago?* "I promise I won't run off to the motel. I would like to get cleaned up and take a long bath."

"Everything you need is in your bathroom. I've got a few things to do outside. Take your time and relax."

Kate grabbed her empty coffee mug

and headed to the bathroom. Brandon reached out his hand and she hesitated before taking it.

When she did, the snapping electricity of their touch went through her fingers and up her arm. She looked at him and the tenderness in his eyes comforted her. "I'm a patient man *now* compared to then. We'll work through this together to understand what it all means."

She squeezed his hand. "I know. We both want answers." She let go, took her mug to the kitchen and made her way to the bathroom, eager to soak in hot water and wash her hair. *Would they find the answers they needed before she had to leave for home?*

* * * * *

Brandon loved the way Kate's fingers trailed over his palm as she let go and walked toward the bathroom. He turned to watch the sway of her slender hips and touched his hand against his heart, praying his dreams might finally come true. This woman had a connection to him neither of them could deny and he'd be damned if he'd lose her now.

Finishing his coffee, he went to the kitchen and put their mugs in the dishwasher. He filled a tall glass with water and then headed out to the deck for some fresh air. Smoke followed him out and Brandon leaned against the log railing to gaze at the distant snow-capped mountains. He needed to think about how to proceed with Kate; he'd love for her to stay but knew she had to return to her job. *What if she never contacted me again?*

Smoke growled and paced the deck.

Brandon set his glass on one of the log posts and scanned the yard to see what might have caught Smoke's attention. He spotted a huge raven perched on a fence rail, its claws digging into the rail. "Go get him, boy!" That's all the prodding the wolf needed and jumped from the deck at break-neck speed toward the bird. To his surprise, the raven took flight and flew at Smoke, pulling up just in time to avoid the jaws that surely would have torn the bird to pieces. "Good job, Smoke. Come here!"

The raven circled overhead and then landed in a tall pine as Smoke returned and sat next to Brandon as he took a seat in one of his over-sized log chairs on the deck in the sun. The heat warmed his face and chest where his shirt lay open. He drew in a deep breath of pine-scented air from the trees that grew close to his home, sheltering it from the weather. Dubois had been his home since childhood and he loved the log home he built five years ago. Much of the furniture he'd made himself. Thanks to his long-time friend, Joe, who owned Absaroka Western Design, where a few of his pieces were on display at the store. Brandon had learned years ago how to custom build logs into furniture. Making the pieces helped him clear his mind as he worked, wishing he had something in his shop to work on now. His mind had too much to contemplate with Kate leaving in a few days.

Thoughts of her, covered in

bubbles, soaking in his tub with wet strands of hair, drifted through Brandon's mind. Imagining her damp, silky skin being wrapped in a soft fluffy towel…*damn*. His groin tightened and he shifted in his chair. Having a woman around wasn't so bad after all. *Or was it?* He patted Smoke's head, scratching the soft fur between his ears. "You knew she'd find us, didn't you, boy? I just wish it hadn't taken so long."

His phone vibrated in his pocket. "Hey, Cody, what's up?"

"I've got news on the movie release. It's planned for three months from now so I hope you'll be around. The reviews are coming in like crazy. The investors are loving you, man. I hope you change your mind about not wanting to do another picture. We've heard from several of the backers and they're already talking about a sequel, so give the movie deal some thought."

Brandon raked his fingers through his hair, pushing it back from his face. Being in the movie had been fun and he'd enjoyed acting, but the thought of being a celebrity with fans scared him. "I don't know, man. Being in the public eye isn't what I want. I've gotten used to being an unknown. The last thing I need are groupies trying to hang out on my private deck back here. Don't be giving out my location!"

"I'm guessing the money helped, yes?"

"No shit! Thanks, man. But if I lose my privacy in the process, what good is that?"

"With the money you could make on the sequel, you could afford guards and a bigger fence! Come on. At least think about it."

Leaning forward, Brandon rested his elbow on his knee and Smoke stood to face the patio door, wagging his tail. Brandon turned to see Kate in the kitchen. "I'll think about it and give you a call in a few days."

"Fair enough. It's not something that'll happen right away. The first movie will explode on the big screen soon, though. Talk to you later, Brandon."

He shut off his phone as Kate opened the patio door. Taking a bath and slipping into clean clothes had put a beautiful smile on her face and the warm breeze carried the scent of her body. He laughed at the hat she had put on. "That looks pretty good on you. Smoke even thinks so." His old straw hat hung on a peg by the back door near her luggage. He'd not worn it in years. "If you don't mind a hat with a few holes in it, I guess it works."

"I don't mind a few holes. It gives the hat character."

Worn jeans fit her like a glove and so did her white tank top. "You look one hundred percent better after a good breakfast and your smile brightens my day. Come have a seat and get a little sun. It'll do you good."

When Kate sat down and rested her bare feet on the footstool, her long slender legs caught his attention. Something about a woman going barefoot in jeans made his own toes curl.

Dark painted toenails only drew

more of his attention. The length of her toes was perfect…just like the rest of her, in his eyes. She tipped her cute little head and smiled at him. "This is really a nice place you have here. Is it always this quiet?"

"It is. Smoke likes that he can roam the property. I'm far enough out of town that traffic is minimal and I can do what I want without a lot of interruptions. Being a loner helps, too."

"You do have admirers in town, you know. The little sales girl at the Mercantile Store is quite taken with you. I don't blame her. She said many of the women in town talk about you."

Her wink made him smile as his cheeks burned. Women normally didn't cause that type of reaction in him. "I don't go into town often, but they all seem to know who I am."

"Women make a point of finding out who the single, good looking guys are, especially if they've grown up here and are still available." She stretched her arms in the sun. "This feels wonderful."

Like out of a nightmare, the raven flew from the pine tree directly toward the deck and smashed into Brandon's glass of water on the post, getting Kate wet as broken glass flew everywhere. Smoke yelped at the same time Kate tipped her hat to cover her face. The bird landed in another tree and screeched as though it were injured.

Brandon reached out for her. "Shit! Are you okay? Don't move. I'll get some shoes on and grab a broom." He checked his side of the deck for glass and hurried into the house. Maybe he should grab his gun. That damn bird had been hanging around since he brought Kate home. *What the hell?*

Back on the deck, Kate had pulled her feet onto the chair and hugged her knees. "So much for peace and quiet, huh?" She dropped three pieces of glass onto the deck.

Sweeping the glass into the dustpan, Brandon then gave the deck another sweep to make sure no tiny shards would cut her feet. "I'll grab your sandals on my way back out. Don't move."

Returning with her shoes, Brandon dropped them beside her chair and noticed that she watched the raven perched on a deck rail at the far side. The bird seemed to stare at Kate and he stepped between them to block Kate's view of the bird. "Don't stare into the raven's eyes. An old legend of skinwalkers who are shapeshifters tells of them taking over the soul by creating a trance with an individual they want. Eye contact is how they do that."

"Seriously? That still happens?"

Brandon helped her up from the chair and she stepped into her sandals. "Let's go inside. I'm not taking any chances." A shiver ran down Brandon's spine as he recalled the creepy legends his grandfathers had passed on around the campfires. No doubt the raven stared at his back. He turned to make sure the bird still sat perched on the rail rather than flying at them and then stepped into the house with Kate.

Memories of a raven's beady eyes

staring at her formed in Kate's mind as she touched between her eyebrows. Like DeJavu, she'd been through this before. Closing her eyes for a moment, the beady black eyes got closer and the raven almost pecked out her own eyes. "No!" Kate forced her eyes open and from the inside, searched the deck for the bird. It screeched at her, flew to the top of a pine tree and landed out of sight. She turned to Brandon, whose eyes were as wide as her own.

"You've had a vision. I recognize that look."

She nodded and stepped away from the patio door. Sitting on the leather couch, she pulled her knees up and hugged them. "Was it a dream or did it actually happen? A black raven used that same technique to take over my soul so she could be closer to Taima. She fooled him by actually changing into me around him, but she'd slip up once in a while and say something that alerted him to the differences between her and me. There was a shaman who knew about these skinwalkers and it took a long time to kill her; she nearly destroyed the relationship Taima and I had." Kate sorted through her memories as Brandon's features softened while he listened to her story. "She would watch me as I moved around their small village and many times I could feel being watched even when she wasn't around. That's when I noticed a raven on many occasions. I remember a medicine bag she'd given me to wear around my neck and the pouch rested over my heart."

Brandon shifted on the other end of the sofa. "That's how they work. It's very scary from what I've been told."

His eyes searched hers, wanting to know more. "It's very scary. Taima would find me caught in her trance because I would freeze where I stood. She'd wipe my mind of my own thoughts and I'd become her, yet never remembered anything when she left my body. I think her father was a known skinwalker or something." Kate gasped and covered her mouth; goose bumps covered her arms and legs. "She's back,

Brandon. I can feel it. It's Mai and she wants you!"

"I've noticed the bird around for the past several days." His eyes narrowed. "Ever since I brought you here after hitting your head. We'll need to talk with my grandfather. He lives down river. Are you up to that today? If not, we can wait a few days."

"How do they find us so many years later? Brandon, this is crazy." Kate brushed at the damp legs of her jeans. *Damn ravens.* "I can't believe this is happening again."

Brandon got up and headed to the kitchen. "Jack Daniels™ or a beer?"

3.

"Jack, on the rocks, please. Thank you." Kate tried to shake off the eerie feeling of the past. "If the attacking raven is *indeed* a skin walker, she has to be a woman in this area, wouldn't she?" The sales girl at the Mercantile came to mind. She'd been the only female in town who'd stood out and now Kate wanted to go into town to see if Brandon attracted any other females.

"Do you know the sales clerk at the Mercantile Store?"

"Her name is Shelly. She harmless."

"That's what Taima said about Mai." Kate paused, surprised that the woman's name slipped off her tongue as though she spoke of her often. "Taima denied having any feelings for her, but *her* feelings went deep enough for both of them. Bitch! Please be careful of women around you in the future."

"Besides you, you mean?" Brandon laughed as he handed her a tumbler of Jack. "Had I not had past visions of you, I'd certainly make sure I got to know you better…which I still plan to do."

Kate sipped the amber liquid as she and Brandon got more acquainted. His resemblance to Taima still stunned her; it was as though he sat across from her. All the times she and Taima had made love drifted through her mind, of the way he'd touched her so tenderly, the memories of his warm, passionate kisses and how he held her face in his hands. Her toes curled just thinking of Brandon being Taima. She wanted to crawl onto Brandon's lap, pretend he was Taima and cuddle within his strong, protective embrace. Couldn't she pretend, even for a short while? Reliving the raven/Mai incident wasn't something she wanted to do right now, but circumstances being what they were, Kate knew she had no choice.

Over the next two hours, Kate

asked questions and Brandon skirted around anything too personal, but he loved talking about his home, how long it took to take shape, and his love of building the log furniture that matched the home so well. She felt as though she belonged here, which Kate found strange, since she'd never been here before. "Your home is comfortable. I like it here. I love the log interior and furniture."

"You'd like Absaroka Western Design. It's a shop in town where he sells hides along with deer horns, cupboard knobs made of horn and my furniture pieces are there. In time, I'd like you to meet Joe. He and I go way back. He does taxidermy for hunters all over the world."

"I don't even want to consider going back home yet. Tomorrow I'll make a decision on how many more days I'll stay. I would like to talk with your grandfather before I go back."

Brandon winked at her. "He's anxious to meet you. I have to admit…the second day you were here and still not awake, I called to tell him I'd found you. He knows of my visions over the last few years of you and he knows of things I'm not sure how he knows…abilities to see past and future. It's strange."

"He'd get along well with Monica! She has the same abilities." Kate laughed. Her excitement bubbled, her thoughts going in too many directions. "Thank you for all you've done for me, Brandon. You've been amazing."

"You should be getting hungry by now. We could eat an early dinner. I have steaks all seasoned, potatoes are ready to pop in the oven and there are veggies for a salad."

Finally, something she could do. "I'll throw a salad together for us. What don't you like in your salad?"

"I love veggies so make it up however you like." He stood and headed for the deck. "I'll get the grill going while you work on the salad."

Glad to have something to do, she made her way to the kitchen, pulled the salad items from the fridge and found salad bowls in the cupboard. After stabbing the potatoes with a fork, she put them in the microwave to pre-cook while she tore the lettuce and cut tomatoes. Smiling to herself, Kate thought cooking for Brandon would be fun and imagined herself living here, then chastised herself for being so silly.

Brandon came in, grabbed the aluminum foil, wrapped the potatoes and put them on a plate. He peeked over her shoulder while she sliced the cucumber, playfully pressed on the top of her hat and sniffed the air. "God, you smell good." He held out his hands. "I'm just sayin'…."

Laughing, she turned to look at him and their lips were mere inches apart. Her inner muscles tightened, a reaction she couldn't control around him. His cologne drifted into her space and into her mind, creating sexual images she shouldn't be thinking yet about him. "Thank you. Your cologne affects me, too. Funny how that is."

"I'll get the potatoes on the grill. I need some air." He grabbed another beer from the fridge. "The Jack's on the counter there if you need a refill."

Kate peeked over her shoulder as he stepped onto the deck and she let out a breath. How would she make it here three more days without jumping his ass? Damnit! She couldn't believe her luck in the connection they shared and wondered where it might eventually lead them. Turning her attention back to the salad, she finished them off with sunflower seeds and croutons, refilled her glass and joined Brandon on the deck, now clear of all glass. His jeans covered his long legs and his bare feet rested on the center railing of the fence. A good-looking man, barefoot in jeans, had always sent her mind into the gutter. She took a seat, put her feet up on the railing and looked over at him.

His blue eyes met hers. "What? I can see those wheels turning in that pretty little head of yours. I think you could be dangerous to have around twenty-four-seven."

She laughed. "I'm sorry you think that. It wouldn't be my fault, I'm sure."

"I'd be tempted by you on a daily basis. Then again, that might not be a bad thing."

"You'd have more company than you do now."

He stared at her for a moment. "My friends know I'm a loner. They usually call before they drive all the way up here."

"I'm not sure I could spend so much time alone. At work, I'm with people all day and don't go home until late. But I do enjoy the peace and quiet, if you can call city life in Pittsburgh quiet. Now that I think about it, out here is quiet…nothing at all like what I consider quiet at home." She looked toward the snow-capped mountains as she sipped her drink and let her mind wander over several possibilities. Her life back home began to take on a hectic memory of the time she spent alone. This type of lifestyle would be way more relaxing, but what would she do for work if she ever had the opportunity to move?

She breathed in the pine-scented

air. Instead of invoking a relaxed inner peace, memories came back of traipsing through the wooded mountainside with Taima, of jumping on a horse in hopes of escaping into the trees…that was when she'd been unaware of the cougars lying in wait for unsuspecting prey. Real or not, her time with Taima had taught her so much…about life and her own heart. She missed Sakima, too. Talking with the older shaman about his visions and how much he'd seen in his own lifetime, made her consider Brandon's offer to meet his grandfather. He'd told Brandon of the visions he'd seen that were close to Brandon's…they both had visions about *her*. She thought back on her dreams, of sensing that someone had stood in her room in the dark. She still swore she had smelled a man each time that damn dream had awakened her.

"I'll grab the steaks and get them cooking. The potatoes should be done when the steaks are."

Brandon's jeans hugged his thighs and ass, leaving nothing to the imagination. His muscled thighs moved beneath the material and teased her senses. *He's just a man, calm down!* Kate laughed at herself and turned her attention back to the distant mountain ranges. Her eyes scanned the hillsides for an elk herd or a lone bear roaming for food. The growing grizzly population in the Rockies was something those back east had no clue of, but she'd followed the articles on-line about it. Local ranchers were in an uproar over losing so many cattle to the grizzly yet the government had turned a blind eye to their ever-growing problem.

The grill lid opened and Brandon placed the steaks next to the potatoes and then turned them. "It shouldn't be long. I'm starving so I know you must be hungry. How's your drink while I'm up?'

"I'm good. I'll wait until I get some food in me to have another one. Not eating for three days has lowered my alcohol tolerance big time and…I don't trust my conversation with you if I have any more right now." Brandon had buttoned his shirt, leaving the top two open and his sleeves were still rolled part way up his forearm, making her squirm in her chair, hoping Brandon didn't notice her reaction.

"Are you implying I would take advantage of you?"

"You're too much of a gentleman for me to worry about that. I've been thinking about meeting your grandfather later if that invite is still open." Brandon seemed easy to talk to yet didn't talk about himself much and she wondered what he did when he wasn't working on his furniture.

He sat back down and replaced his feet on the rail. "That decision is totally up to you. We can go after we eat."

Again, the raven flew overhead, cawing like crazy and landed back in the pine tree. "I hope that damn bird doesn't follow us to your grandfather's. I don't think that would go well."

"Perhaps he'll have answers about the raven. He and I have never discussed skinwalkers in detail other than to mention them in folklore stories but he *has* talked about you in great detail to me."

"Now that interests me. I'd love to hear what he has to say about your visions. Maybe he can tell me more about you since you've not told me much."

"There isn't much to tell. I'm a simple guy." He tipped his beer can for a drink. "Simple guys lead simple lives."

"Whatever. I'm interested to know more of what you do besides building furniture. You can't sit here and look out over the land all day."

He nodded. "You're right. I spend time online once in a while. I run a website for my furniture and Joe has it on his website. A few orders come in. You'd be surprised what people are willing to pay when they really want something…then there are the shipping costs that they never complain about, so things like that keep me busy."

The sizzling grease on the grill sent up a wonderful smell of rib eye steaks that drifted past Kate's nose and her stomach growled. The Jack Daniels™

on her empty stomach made her too talkative. At least she realized it before she said too much more to Brandon. Kate rested her head back and enjoyed the warm breeze. What a great day. Right now, she didn't have a worry in the world…or at least she didn't let them bother her right now. She cleared her mind and enjoyed her view of the mountains.

Brandon removed the steaks and potatoes from the grill and she followed him inside. While she got down a few plates and silverware, Brandon made a call to let his grandfather know they were coming over and then cut into his steak. The flavor of grilled steak only made her stomach growl more and she lifted a forkful of potato covered in sour cream, the tangy flavor bursting in her mouth. She sipped her iced cola and glanced at Brandon. A quiet meal with a handsome man and a future that could go anywhere made Kate happy. She wondered how much of what his grandfather would tell them might actually happen.

With dinner over and the dishes cleaned up, she climbed into Brandon's four-wheel drive Dodge pickup and they headed down the mountain through town. His grandfather lived along the Wind River on the other side of Dubois and the scenery fascinated Kate. "I bet going up into the mountains is a beautiful drive, looking for wildlife and smelling the pines."

"There are more cattle up there than wildlife but once in a while, if you go early enough, you can watch a herd of elk roaming the DuNoir Valley over the mountains. Bighorn sheep roam this area a lot. We have an interruptive center here for them and the kids love it. I think you'd like it, considering your background at the museum. The center is always looking for good people to help with the work out there." Brandon's fingers extended from the top of the steering wheel. "I'm just sayin'…it's something to consider if we decide to pursue these visions we both have and you move here one day."

Kate looked at him, seriously

considering what would happen for them if she moved here. It had nothing to do with the fact that they'd actually just met…their past went deeper than that and they both knew it. People around them didn't have to understand; it was none of their business. "A visit or two in the future isn't out of the question. I'd love to come back. Moving here would depend on what your grandfather's visions tell me. I think we have a lot of talking to do in order to make sense of all this. You have to admit, this type of thing doesn't happen."

The sunset beyond the mountains and dusk settled over the small town. The closer they got to his grandfather's, the more her stomach twisted. *Was she ready to hear all he had to say?* Anxious, Kate had waited years for this moment to arrive and now pins and needles poked at her every thought. So many questions, so many feelings…the inner turmoil tugged at her heartstrings. She wanted to be back with Taima, damnit. Kate glanced at Brandon. When he met her gaze, he slid his open hand across the console between them and Kate laced her fingers with his.

He gently squeezed her hand. "I feel confident that things will work out for us. Granted, it won't happen overnight, but I don't think either of us is looking for a quick resolution to this. We need time…but finding you is the best thing that's happened to me in a long time." He winked at her and set his gaze back on the road. The truck slowed and Brandon turned onto a long winding driveway.

When she tried to pull her hand from his, he held tight. "Promise me you'll give this a chance."

Kate took in a deep ragged breath. "I promise, but…what if he doesn't like me?"

Brandon tipped his head back and laughed, the brim of his Stetson hitting the rear window. "He already knows all about you. He's seen you so many times in his visions that he could spot you in town if he had to."

Several people sat in lawn chairs

around a fire pit being prepared with kindling. She did love a good fire and prayed all would go well. What she hadn't expected were so many of his friends and family to be around. Brandon parked, got out and opened her door to help her out. At least he had running boards for her to step on. Walking toward the crowd, Kate looked into as many faces as she could, given the lack of daylight now, though it was about nine o'clock. A young woman with long dark hair came running toward Brandon and jumped into his arms. He swung her around and Kate didn't miss the kiss she planted on his mouth.

The woman held his face so he couldn't pull away and eventually he set her on her feet. "I'm so glad you came out to see me." She looked at Kate, up and down, cocked her head with a snotty attitude and her lip curled ever so much, but Kate stood close enough to see it. "I don't know who you are…but he's already taken." The girl's eyes appeared to turn black and widened as she stared at Kate.

"Shelly, that's enough. This is Kate."

Recognition hit Kate and Mai came to mind…the skinwalker who tried to take Taima from her. It couldn't be. Yet, she and Brandon were here, why not their enemies from the past as well? Kate pulled her gaze away and looked at Brandon. She was the little bitch from the Mercantile Store the day she arrived in town. Without a how-do-you-do, the young woman spun on her heel and strode past those sitting around the fire. *Good riddance!* Kate didn't care if she ever joined them tonight.

"Ignore her. I'm sorry. She's a good friend, but not as close as she'd like to be. The others are more accepting. They've listened to grandfather and me as we talked about our visions of you so they're as excited as you and I, which is why they showed up. I'm sure he told them all that you're here. Come on."

A frail old man sat beside another old man, likely his son and Brandon's grandfather. She watched as Brandon hugged them both and then helped his great-grandfather to stand. Brandon held out his hand toward her. "Kate, he wants to hug you if that's okay."

Carefully Kate stepped forward but she was afraid to hug the frail old man too tight. He gently embraced her for a few moments and then stood looking at her as if he knew her. To her surprise, he cupped her face and looked into Kate's eyes. In turn, she placed her hands over his, but the shock slowly took over, as did the recognition. It seemed impossible, yet he stood before her. The fading blue eyes were almost too much and she had to concentrate on his words. "We have waited many moons for you to return to us." Then he took her hands in his and lifted her finger closer as his hand shook. "I held this ring in my own hands and prayed so many times that I lost count, yet you never returned." He took in a slow, raspy breath. "Now…here you are."

The world around Kate spun and made her dizzy as the old man's words repeated in her head. The deep lines in his face told a story of age. His gray hair lay in braids past his shoulders, but the blue eyes held her attention. He couldn't possibly be who she thought he was. "I don't understand. How could you have held onto this ring in the past?"

"I'm an old man. I need to sit now."

Kate helped him back into his chair and waited for him to get comfortable. He waived a gnarled hand at Brandon who grabbed two empty chairs. Even though the other chairs formed a circle, the old man wanted her and Brandon to sit right in front of him and his son.

He stared at Kate and slowly shook his head. "It's been so long now." He paused to breathe and Kate waited, but she was dying to know what he had to say. His eyes drilled into her. "Kelee…was my father…Taima would have been my grandfather. I wish I would have known him."

Kate gasped. Chills like Kate had never before experienced covered her arms and ran down her back. She couldn't look away.

"Sakima…was my great-grandfather."

Kate covered her mouth and her stomach flipped. "Oh my god." She stared at Brandon, her eyes so wide they almost hurt. A tear slipped down her cheek as more pooled in her eyes. Her vision blurred but memories flooded her mind. "Brandon, tell me you know about this."

The heat of his hand warmed her through her shirt as he caressed her back. "Of course, I do."

The old man reached out to wipe away her tear. "You look exactly like both of them used to describe you. They said your eyes matched the stones in the ring." He reached for her hand and held it up for all of them to see. The fire reflected into the stones.

Kate jumped when the cheers rang out. She looked to Brandon's grandfather who smiled and nodded his head. His words came in a slow whispered tone. "Welcome home, Kate. We have all waited a long time for this day."

She could only look at the stars dotting the night sky as she tried to sort out so many memories. Now even the stars blurred. She'd not yet explained everything to Brandon; he didn't know all of the details...or did he? She snapped her head to look at him and met his gaze. "You know who Sakima was? And Kelee?"

Brandon waited a moment before answering. "I do. My elders have talked often about them."

Wiping her eyes, she tried to make sense of it all. Looking back at the old man, he sat quietly watching her, still holding her hand, his fingers touching the ring. If she didn't know better, she'd think his touch alone heated the gold ring. His lips moved before he spoke. "...Always with you...that's what it says inside the ring. I used to chant that in my prayers. My father, Kelee, loved you very much, as much as he loved his own mother Witashnah and...I wanted you to return for *him*. Many times he told me that Taima swore he would return to you through time. I think he's chosen Brandon for that purpose."

More tears came as she thought about Taima's blue-eyed little boy, Kelee, who played as a child. His laughter used to make her and Taima smile as they watched him together. Now she cried harder and rocked in her chair as she looked at the sky, hoping the tears would go away.

"Taima! Why? Why did you leave me alone?" Kate yelled at the sky and choked on her sobs.

Brandon took her free hand. "I'm here now. If I could only take away your pain and sadness. I'm so sorry you have to relive all this."

4.

With her vision blurred by tears, she concentrated on a bright star overhead, unable to look at anyone right now. His grandfather covered their clasped hands with his own. "Nechan, you will take away all of her sadness. Now that you have found her…healing can begin."

Kate blinked at his grandfather when he paused and the warm tears slipped down her cheeks.

The old man rubbed their hands. "Look at each other and concentrate on the feeling in your hearts. Kate…he *is* the man you want him to be…returned to you by the Great Spirit so your souls can be one. It will be a *final surrender* for both of you."

As she stared into Brandon's eyes, an overwhelming love reached out to her that soothed her heart. It was as though Taima looked back at her, silently telling her all would be right. She pulled in her lower lip and refused to cry, but her heart ached for the man she'd lost. Was he inside of Brandon? Did they already share a love that continued through time? She refused to say a word yet. Too many memories fought for her attention.

"You both have had a past together and shared a love stronger than anyone here. You must allow yourselves time to rekindle what is hidden deep inside your hearts. It *will* happen; this reunion proves *fate* is stronger than we give it credit for."

Brandon squeezed her hand cupped within his grandfather's hands. "I've loved you for as long as I've had these visions of you. Please give us a chance to explore our feelings before you have to go back east. Allow me to love you the way I did before."

She rubbed her thumb over the back of Brandon's hand. "I promise I will give us a chance. Even though this is what I've hoped and dreamed for, it's all a little over the top. To think that we were lovers in the past, yet our spirits found each other through time and miles apart…how can we dispute that?"

"We can't. Fate has brought us together and to ignore *that* might be thumbing our nose at fate and cause other problems."

His grandfather leaned close. "You both must kiss and seal what fate has rejoined."

Pulling her hand from his great-grandfather's grasp, Kate threaded her fingers behind Brandon's neck as their lips touched. He cupped her face. Her mouth opened to him and their tongues tangled, explored and reunited a love from the past. New life within her heart rose up and her sadness seemed less than it once was. Familiar feelings sparked to ignite what was buried deep inside.

Hope rose above all in her heart.

Brandon pulled from the kiss and his thumb caressed her lower lip. "This is just the beginning, I promise. Welcome home."

Friends and family cheered. "Let the party begin."

The smell of hamburgers drifted on the night air and the line formed for food. Kate smiled as she wiped her eyes and turned to both of Brandon's grandfathers. "I would love to talk with you more sometime. Thank you both."

The older man leaned toward her. "We have done our part. The spirits are happy at last. Go join the young people and celebrate. We'll talk another day."

"Thank you so much." Brandon still held her hand when someone brought over two beers. He twisted the tops off and gave one to her. Kate took a long swallow and watched Brandon get hugged by his family. She sat with the elders, feeling a vibe from them that comforted her heart. She truly felt accepted and as though she were among friends. Leaving this and driving back home alone wouldn't be easy. Decisions didn't have to be made tonight, but many lay ahead of her.

Hours later, after she and Brandon ate and enjoyed a few beers with family and friends, she hugged Brandon as they walked toward his pickup to go home. He opened the door, she got in and buckled her seatbelt. Moments later, he backed out and headed down the driveway, his high beams lighting the way. Brandon hit the brakes and Kate grabbed onto the dash in front of her. A slender woman stood in front of his truck, her hair looking like it hadn't been combed in weeks. Brandon reached toward Kate, but didn't take his eyes off the woman who stood in the truck lights.

Kate screamed as the woman scrambled onto the hood of his truck and clawed at the windshield with her dirty fingers and ragged nails. Her dark eyes widened and she showed teeth that were more like that of a wolf.

The creature stared at Brandon. "She doesn't belong here and you both will pay for this! Get rid of her…you are already spoken for!"

Brandon shifted into reverse and stepped on the gas. The woman flew off the hood of his truck and disappeared into the darkness.

"Holy shit!" He shifted into drive and sped ahead toward the main road.

Kate reached out for his shoulder, hoping he wasn't too shaken, but her heart raced as the image of the crazed woman stayed in her mind. *Who the hell does that?* They headed toward town and she tried to breathe slower and make sense of what just happened. *Who didn't want her here? Shelly?* That certainly hadn't looked like Shelly on the hood of the truck.

"Are you okay?" He reached over toward her and she took his hand.

"I think so, but what the hell?" Kate put her hand on her chest, still not able to believe what just happened. The look in those beady eyes would haunt her all night, but she didn't want Brandon to know that.

"Don't take it personally. *I* want you here. I have no idea who, or what, crawled up to the windshield. I know *I* won't be sleeping anytime soon."

Brandon squeezed her hand and looked over at her.

"Me neither and it's been a damn long day for me. I'm exhausted."

"We probably should have come out here tomorrow. This was a lot for you take in after what you've been through. I'm sorry. I should have waited until tomorrow. My luck, you'll sleep for two more days now."

"I hope not. We have a lot to talk about and since we may not fall asleep tonight, we might find some answers for us." Kate adjusted her hat and rested her elbow at the edge of the window, her eyes scanning the dark side of the road for glowing eyes in case something else jumped out at them. Brandon's warm fingers caressed the back of her hand as he drove in silence the rest of the way home. His floodlight came on as he drove up his driveway closer to the house and he hit the garage door opener on his visor.

Brandon dropped his keys on the counter and patted Smoke on the head. "Did you miss us, buddy?" He watched

Kate pet Smoke, worried he'd put her through too much today. "How about we grab a glass of Jack and kick back on the couch with some music. I think my nerves need that right now. I'm pretty sure *you* do."

"It'll help me sleep if nothing else."

She removed his hat and hung it on the peg by the back door. When she ran her fingers through her hair, Brandon wished it were his fingers. He wanted to rub the soft strands between his own fingers. How many times had he thought of doing that before she'd even arrived? Dreams of Kate used to keep him up for hours wondering where she lived and if he'd ever get to meet her. Before he took her in his arms for a kiss right here in the kitchen, Brandon took a deep breath and turned to get the glasses. He filled them with ice and poured the whiskey in.

When he handed Kate her glass, the seductive look in her eyes was that of a woman begging to be kissed. Her lips were parted and her tongue made its way over her lower lip. Without losing eye contact with him, she took her glass and a long sip of the amber liquid. She swirled the drink over her tongue, teasing him, and he knew she'd taste good now. His groin tightened at the thought of holding her in his arms, smelling her hair and finally tasting her.

Kate turned before he moved and walked into the living room where she sank into the center of the leather sofa and put her feet up on the ottoman, making Brandon smile. At least she didn't sit on the opposite end tonight. After hanging his own hat on the peg at the back door, he joined Kate. Pressing the power button on the stereo, he turned down the volume so the Native American flute music played in the background. He sat down beside her, put his feet up next to hers and turned to look at her.

She winked and took another long drink. "This better kick in fast. I've had a stressful day, damnit! It didn't end like I thought it would, but I enjoyed talking with your grandfathers today…and I enjoyed kissing you."

God, he loved that look. "Your day's not over yet…and I enjoyed kissing you more." He put his arm around her and pulled her close, liking the way she blushed. "I'm glad you're here. I think we heard some good information about our pasts tonight. It's a lot to think about." He rested his head back against the over-stuff sofa that molded around them and held his glass on his thigh. Kate rested her head on his shoulder and scooted closer. Right now, Brandon didn't think life could get any better.

Kate finished her drink and handed him the glass to set on the end table. "That's what I needed to calm me down after that crazy woman crawled on the hood of your truck. I think those eyes will haunt me a long time. Now that I think about it, they were a larger version of the raven's eyes! Black and threatening."

Brandon knew the woman had to be a skin walker…perched on the hood of his own truck. That's exactly what she was. Kate was too smart for her own good and he had to stay ahead of her or she'd tempt the raven on its next attack.

Smoke growled and got up to stand at the patio door, pacing back and forth. The hairs on Brandon's neck stood up. "Easy, boy."

"What if she's out there? Are all of your doors locked? I knew tonight wasn't going to go well. It's not good for you that I'm here. You heard what she said."

"All of the doors are locked and the patio door has a safety bar. Let me close the drapes. Then we probably should get some sleep. Tomorrow will be a better day."

"This might sound stupid, but I really don't want to sleep alone tonight."

He couldn't help but snap his gaze to look at her. "Smoke will keep you company."

"I'm sure he's good but I'd feel better if you were in there with me. Just for tonight?"

How could he say no to such panic-stricken eyes? Did she not realize what she asked of him? "I'm not getting under the covers with you. That's my condition if I go in there."

"I'm fine with that. Thank you."

Brandon shut off the stereo and the lights in the living room. "Smoke, come on, out the back door before bed."

Kate took her glass into the kitchen and waited until Smoke came back in. Brandon turned out the kitchen light and followed her down the hall to her room. She turned on the bedside lamp and went into the bathroom. He removed his boots, adjusted the covers so Kate would have enough to cover up with, and then pushed the bedspread between them in case he got cold later. He stretched out on the top sheet, like that would keep her away from him and laughed at himself. This wasn't the way he'd imagined their first night in bed together, that was for damn sure.

Dressed in a nightshirt, Kate tossed her jeans and top in a chair. "That doesn't look very comfortable for you."

"I'll be fine. Come on, you need your sleep. I hope you get some tonight." Her day had been too busy but she'd insisted on doing so much, how could he say no?

She slipped beneath the covers, rolled over to face him and then scooted closer. Her green eyes were his weak spot. She might fall asleep but he'd be awake for a while yet. Brandon rolled over to face her and reached out to caress her cheek. Soft skin met his fingers. "You have no idea how many times I've dreamed of touching you. Perhaps I'll wake up in the morning and you won't actually exist. Maybe today has been a dream for me."

"I'm here and you aren't dreaming." She turned her face into his hand and kissed his palm. "Thank you again."

Could he trust what he saw in her eyes? Leaning closer and threading his fingers through her hair, Brandon kissed her and pulled her close. A kiss that he'd thought about for years. Kate kissed him back and her fingers curved over his bicep. Their tongues met and passion ignited in his body. Sensations sparked that had lain dormant for too long, but tonight was not the time to let them loose. He cupped her face and pulled back to search her eyes and make sure she felt the same things. The dim night light surrounded them and he couldn't see well. Touching her forehead with his, he breathed in her scent, locking it away in his memory. "I will always protect you. Tonight, you need sleep. Good night, Kate."

She adjusted her pillow, rolled the other way and leaving the night light on, scooted her back against him. Instinctively he put his arm around her waist and held her close. In a matter of minutes, she slept, her breathing now even and Brandon prayed for protection for them both.

The smell of bacon and coffee woke Brandon. Kate's side of the bed had been made and Smoke was gone. He raked his fingers through his hair as he padded down the hall to the kitchen where Kate turned the bacon and eggs sat ready to be cracked. A gorgeous woman in your kitchen was a pretty good thing to see first thing. Her smile brightened the day as he sat in a chair at the counter.

"Good morning, sleepy head." After filling a mug with coffee and cream, she sat it in front of him.

"You look like you slept well. I'm glad." The coffee tasted amazing today but he'd need more than one cup.

"The bacon won't be done for a few minutes yet if you want to jump in the shower."

"That was my thought. I'll only be a few minutes." Uneasiness crept over him that he couldn't set aside, like something bad would happen any minute. Without mentioning that fact to Kate, he headed up to his bedroom for a shower and to think things through. These feelings were from last night, he was sure. Images of the crazy woman on his windshield had hit him harder than he wanted and he tried to push them from his mind.

This was a new day and if Kate were up to it, he wanted to take her for a ride around town, lunch at the Cowboy

Cafe on the deck and just talk about their future. Maybe later they'd stop by to see Joe at Absaroka. He laid out clean jeans and a denim shirt and headed to the shower.

When he returned to the kitchen, Kate was just serving up their eggs at the table. This was nice; he could get used to this, but how could he convince her to move out here from Pennsylvania? Their relationship was too new for such a conversation, but he could dream of the future all he wanted. He'd love to know that one day she'd join him.

"This is so much easier. It seems like only last week I was cooking meals over a fire, dressed in doeskin and tanning hides. I'm not quite sure what happened to me while I slept for those three days, but months went by during that time."

Brandon laughed. "I'm sure Joe would be happy to show you an easier way to tan hides than what you dreamed about. What would you like to do today?"

"I think I'd like to meet this Joe…and I'd like to go back to Whiskey Basin. I promise to be more careful this time." She cocked her head to one side and gave him a pouty look he couldn't resist. She was so cute when she pleaded with her eyes.

"If that's what you want to do. We can drive your rig today. It's been sitting for a while. I hope you like it out here enough to want to return someday." There, he'd said it out loud and prayed Kate would at least give it some thought. "I'm liking the idea of you living here already." Thoughts were going around in her head. He'd learned to read her in a short time, along with a few of her mannerisms and when she was trying to figure things out.

"I don't have enough money saved up to move out here." Her laugh lightened the mood.

Sipping his coffee, he wondered when to tell her exactly where most of his money came from, but he wasn't ready to get into that today. The fact that he happened to be the lead character in an upcoming movie was scary when the producers weren't sure of its success, although what he'd already received certainly put more money in his account than he'd ever seen. "You don't need money if you come back to stay with me. I make enough for both of us. Your room will be waiting for you whenever you make that decision."

Kate's head snapped up. "Are you serious? That's a big decision…taking on a full-time roommate."

"I think we both know we're more than roommates. It would give us time to get to know each other and you could get a job if you want later on. Give it some thought. You've had a lot thrown at you in a week."

She nodded as she watched him and her emerald eyes fascinated him. "I will definitely give it some thought once I get back home and take care of a few things. I do have a job I need to get back to, but the thought of moving…wow. Monica would be all for it. I'll get back to you on that."

Riding into town an hour later as

Brandon drove her Blazer gave Kate time to consider life out here. A life with a man she barely knew, yet the similarities between him and Taima couldn't be questioned. The chance that souls could travel through time to choose when and where they were born had reached out to her on a daily basis since the day she woke up.

Granted, they'd only spent a few days together, but she trusted her gut. His great-grandfather told her more last night than she thought she had ever heard. When he made them share a kiss as a reminder of their past, visions *did* return to her that were similar to her three-day dream. Soul mates existed and they both believed in that. Brandon was still a stranger whom she wanted to know better. Today might give her more insight into his personality as well as more of the people he interacted with.

Smoke was a perfect example. Kate turned to watch the wolf take in the passing scenery. He seemed familiar to Kate and acted like she should know him. At times, the animal sat watching her when she least expected it. At others, she caught him protecting them both. If he could only talk, she'd probably learn even more from his old soul. Smoke sat in the backseat behind Brandon, with his nose out the window, enjoying the ride.

Sagebrush grew everywhere and the scent drifted through her car bringing more memories of how she rubbed the velvety leaves over her skin after bathing when she lived with Taima.

Taima.

Kate bit her upper lip to keep from crying, from missing the man she'd grown to love…and lost all too quickly.

A man from her past, yet it was as though she'd been with him only a few days ago. Her dream has been so real.

He'd been so real.

Kate glanced at Brandon and saw the same sculpted jawline she was so familiar with. Turning her attention to the approaching town did little to get Taima, and the relationship they'd shared, off her mind. One day at a time is what would get her through all of this.

Brandon parked in front of the tannery-furniture store. "Joe said he'd be here today and would be happy to show you where he does the tanning. Come on."

Before they got out, she grabbed his arm. "You didn't tell him I was a nut-job who thinks I lived a hundred years ago, did you?"

He laughed and tapped her nose. "Of course not. I'd never say something like that. Only a few of us know our souls are reconnecting from a past life." Brandon made sure to leave the windows halfway down for Smoke.

"Thank you." Shutting the car door, she followed Brandon to the door where he held it open for her to the rustic store with a wooden porch.

5.

The smell of leather permeated the store but didn't overwhelm Kate as she eagerly surveyed the knobs and pulls made of horn, animal hides that hung on the wall, lamps decorated with the cabin feel of pine cones and elk, and the log furniture with moose and bear designs on the cushions. "Is this your work?"

A man joined them. "Yes, it is. Our customers love his pieces." The man held out his hand. "I'm Joe. It's a pleasure to meet you."

She gave him a firm handshake and instantly liked Brandon's friend.

"I understand you have an interest in tanning hides and the different ways it can be done. Follow me to the back room. I tan on an open wheel because it gives me more control over the hide, but one has to be careful; a wrong move and you cut right through the hide."

The odor of raw hides and chemicals made it hard for her to breathe. "You work in this smell every day?"

"You get used to it. I've been tanning for over twenty years and have trained a few others who asked me the same thing." He laughed. "I once trained a blonde to use the open wheel method. She got pretty damned good at it and worked with me for a few years. She ended up having to move back east. They weren't familiar with this method back there. She told me as she interviewed back home for tanning jobs, many of them already knew her as the 'blonde who tans on the open wheel from Wyoming' and were glad to finally meet her. She got a kick out of hearing that. Strange how word travels within a trade."

Over the next hour, Kate understood more about the tanning business, or at least how it worked. She couldn't help comparing it to the procedure done by the women in

Taima's village, staking the hides to the ground and using sharpened stones.

A shiver ran down her back and her fingers ached just thinking about it. "Thank you for taking time for me today, Joe. It's a pleasure to meet you."

"Likewise. Feel free to roam around the showroom. We've got some great things out there."

Kate enjoyed wandering through the store and as she did so, Brandon took her hand. His nearness gave her grounding while memories swam through her mind.

"Ready to head over to Whiskey Basin?"

Kate's heart skipped a beat as Brandon led her back to the car. She longed to return to the place where, in her dream, Taima had died in her arms. "I'm not sure how I'll react when I get there. I'd like to think I could feel some of the spirits who still roam the area."

"You can look around, but I'm not letting you *touch* anything and risk losing you again." His knuckles whitened on the steering wheel as he headed toward the edge of town. They pulled into the rocky basin and just drove for a bit.

She scanned the high rocks for petroglyphs, hoping to connect with them. "Can we stop for a little while? I just want to listen and feel the warm breeze. God, it's nice here." Kate stepped out of the car and stood to look around until Brandon joined her after letting Smoke out for a run. She held out her hand and Brandon took it. "I want to feel if we both connect…not only to the other spirits, but with our own."

He tugged her toward an area of petroglyphs high on the rocks and she held onto the tattered straw hat she wore that shaded her eyes from the sun. Listening to the breeze blowing through the pine trees and rustling the leaves of other trees sounded like whispering spirits. Breathing deep, Kate let it flow through her. Peacefulness soaked into her bones and she felt more at home here than back in Pittsburgh. Blue sky dotted with white wispy clouds floated overhead on a sunny day.

Brandon pulled her close and she looked into his eyes as his knuckle lifted her face to his. He leaned in and their lips touched before he deepened the kiss, his fingers threading through her hair to cup the back of her head. His arm pulled her close; he still held her hand behind her back, their fingers entwined. Kate trailed her hand around his waist and she hoped he would never let go. Closing her eyes, she would swear Taima kissed her and she didn't want this moment to end.

Pulling from the kiss, Brandon took in a deep breath as he searched her eyes. "There are spirits here creating a connection that I've not felt with you before. It's as though I've known you forever. I've kissed you so many times in my dreams and now all of this is real. My heart aches because I'm not sure where we're heading with our relationship, if we can even call it that."

Kate pressed her palm to his chest and as she felt the rapid beat, she also saw the pulsing at the hollow of his throat. "I'd like to think it's the beginning of a new relationship. It makes me feel sixteen again. Does that make any sense?"

"Of course, it does. I'll try not to dwell on the fact that you're leaving soon, but I don't want you to leave." He kissed her nose.

Squeezing Brandon's hand, she regretted that she had to go back. "It's going to be hard to drive away from all of this."

His fingers brushed her hair from her cheek. "I'm just hoping it's not for too long. You belong here. I hope you know that."

Kate's hat flew from her head and landed on the ground, but her head felt as though a rock had hit her. She looked around. "What the hell?"

Brandon scooped up her hat so quick it surprised her. He waved it at something in the air as Smoke ran off howling like crazy.

Then the caw of a raven sounded above them and she watched it land on the tip of a rock.

It cawed again, as though laughing that it had struck her.

The straw hat came between her and the bird and she glanced at Brandon. The muscle in his jaw went taunt; his temple twitched. "Get in the car. I'm not doing this again today with that damned raven." He settled the hat back onto her head and pulled her toward the Blazer as he ordered Smoke back toward the open car door.

Back in the car, she made sure the raven stayed on the rock. It could only be Mai, back from the dead, to torment her and Brandon. She stared at the bird with such anger that her nails dug into her palms and she hoped Brandon hadn't noticed her momentary episode. Smoke paced the back seat, jumped into the far back, and whined at the raven. Brandon didn't waste time getting onto the main road and headed to town. When Kate looked back, she could have sworn she saw the outline of a woman with tangled hair standing where the raven had been. She blinked, shook her head, and the raven reappeared on the rock. "Drive faster."

"We'll go have lunch at the Cowboy Cafe and eat on the deck. Hopefully, we can have a quiet, uneventful lunch."

Determined to enjoy what remained of their day, Kate absorbed as much of the small town as she could, loving the wooden sidewalks stretched before the small shops. A few horses stood tied outside of the hardware store waiting for their cowboys. Brandon held Smoke on a tight leash and they stopped at the cafe, tying him nearby in the shade, but away from the tables. From their table beneath the red umbrella outside the Cowboy Cafe, she eagerly watched life go by in this tiny laid-back community. Tourists meandered through town as they peeked in the shop windows.

Brandon's hand covered hers for a moment. "Look up the street. The kids love this. Watch."

Two workhorses pulled a stagecoach filled with cheering, waving children as they enjoyed their ride. A cowboy sat on top between two little girls who waved at the tourists and they held on tight so they wouldn't fall. Kate could only smile as she watched, just imagining how much fun they must be having.

"The tourists love that old stagecoach. Charlie's been giving them rides for years. I think it gives him something to look forward to each year after winters over. If you can call it winter. We don't get much snow in town, but the mountains make up for what we don't get. Nor does it get really cold. Don't get me wrong, we get our fair share, but it's still on the mild side. Our town gets those warm California winds as they come over the mountains to keep our temps in the low forties most of the winter months."

"I wish I could say that for the east coast. We get slammed with ice and snow all winter."

"All the more reason to live out here, babe."

Kate met his gaze when he said that. He just gave that one-sided grin of his, yet it melted her heart and sounded so natural for him to call her *babe*. Damnit, he made life seem easy living out here with him. A waitress interrupted her thoughts to take their order.

"Hey, Brandon. Good to see you in town for a change. You do keep yourself scarce, hon. What can I get for you two?"

The girl took their orders and brought back their pops. A thundering Harley slowly came down the street and she felt the roar of the engine in her chest. It was as though he watched them at the table. He parked a block from where they sat, but Kate couldn't ignore the dark-eyed stare-down he gave her before getting off the cycle. He removed his helmet and hung it on the handlebars.

Native American.

God, no!

His hair hung to the middle of his back in a ponytail and when she looked at his face, a white scar ran from his forehead, through his eyebrow, and down his cheek.

Her breath caught in her throat as though his own fingers were around her neck.

Smoke lifted his head and looked around as his lips pulled away from his teeth. A low growl came as he spotted the biker.

Kate grabbed Brandon's forearm.

She held her breath as she saw the biker move his stare to Brandon for a moment and then back to her. Hatred is all she could use to describe that look. His boot kicked down the stand, he got off and swaggered in the other direction.

"Kate, breathe. What is it?"

Pain stabbed through her jaw from clenching her teeth. She stared at the spokes in the umbrella overhead as she tried to contain her fear. "Tell me you don't know him…please."

He paused before answering. "I do, sorry."

She stared at Brandon for a moment. Could she sense a past with the biker deep in Brandon's blue eyes? She hated guessing. "Is he always so filled with hate? He is, you know."

"He's been pissed at me ever since I gave him that awful scar. He came at me with a knife when we were kids. He goes by the name of Bear and always seemed to have something to prove to the other guys we hung with."

She shook her head as her fingers stroked her throat, wishing she'd not just witnessed the angry biker. He brought back too many memories and she certainly didn't doubt his hands would roam her body the same as her previous captor in another life. Her stomach flipped and twisted. "This can't be happening. Too many things are the same, Brandon. I'm not sure I can stay here." Taking a slow, deep breath didn't do much to calm her nerves as she shifted in her chair. Kate watched in the direction the biker went, hoping he wouldn't return until they were gone.

"Talk to me, Kate. What about the memories?"

"When I was with Taima…shit! That sounds so lame, but Brandon, it's like it was yesterday." She searched his eyes for understanding and he listened. "I was kidnapped by an Indian with a scar…exactly like the one he has. My god, it's got to be the same soul. I don't believe it. Just the hatred in his eyes could have been enough to tell me that. Fate made you give him that scar."

The waitress brought their burgers and fries.

Could she even eat now?

Kate shook her head. "So much for a peaceful lunch."

"I'm sorry. This isn't how I imagined our day would go. We don't have many left for us. I wanted it to be a time for us to learn more about each other. In a way, I guess we are, since the people around us seem to come from our past."

Biting into her burger, Kate realized she was hungry after all. "This is delicious. Wow."

"I've got an even better supper planned for us."

Brandon ate his burger faster than Kate and she laughed. "How can you top last night's supper? I don't want anything too fancy. Slow and laid-back. Life out here really *is* different than back east. There, everyone's always rushing off somewhere. It makes me realize how much we take for granted. I don't think *you* take anything for granted."

His blue eyes searched her face, as though he wanted to say so much, yet held back. She sat waiting for him to gather his thoughts and got lost in his eyes in the process. Brandon's lips were full and she thought of his kisses, of how he'd already made her toes curl when he touched her. His tongue wet his lips before he spoke and she wanted to lean over for a kiss but thought better of that right here on the sidewalk.

"One thing I *don't* take for granted…is finding you." He watched her and she held her tongue, wanting to hear what he had to say. "I know we have a connection and I want us to experience whatever that brings us. Our pasts are entwined and so is our future. I know it is. I know you must leave to tie up loose ends at home and I pray you return." Brandon shook his head. "I have to trust in that."

Kate nibbled on a French fry and thought for a moment as he lightly caressed her palm, sending tingles up her arm. This man she's connected to has wisdom beyond his years not yet etched on his face. He was beautiful to her, so like Taima. Brandon looked at her the same way.

When he talked, if she didn't look at him, it sounded as though Taima were right there with her. His mannerisms were spot on, the way he held his head, the way he touched her, the way he *kissed* her, for god sakes. "There are so many things I need to clear up at home, but I do see me coming back out here. I want you to trust that I *will* do that."

"The Great Spirit has already shown me that you'll return. My grandfathers have seen it, too. We have all waited a long time for you. A bit longer will mean nothing."

A shadow fell over their table at the same time she heard Smoke growl.

When Kate looked up, she saw the long white scar first.

Bear stared down at Brandon and then at her with a curl to his lip. It was as though he'd sucked all the air from the entire town and she couldn't breathe. "I'm not sure what you see in this half-breed, but rest assured, I can give you a better ride than he could any day. When you change your mind, he knows where you can find me."

Brandon stood and Kate grabbed his arm.

"You better hold him back because next time, he's a dead man." Bear laughed and strode toward his bike.

"Please Brandon, he's not worth it." Her heart raced, glad that a fight didn't happen. The image of Bear killing Brandon flitted through her mind too quickly. Just like Scarface had killed Taima. "His kind doesn't interest me in the least…just so you know."

He stared after Bear until the biker drove out of sight and then sat back down. "Some days there is just too much to deal with when I come into town, which is why I don't. It's easier to ride in the mountains or build furniture. At least at home, I'm not bothered by the outside world."

"I'm sorry I've brought bad happenings to you. Since I've been here, you've had nothing but bad luck, from dealing with me, to that damn raven following us, to Bear and his anger. I'll never understand why people can't mind their own business and leave us alone."

"You've brought nothing but joy to me since you arrived. My dreams have come true, my grandfather's visions are coming true and together, we'll get more answers to what we question." Brandon pushed his plate back and stood. "It's early yet. I'd like to drive out to Brook's Lake and show you around out there. Is this too much in one day?" He laughed and gave her a quirky grin.

Kate smiled, loving the sound of his laughter at the same time. "As long as I can spend the rest of the day with you and learn more about the area, we can explore until we drop." She took Brandon's hand and headed to the Blazer, untying Smoke on their way. Once in her seat, Brandon stood beside her at the open door. His hand touched the top of her hat, tipped it back, and leaned in to kiss her. Warm fingers laced into her hair at her neck as his tongue touched hers and swept her mouth. Her back arched as she leaned into his kiss that ended too soon, yet left her breathless. Brandon stepped back, closed her door and got in on the driver's side.

After he backed into the street and headed for the highway, he reached out to her. She laced her fingers through his and squeezed. "Thank you for showing me so much of your town. I'm recognizing some of the places and feeling the others. Does that make sense?"

His left wrist rested on top of the steering wheel as he drove. A quick glance in her direction and a wink made her smile. "I love your smile. I saw it often in my visions. Yes, it all makes total sense to me. When you told me about your dream of the Indian on horseback near two mountains and about the lake in front of him, I knew I wanted to take you out there. I hope it jars more memories of our past life for both of us. I'm anxious to see if it does because I want to know more about what you experienced. Tell me each time something reminds you of that."

She breathed in the scent of pine and sagebrush. If she moved here, she could enjoy this every day. Antelope played in the distance without a care in the world, chasing one another before taking time to munch the grasses. She and Taima used to sit watching the wildlife, not saying a word, just enjoying the fact that they could be so close with nature.

Could she and Brandon rekindle that kind of relationship if they were true soul mates?

More memories seeped into her mind's eye.

Death and sadness.

Loved ones lost that she'd never get back.

Again, walls closed in around her heart. If she let herself love Brandon, she'd lose him too, in time. History had already taught her that. Her beloved grandparents, one of her best friends, her fiancé, Taima. How many more would die because she dared to let her heart love them?

The pines trees grew thicker and Brandon turned off the main road to head toward the lake up ahead. The huge log resort lodge on the left beckoned to her but they could stop there later. Brandon followed a dirt road around the lake. Images began to form and she could almost hear the laughter of a young boy who drifted through her mind.

Kelee.

Kate smiled. His blue eyes sparkled back at her. She so wanted to reach out and hug him. At least the memories would never fade of their time together. Kelee looked so much like his father and a blue-eyed warrior came in behind

Kelee. Even taking in a deep breath didn't calm her heart.

She looked at Brandon and he turned toward her, his blue eyes wanting to comfort her, yet unsure how. "Taima, no, *you*…you and I used to fish here with y*our* son, Kelee." Kate scanned the shoreline almost wishing Kelee would run out and wave at her. "Taima…you, had taught him so much. I know Kelee must have grown into the man his father would have been proud of. I wish I could remember that part, but I draw a blank when I try to remember beyond that time…that time after Taima died in my arms."

"I'm so sorry you had to experience that. I'm hoping we can build new memories to continue on for us."

Looking out the window into the mountains, her vision blurred as tears threatened to spill down her cheek. "If I let myself get close to anyone else, they will just die, too. That's what always happens, Brandon."

His grip tightened on her fingers and hand. "We will get past that. We're different. I've seen it, Kate. Give us a chance…please?"

She pressed a finger against her upper lip to ward off a sob that tightened her throat. Taking a deep breath was a struggle.

"What do you feel here?"

Looking out over the lake, then toward a huge dead tree laying on the beach area, Kate let her mind go, hoping for more images. Her mouth turned up on one side. "I feel happiness. I'm trying hard to remember so much but we *were* happy here. Taima and Kelee bonded as they fished together over there by the log. Brandon, we were here…so long ago. My god. How can this be? For us to feel and remember so much of the past. I know you probably don't see this because it's so fresh for me. This is a good place."

"Are you up to getting out and walking on the very sand we walked on one hundred years ago?"

Her eyes widened at his question. Could she feel even more if she stood out there?

6.

Kate opened the door and stepped onto the same ground where she had walked with Taima and Kelee so many years ago. As she closed the door, she glanced around for anything familiar besides the dead tree on the beach. In the distance stood the familiar majestic snow-capped mountains covered in pines and the scent lingered in the breeze around her. Brandon must have let Smoke out of the car because he ran directly toward the water's edge.

Brandon stood beside her and took her hand. "Maybe if you close your eyes, it will help bring back the memories."

Holding tight to Brandon's hand, Kate did as he suggested and pressed her fingers between her brows, wanting so bad to see images of her past. She searched the darkness for Taima, Kelee or even Sakima. His name easily came to mind as she remembered Taima's father and his words of wisdom whenever she had needed them. His eyes were the eyes of a wolf, always wary, always knowing, and she realized why now. Smoke was her guardian, just as Sakima had been. Kate listened and soon words echoed in her mind...*I will find you through time and our souls will reunite. Always remember that.*

Goosebumps covered her arms.

At that moment, Brandon's knuckle touched beneath her chin and lifted her face. When she opened her eyes, she could have sworn it was Taima's eyes she searched.

"I will always be here for you and when you're ready, you'll know. I've waited more than a lifetime to find my way back to you."

He removed her hat, pulled her up within his embrace and his mouth demanded hers, his tongue sweeping her mouth. Her arms went around his shoulders and her fingers into his hair, wanting him to be the man she'd longed for. She sucked his tongue to swirl with hers and her breath caught as sparks tingled along every nerve all the way to her toes. Brandon's hand caressed her lower back and then cupped her ass, pulling her tight against him. Memories flowed through her of a love so strong it might go on forever and it made her a bit dizzy.

Brandon pulled from the kiss and Kate looked up at him, their eyes searching for answers neither of them had. She caressed his lower lip with the pad of her thumb. "One day at a time is all I can promise right now."

"I'll take that. I just need to know you'll not give up on what we could have together." He put her hat back on her head.

"I won't. I promise. Let's walk along the shore over to the log. I feel happiness here. Can you feel it? The three of us were a family, with no intruders. This is the lake that I saw in my dreams each time it came to me. How strange." Goosebumps again tingled along her arms. Down river,

Kate saw that Smoke stood still, watching and listening to children fishing on the other side by the main lodge. "Kelee loved to fish here with you." She looked at Brandon. "Have you seen children in our future?"

"I haven't, but it's fun to dream about children with you. They would be beautiful." Brandon laughed again.

She could listen to that all day. "I hope the boys have blue eyes. Kelee and Taima used to try to get me to fish with them, but I don't remember ever doing that. I do fish back home though."

"That's good to know. Fishing relaxes the mind and body. The trout are good out here."

Kate climbed up and sat atop the huge dead tree log and placed her hands flat against it, hoping the past would flow through her palms as she closed her eyes again. A life with Brandon would be different than the life she had back east, alone, working so many hours she didn't have time to contemplate her past. *Could all of this be the reason I am so drawn to the museum and the Native American culture?*

Kate…I will find you.

She opened her eyes to find Brandon watching her. His stance so much like Taima's. The muscular build of his body could make him Taima reincarnated. So, what held her back? A stupid superstition of the damn raven? The thought of those she loved dying before their time?

"Tell me what message you just got." He strode toward her until he stood between her thighs and took her hands in his. "I sensed it, too. Taima's spirit is pretty intense here. He brought you out here, you know. Being here has helped make sense of some of the images I've dreamed of, too. I hadn't put them together before with this whole area, but I can feel a past here."

"Smoke is from our past. Haven't you felt a nearness to him? It's in his eyes and I think his soul is Taima's father, Sakima." More goosebumps crawled over her arms. Pulling her lip in, she met Brandon's gaze. She couldn't help but think of all the signs that led her to this area…the petroglyphs, the mountains, the dream, the lake. "Perhaps it wasn't Taima at all, but you. The dreams you've had of me could have unknowingly sent those dreams to me, even over so many miles that separated us. The more I learn, the more I realize I can't ignore the signs. Your grandfathers even know all that has transpired." She shook her head. "It's like we're puppets in a game of the past."

"Is that so bad?"

"Not at all. But I wish there were some guarantees that no more men that I love will die on me."

"No one can give you that guarantee."

"The man in town with the scar…he's from our past and he scares me."

Brandon cupped her face with both hands. "I will protect you from him."

Kate wet her lips. "Taima said the same thing and yet scar face continued to torment us and in the end, is the one who killed him."

"Life holds no guarantees. If we let those types of things cripple us, we can never move forward."

"I *do* want to move forward. I have to let go of the bad things in the past if I want to move on. Monica continually chides me for that." Kate stood and Brandon wrapped his arms around her. His strong embrace made her feel protected and she moved her hands over his muscled upper back. "I'd love to stay right here forever."

"We *can* make that happen but…you have things back home to take care of first. Speaking of you going back, I hate to think you'll drive alone. I'd like to drive back with you if you'd let me. I can fly home, that's not an issue. I just don't want you driving four days by yourself."

Kate stepped back. "Honest? You would do that?"

"Yes. I don't have anything keeping me from being gone a week or two."

"What are you, independently wealthy or what?"

He looked at her for a moment, as though he contemplated not telling her something. "I'm not hurting for money, if that's what you're asking. I have many different avenues for income." Brandon sat down on the log and she sat with him. "On a bet from a friend, I took a part in a movie he produced and it's getting better screening reviews than we'd hoped it would. I didn't take it seriously and didn't pay attention to the movie critics. The film will be released in three months and Cody said he's already gotten more investors who want him to do a sequel. He called the other day…asking if I'd be interested."

"Again, you're serious!" Kate hoped her dropped jaw didn't tell him just how surprised she was.

Brandon's cheeks flushed.

"You're blushing. You should be proud. Wow. This could be a good thing for you. I hope you told him yes."

"I told him I'd not decided yet. I'm not sure if it fits in with what I'm seeking in my life right now. *You* are what's important to me."

Smoke ran up to them and put his feet on the log next to Brandon. He nudged his master for a pat on his head.

Kate patted Smoke's head. "I don't want to be the reason you don't take what's been offered to you. Brandon, this doesn't happen to just anyone. This could be a once-in-a-lifetime opportunity."

"So are *you* and I'm not screwing that up for a few extra bucks." He reached out for her and she took his hand, reigniting the tingling connection each time he touched her. "Well filming doesn't happen here and I'm not sure *when* it'll begin if I tell him yes."

She stared at him, unsure what to say. *This crazy man would rather give up a movie career than take a chance on losing me.* "I think I'd like it if you came back with me to Pittsburgh, on one condition. You call your friend and find out the specifics on this sequel. Please?"

He nodded. "Deal. I'll call him tomorrow and we'll decide when we head back east. I can fly back here later. When you decide to come back for another visit, I'll get your airline ticket. Nothing is written in stone and we'll play it by ear." Brandon squeezed her hand. "I just want to see you come back again."

"Deal."

"Ready to head for home? I think we received more insight here today. I'm ready for a beer."

Kate followed him to the SUV while Smoke ran ahead of them. Her mind swirled as they drove back to Brandon's place. All of this could happen if she'd open her heart and accept what he offered…a life being doted on by someone who loved her unconditionally. *What more could one ask for?* Against what she'd told herself earlier today, living out here was becoming more of a reality and it felt good. Brandon was a good man, ambitious, and made things happen. They could make a good team.

Brandon pulled into his driveway with his mind racing faster than the engine. Glad that he'd told Kate about the movie deal, he didn't have to feel he was hiding something from her anymore. Driving back east would keep her safe and he wouldn't have to wonder for five days if she was okay or not. And it'd give them more time together which is what they needed right now.

He parked and got out, freeing Smoke from the back seat. "Would having steak again tonight be too much for you?" He put his arm around her shoulder as they walked up the steps of the porch.

"I'd probably eat half of one with a salad. We have potatoes. I could slice them with onions and butter, wrap them in aluminum foil and put them on the grill before the steaks if that works for you."

"It does." His mouth watered just thinking about the buttery potatoes. They liked many of the same things already and Brandon smiled at that. His grandfathers had warned him to be patient for his future. It seemed he'd waited forever for this day to arrive and now it was here. He prayed he wouldn't screw it up. Kate seemed fine with him driving back with her; he'd not seen any telltale expressions that she might be against the idea. She'd said something about looking for work if she came out here, but that wouldn't be necessary unless she wanted to work. He had enough money to keep them both comfortable and wanted to share it all with her.

Opening a beer for each of them, he leaned on the counter and watched Kate slice the potatoes and onions, then wrap them in foil. Watching her work was a delight in itself. She moved with grace and confidence, no matter what she did. Going back east with her was more selfish on his part because then he wouldn't have to say goodbye when she left. Having her around all the time would be like living with your best friend. Sexy images of her in his bed invaded more than his thoughts and he shifted his stance at the counter. Making love to Kate would never get old. She excited him without even realizing it each time she smiled or glanced at him with those warm green eyes of hers.

He'd have to be careful where that part of their life was concerned. A woman didn't make love to just any man, at least not Kate. She didn't seem that kind, but he hoped as they got closer, things would change for them.

I can only hope.

There was that sexy smile again and those searing eyes. "Is the grill ready or were you just enjoying your beer?"

"I was enjoying the company and the scenery. Thank you for being here. You have no idea how happy you've made me in just a few days. I'll go light the Traeger." He set his beer on the counter, glad to move before she noticed his jeans were tighter. She'd hardened him to the point of near-pain and he shook his head. After lighting the grill, he stepped back inside to find Kate in the open living room, looking at everything. She tossed her hat on the end table and combed back her hair. Later, her fingers caressed the back of the leather sofa and he couldn't help thinking of her touching his body like that.

He took in a ragged breath, but it did little to calm his emotions. His blood ran hot with Kate in his home. Or perhaps it was tonight's beautiful sunset and the approaching evening alone with her.

"I love your home, Brandon. The light lodge pole and stone give it a ruggedness without making it a man-cave. That antler chandelier is gorgeous, but then again, I love this kind of decor."

"You can move in whenever you're ready. Always know that." He took a long pull on his beer hoping to cool his insides.

Nope, not a chance.

His blood still hit the boiling point.

The steaks would take his mind off bedding Kate and he pulled them from the fridge, already seasoned. He took out a large platter from the cupboard and reached for a knife to test the steaks later when, from behind him, warm hands slipped beneath his shirt and made their way around to his abs. Soft breasts pressed against his back and Brandon flattened his hands on the counter. If she'd had more than one beer, he could assume it was the alcohol making her do this, but that wasn't the case.

Nails dug into his abs ever so gently, and he swore under his breath.

Brandon sucked in air and groaned it out. "Be careful…I'm already craving to take you right here."

Teeth teased his shoulder and she breathed in deep. "You even smell like *him*." Kate toyed with his nipples. "You're making me crazy, you know."

"Then…mission accomplished." He turned in her arms and cupped her face with hungry lips mere inches apart. "If you belonged to *him*, then should I assume you belong to *me*?"

Kate searched his eyes and he saw how dark her pupils were. Then her tongue moved along her lower lip, making his jeans tighten again and he moaned, imagining where he'd love her tongue right now. "I'll take that as a *yes*."

Almost begging to be kissed, he leaned down and took her mouth with his, their tongues tangling, searching and teasing. He sucked hers into his mouth as his arms embraced her and his hands cupped the ass that fit perfectly into them. Pulling her against his hips, she'd feel his hardness meant for her. His fingers moved up to fist in her hair and he kissed her deeper. After several lengthy kisses, he pulled her head back by her hair so he could see her swollen lips. "I'm glad to know the feelings are mutual."

She breathed in slow. "I knew you wouldn't make the first move and I wanted to feel how warm your skin was."

He chuckled deep. "I think you wanted to see how hard you could make me."

"…that too. Sorry, but I had to know."

"Well, now you do. I want to make love to you, but I don't think we're at that point yet. I'll leave that up to you…whenever you're ready for that step."

"You're such a gentleman. Just don't make me beg." Kate's warm lips pressed against the hollow of his throat. The heat of her tongue made his groin twitch.

Holding tight to the fist of hair in his fingers, he tugged her head back so he could look at her. Within those murky green depths, he saw a hunger he'd not seen before and his heart raced. "Perhaps making you beg would be more fun. We'll see." He slapped her ass. "We'll never eat if I don't get the potatoes started. Get us two beers while I throw these on the grill?" He grabbed the foil package before he grabbed Kate and headed for the bedroom. His mood had stepped up a notch and the future looked hopeful.

"I'll bring them out. We can watch the sun set."

Kate peeked over her shoulder at Brandon heading toward the deck, the muscles of his forearms drawing her attention below his folded sleeve. She loved how the veins popped over the taut muscles…and those strong hands could be so gentle when he touched her. *Just how tender could he be? Damnit, I want to find out but would he think I was too bold?* He didn't think she was too bold when she ran her hands over his abs. She should have let her fingers wander where they *really* wanted to.

In due time.

Let your inhibitions fall away and enjoy what he offers you!

If only she could ignore her conscience and let that happen. Work on it, she would.

Here was a man wanting you no matter what. He doesn't know much about you and wants you anyway…you had him in your arms, crazy woman!

She shook her head, more to lose the devil on her shoulder who tempted her to get into trouble. Her bad-girl side wanted out something fierce and if she let Brandon continue to tempt her, she'd find herself in his bed anyway. Kate bit her lower lip and glanced in Brandon's direction again as she opened the fridge for two beers. At least these were safer than drinking Jack Daniels™. That went straight to her head and made her mind go right into the gutter.

"What's the hold up on those beers, woman?"

"Coming." Kate grabbed her hat, set it on her head and scurried to the door. On the deck, sunlight faded fast and the pink-orange horizon tinged the skyline. Brandon took his beer and sat beside her. Was he thinking of what happened in the kitchen the same as she was? Kate wished it hadn't ended. When he fisted his fingers in her hair, her inner muscles tightened like a coiled spring and were still tight. Being close to him today set those thoughts in motion, unlike yesterday. The more time she spent with him, learning more each day, made feelings for him ignite like the flare of a sparkler, getting hotter as well as brighter. The fact that their paths were destined to join was a little scary, yet exciting at the same time. Not only had he dreamed of their future, but his grandfathers had seen the same visions.

Should I just accept it and forget about worrying that if I loved him, he'd die?

Damnit all!

Brandon opened his hand toward her, but kept his gaze straight ahead as they sat in the large log Adirondack chairs. "Thank you for opening yourself up in the kitchen. It does mean something to me."

She lightly traced her fingertips over his palm until her fingers slid between his, loving the feelings that melted her insides. Her hand looked small compared to his. "I can't believe it's only been three days between us and I feel the way I do this early."

"It's not early and it's not been only three days." He swigged his beer as he squeezed her hand. "Our past gave us the love of a lifetime and more. We have to trust in that and let it happen. I've accepted it and I understand it may take a little longer for you. My visions showed me you coming in search of us…and you're here."

His gaze met hers as though he

spoke facts and, in a way, she knew he did. Her inner struggle came from past relationships that she had to release if she wanted to move on. "Our dreams brought us together across so many miles. I'm not sure how I got to re-experience my time with Taima, but it's like it was meant to be, to show me a love so strong that it had the power to travel through time and bring two souls back together. Who would believe this?"

He squeezed her hand again and did a half turn in his chair. "We don't have to make anyone believe it. Those close to us already know how it works and believe in souls finding one another again. The fact that you're here has to outweigh any inner battles you're struggling with. Let them go. I know you're fighting your conscience about making sense of it all. I'm sorry the men you loved in the past have died. I don't want to dwell on that. Let's enjoy what *we* are building on here. Can you do that?"

Brandon spoke sense to her. She

knew that, otherwise why would she have driven two-thousand miles to find answers. Now she had them and refused to believe in the process. "I know I need to let go of the past if I want to build a future, and I do. Worrying about losing a loved one kills the present and doesn't solve anything."

"Exactly. We can be happy, we both know it. We've both seen it. Fate has put us in each other's path and…I loved being in your path in the kitchen."

Her cheeks lit on fire and the heat moved down her neck. He knew exactly what to say to her.

A smile grew on his lips. "How far down does that blush go?"

"Don't!" She cracked up laughing at herself.

"I love making you blush. You're so cute." He set his beer on the arm of the chair. "I'll turn the potatoes and throw on the steaks. When I come back, I want to find you on your knees begging me to love you tonight." He winked and turned away, not waiting for an answer.

Kate gasped at the thought of kneeling before any man to beg for anything.

Oh my god!

She stared out over the pines as they made their way up the mountainside.

"I guess you've chosen to sleep alone tonight. I'm fine with that."

She jumped, not realizing Brandon had turned to watch her. "What?" He made her laugh too easily.

He laid the steaks on the grill, closed the lid and sat back down. "I'm not sure I can control myself sleeping next to you tonight so it'd be best if you slept alone."

"The other night was *scary*. You have to agree."

"So, I just need to scare you to make you come into my bed...or me into *your* bed? Trust me...that *can* be arranged."

"Don't you dare. We'll see how the night goes." Kate took a long drink of her beer, hoping Brandon would change the subject, but the thought of slipping into his bed tonight did cross her dirty little mind.

7.

Carrying the supper dishes to the sink, Kate thought about their conversation before dinner. She decided that whenever she thought about Taima or her fiancé dying, she'd stop herself right then and there to change her thoughts. That's what they would want her to do also.

She couldn't quit living. A life with Brandon in it could be bright, sunny and full of love.

Hot loving at that.

A shiver ran down her body, zapping every nerve ending she had.

Strong arms embraced her and she leaned her head back against Brandon's shoulder. "Mmmm…shiver again!" He nuzzled at her neck and circled his tongue on her skin, making her shiver once more. "Thank you…I love being the reason you do that." When his fingers lifted her face toward him, she turned in his arms and accepted his deep, demanding kiss. Large warm hands cupped her ass and pulled her hips in, pressing his hardness between them. "God, woman…." Brandon lifted her onto the counter and stood between her thighs as his thumb rubbed down past the zipper of her jeans and pressed on her center.

Tipping her head back, Brandon kissed her throat. A moan slipped out. He squeezed her breast and tweaked a nipple through her shirt. Every one of his touches woke up her sexual needs. Each heated touch made her body betray her thoughts. If he kept it up, she wouldn't be able to stop him, but she wanted him to continue. "Brandon…"

He lifted her shirt and pressed her breasts together, mounding them inside her bra and he met her gaze. "Come on…beg me for more."

"Keep this up and I might."

Fingers reached around and undid her bra and quickly lifted it, with her tank top and hat, over her head, tossing them on the counter. Blood flowed like hot molten lava through her veins, melting her resolve. Brandon could make love to her on the counter for all she cared right now.

Too much beer.

She didn't care.

"Put your hands on the counter behind you."

She did and he cupped her breasts together so he could lick each nipple into rock-hard pebbles. His teeth teased each one and then thumbs and fingers pinched them, getting her attention and she met his gaze.

"You are so ready, aren't you? I know you want this as bad as I do."

If she didn't slow down her racing heart, she'd be panting soon. "You're hard to resist."

"Tell me what you want or I'll stop." His hands went behind her and scooped her ass, pulling her into him. "You want me to make love to you, don't you?"

Her heart raced and throbbed in her

throat. Short shallow breaths were all she could take in. "I do."

"You do, what?" His thumb moved around to caress her again, harder this time.

"I want you to make love to me, Brandon." He had her so hot she'd agree to anything. "Please? God please. Now."

"I knew you'd beg. I just need to get you on your knees and beg for it again." Fingers tightly fisted in her hair, tipping her face up to his. "Trust me, one day that *will* happen."

He kissed her hard this time and she didn't care. Her nails dug into his upper back as her tongue swirled with his. Out of breath minutes later, the kiss broke and he pressed his forehead to hers. Lightly caressing the curve of her breast, Brandon took it full in his hand.

A moan slipped from her throat. "You know exactly what you're doing."

He let out a low sexy chuckle. "You tempted me and I warned you. But I've not gone beyond the line I drew for myself where you're concerned."

Smoke put his paws on the counter and tipped his head at both of them, panting like he was ready to play. Kate patted his soft head. "I don't think you can play this game."

His tail wagged, not understanding. Brandon brushed him off the counter and slipped Kate's top over her head. "There, you don't need to put the bra back on, not on my account. I like you this way." Before she knew it, Brandon scooped behind her knees and held her in his arms. He strode to the sofa and set her down where she sank into the cushions. "I'll get us another beer. Don't go anywhere."

"Yes, sir."

He laughed. "I doubt you'll keep *that* up, but was that so hard to say?"

"No, but I'll work on it and keep *you* hard."

"That's a given where you're concerned, white woman." He handed her a beer and sat next to her.

Kate snapped her head around to look at him, surprised by his choice of words. "I remember Taima using that phrase with me. He used to call me that, too."

"One more reason to believe in our fate."

She cuddled closer when Brandon put his arm behind her, the television came on and Smoke lay on the floor near the door. The day had been a happy one yet filled with information from their past. All of it would mean something for their future, she need only stay sharp enough to recognize how.

Brandon reached over her shoulder and his fingertips caressed the curve of her breast. "I thoroughly enjoyed being with you today. I hope you feel how right this is."

"I do. I'm comfortable around you and don't have to explain every detail when we talk. You understand what I'm trying to convey when I say things."

He kissed her hair. "That's because I *do* understand. It's as though I already know what you're going to say sometimes. I find it almost eerie."

"Like the dreams and visions we've had without ever meeting."

"I know. That day you came into the Mercantile store, I remember feeling something familiar as you walked by me. You were far from an ordinary customer. I don't think you noticed me but I felt you to my bones. I picked up my bag and when I stepped outside, I watched you talking with Shelly at the counter. I let it go, went into the next store and fate brought us together again. I knew I couldn't ignore you that time. You looked like the woman in my visions but I had to know for sure."

"I'm glad you did." She laced her fingers with his at her shoulder. "It wasn't smart of me at the time to let a total stranger in my car. You could have killed me. Not smart on my part."

"You felt it too, that's why you agreed to let me show you around. The winds surprised me at Whiskey Basin that day, as though they were trying to send a message."

Kate traced the denim on his thigh, feeling the tight muscles there. "Making me blackout was a pretty strong message. Then they fed me images of our past in three short days. Damn."

"You did have me worried and I'm glad that's over now." Brandon pulled her closer. "A day filled with new information, a good meal, and a few beers has made me relaxed and sleepy. Tomorrow I'll give Cody a call with my decision on the movie and we'll decide if we leave in a day or two to get you back home. I don't want Monica thinking I've kidnapped you. That'd not be a good way to start my relationship with her."

"I can't wait for you to meet her. She'd love to meet your grandfathers."

"Perhaps one day she will." He winked and she settled in to watch the local news with Brandon. Sleeping in her own bed *would* be a good idea after what almost happened in the kitchen tonight. It was too early for that to be happening between them, even as bad as she wanted it. He'd been right and didn't want to cross that line either. After all, it'd only been three days yet felt like a lifetime that they'd known each other. She'd never understand fate and that finding a soul mate could make your heart lighter somehow. Kate sighed with a smile and finished her beer, resigned to a night of sleeping alone.

The clock on the Bunn blinked six-thirty as Brandon poured a cup of morning coffee. Smoke begged for a head-scratch and nudged his empty water bowl. Brandon filled it and grabbed his coffee. Out on the deck, heat warmed his bare feet as he settled into a padded chair and Smoke lay nearby sniffing the cool breeze. Brandon lifted one sore shoulder and then other, trying to stretch the knots from his back. As he closed his eyes and tipped his head back, the sun's rays welcomed him to a new day. Images of Kate danced through his mind while he thought about his future with her. Even though he knew not going to her room last night was the right thing to do, didn't mean it's how he wanted his long night to go. Tossing in his bed knotted his muscles tight as his clock glowed hourly until he fell asleep at three-thirty.

He hoped Kate had slept better.

The creamy coffee teased him awake with slow sips of the hot brew. Beautiful pine trees on the mountains drew his gaze and a single eagle flew overhead, graceful and care-free. Brandon summed up his life that way so far and now he wanted more. Although the eagle flew alone, Brandon no longer wanted that. A partner for life to ease the loneliness is what he saw in Kate and he prayed to the Great Spirit that her wishes were the same.

Living alone had served its purpose until she came along. The last few days, with laughter and happiness filling his home, were an eye-opener for Brandon. When one doesn't have those things, one doesn't realize what's missing in life. She'd changed all that for him. His visions had hinted at that. Now they were coming true and he wanted it all.

An hour later, Smoke lifted his head and looked toward the patio door. His tail dusted the deck. The slider opened so Kate could join them with her own mug of coffee and wearing her sunglasses. "Good morning, handsome. What a gorgeous day."

She reached for his hand and he pulled her in for a kiss. Soft warm lips touched his own and he took in a deep breath as she sat next to him. "Morning. I hope you slept better than I did."

"I don't know. If you tossed and turned all night like I did, you're probably just as tired." Kate sipped her coffee and looked his way. "If you'd have slept with me last night, I would have lain still and not tempted you."

Brandon swore under his breath as his groin tightened against his jeans just thinking about that. "You laying still would have had nothing to do with me wanting you. Trying to control my urges with you in my arms would have been the problem. Be right back. I need a refill." He stood and stepped to the door for more coffee. "I can't wait until I can hold you in my arms every night though."

With a full mug, he sat back down

and put his feet on the railing next to Kate's feet. Cute little toes, all polished in a reddish brown, wiggled as he admired them.

Kate giggled and he smiled at her. "What?"

"My feet look so small next to yours."

"You're supposed to be smaller. I like it that way. So, when should we head back east?"

"I think in two days. If we leave early, we could get far in twelve hours and perhaps be home in four days. That's how long it took me to get here. Will that give you enough time to get business in order here?"

He nodded. "I can do that and be ready. We should make good time."

"You'll call Cody today, right? Don't miss out on that opportunity. I can't wait until the movie hits the theaters."

"Cody said it's three months out yet. The editors are still putting things together but the backers seemed to like what they've seen so far and want more.

Close friends of mine watch Smoke when I'm out of town. I know he's well taken care of don't have to worry about him. They come here to feed him. Once in a while, they take him back to their place so he can run." A raven screeched in the distance.

Hairs on Brandon's neck stood up and Smoke jumped to his feet. "You don't like that sound either, do you, boy?"

The bird perched in a distance pine tree, not even trying to hide.

Kate looked at him. "I don't want to spend another day being stalked by a bird. At least I'm not wearing a medicine pouch. Mai had given me one to wear before I knew how much damage they could do. She said it would keep me safe from the evil spirits around us and that I needed to wear it close to my heart every day." Kate shivered. "She'd put the eyes of a raven inside of it to help lure my spirit into giving into her powers. God, it all seems so real."

"Let's go inside, make breakfast

and plan our trip. It'll be safer in there." Brandon slid open the screen door. Kate and Smoke went in and he turned toward the raven, his blood near the boiling point. "You'll *not* win this time!" He went in and closed the screen behind him, but the edginess that sparked along his nerves didn't go away. A need to protect Kate kept his guard up. Perhaps his grandfathers would know of a way to be rid of the raven. He didn't want Kate worrying about it every time she turned around.

Kate sat in one of the chairs at the counter and he put his arms around her. She hugged his waist and her hands pressed against the muscles of his back. Her hair smelled like heaven as he held her close, feeling another shiver go through her body. Brandon closed his eyes, wanting to be left alone in their own little world so they could have their happiness without intruders. "We'll get through this, babe. Mai will not win *this time* either." Brandon didn't want to let go of her, but breakfast wouldn't cook itself and his stomach had growled again.

After breakfast, Brandon drove with Kate and Smoke to his grandfathers. With plenty of daylight ahead of them, there'd be no need to worry about leaving in the dark like last time. He and Kate joined his grandfathers in the shade of a huge pine, frustrated that the raven was out of his control. He'd like to shoot the bird. Perhaps that's all it would take…one bullet straight through the heart.

But he doubted the raven had one.

His grandfathers sat in the warm sun and gazed over the mountains. "Nechan, my son, one must always keep positive thoughts up here." He tapped an old finger against his temple. "If fear is allowed to invade the mind like an enemy, it also invites the skinwalkers such as you're both seeing. The raven is alerted to the fear and feeds on it. Sage will help keep them at bay so burn some inside your home."

Kate nodded. "We can do that but I don't understand why bad spirits have followed us. I feel there are more than just the raven. I saw a man in town yesterday with the exact same scar as a man from my past. When he looked at me, it was though he were the same man."

The old man nodded. "Fate sends good and bad. It's up to us to determine how these things will affect us. Then again, we may have no control over that. If in fact, they are skinwalkers, they must be dealt with. Good spirits follow each of you and will guide you as best they can. Take your wolf for instance. He has an old soul from both of your pasts…sent here to protect you. I hope he doesn't have to work overtime."

"You always alert us to danger, don't you, boy?" Brandon patted Smoke on the head. "Grandfather, talking with both of you gives us peace. Kate's anxious to hear more of what you know of the past legends that were handed down to you."

Brandon's great-grandfather held out his gnarled hand to Kate, who sat next to him and she placed her hand within his. Knowing that they accepted her made it easier for her to be here. Brandon wasn't sure how much longer his great-grandfather would be with them but to see him this happy was good.

The old man's eyes seemed to search her face, as if taking it in for memory. "Kelee was my father and he spoke of you often. You look just like he described you. Like an angel among us. He said you made him and his father happy again. Thank you for that." He struggled to breathe but didn't let go of Kate's hand. "It meant a lot to my father that you were such a loving mother to him back then. His mother was only a memory made possible by stories from his father Taima. So often, his stories of you made us laugh when he spoke of you learning the Shoshone ways."

Kate squeezed his hand. "It surprises me how recent the memories seem because of the visions I experienced a few days ago."

"Those visions were intended to remind you of the timeless love you and

Brandon share. Your souls have searched for one another for a long time. You must nurture those feelings and let them grow. Not everyone is granted a love that travels through time to seek us out."

"I promise I will not take it for granted."

Hours had passed since Brandon arrived to talk with his family and he didn't realize it. "We need to get home so we can pack. Tomorrow morning we're driving Kate back home. Her family is worried about her, too. Thank you for the stories."

Early the next morning, Brandon tossed in the last of their suitcases and the cooler with enough water for them. He climbed into the driver's seat, backed out and headed for the highway. "Anxious to get back? We have a long drive ahead of us. I'm glad you're not driving this alone."

"I'm glad that you wanted to join me. It won't be so lonely and we have a long way to go. I called Monica and she's excited to meet you. Mom and dad are, too."

"Will they understand our relationship?"

Kate nodded. "They do. Mom knew I had to find the answers to those dreams. We used to talk about what they meant, yet still never had answers. Now we do. I'm happy about that."

Brandon reached for her hand, loving the connection. This trip would give them more time to connect and discuss where they wanted their lives to go. He prayed her goals were to give their relationship a chance and that she saw a future for them. Kate had already told him she'd give them a chance. Actually, meeting the woman who'd invaded his dreams for so many years had given him hope for what he wanted. IIe needed to be patient, take one day at a time and give Kate space.

Once they arrived at her home, he'd stay a few days and make sure she was going to be fine before he flew back to Jackson Hole, the nearest airport. One of his friends would pick him up, he had no doubt. Kate would love Jackson Hole. He couldn't wait to show her around that city but again, patience is what he needed. This was just the beginning for them.

The third night on the road, Brandon pulled into a hotel in Joliet, Illinois after a grueling thirteen-hour drive. Exhausted and hungry, but happy that he and Kate had become closer with the drive, he turned off the car. "Let's go find a room and then grab something to eat. I need a beer."

After dragging their luggage to the room, Brandon put his arm around Kate on the way down to the hotel bar and restaurant. The muscles in his legs and back took advantage to stretch out. He ordered them a beer and dinner, happy to enjoy a dimly lit quiet corner with his woman.

Kate held out her hand across the table. "Thank you for making this drive with me. We've got about an eight-hour drive tomorrow and we'll be there. I really didn't look forward to doing this alone. It gave us time to get to know each other better."

"I didn't want you driving this far alone either." He squeezed her hand, not sure he'd have the will-power to sleep beside this gorgeous woman for another night without making love to her. "I'm learning to read you a little better. I can tell you're exhausted, too. My back is killing me. I probably should have stopped more often than we did."

Tipping her head in such a sexy way caught Brandon off guard as the lights sparkled green in her eyes. "Perhaps I need to give you a good back rub tonight and relieve you of some tension."

Keeping eye contact with Kate, he took a long swallow of his beer. "Be careful what you offer me. That line I drew for myself is beginning to disappear, woman."

She winked. "Maybe it's time it did."

His heartbeat picked up the pace. His brain went into overdrive as his muscles knotted even more. "Be careful.

Do not tempt me with implications you won't follow through with." He had to laugh.

"I think I can handle whatever might transpire during a soothing back rub for you. Sleeping with you and not doing what we both know we want, is making me crazy. I'm not going to lie." She watched him closely. "I've given it a lot of thought in the past thirty-six hours. I like the man I've been traveling with. I like the gentleman he is, but…I'm done being prim and proper, hon."

Brandon didn't want to hide his reaction to her offer. A back rub would be heaven after sitting for three days in a vehicle. Having her hands on his body made him shift in his chair. "The vixen I've been traveling with has made sitting a real challenge. *I* won't lie. And I'll look forward to a relaxing back rub. Thank you."

"The pleasure will be all mine, I'm sure."

8.

Kate dried her hair while Brandon took his turn in the shower. Dinner had been relaxing after the long drive but tonight, she had other plans for the man of her dreams. Not many other women could say they'd found the perfect man. She had. He was handsome, well-built and a gentleman.

And he wanted *only* her.

Finished with her hair, Kate turned out all of the lamps except a small one over on the desk. She pulled out the sexy nightie she'd brought, tossed the towel on the bed and slipped the nightie over her head.

A groan came from the doorway of the bathroom and Kate looked up to see Brandon watching her as he leaned his head against the doorjamb. The look in his smoldering eyes set her needs on high alert. Imagining him making love to her melted her insides and she wanted him *now*. His towel hung from his hand, hiding her prize behind it and she wished he'd drop the towel.

"Dark green is my favorite color and you look amazing."

His deep sexy voice touched her core. Kate took in his naked body as he turned back into the bathroom. The muscled thighs formed into a tight ass and narrow waist. The muscles of his back and shoulders weakened her knees and tightened her inner muscles. *God, they'd be good together.* She couldn't wait to feel him inside of her, full and tight.

Damn!

Oil! She packed it in her bag. The bottle wasn't large, but they wouldn't need much tonight. Tossing her towel toward her pillow, Kate tugged down the covers and waited on her side of the bed.

Brandon came toward her in black silk boxers and she pulled in her lower lip as she admired his corded chest and arms. He didn't need a gym as long as he had wood to chop. A tingle worked its way down her spine. Those same strong arms comforted her when she needed it and made her feel safe. She patted the center of the bed. "Lay on your stomach. You'll probably fall asleep on me though."

He raised a brow. "Don't count on that. Someone got my hopes up for later and that's likely to keep me awake. I'm not sure those tiny hands and fingers of yours can do much in the way of massaging the knots out of my back." He laid on his stomach in the middle of the bed and twisted his long hair out of her way. "But I know they'll be good on other places later…after you beg for it while you're on your knees."

Grabbing the small bottle of oil, Kate straddled Brandon's thighs, her knees alongside his hips. She poured the oil into her hand, closed the lid, and warmed it before spreading it up Brandon's back from his waist to his shoulders. Her fingers pressed into the muscle cords as she made long strokes, searching for knots. Using her thumbs, she pushed up, found knots and massaged until they disappeared and then repeated on the next one.

The massage was intimate and her mouth got drier as she anticipated what the night might hold for them. She wanted Brandon and was more than ready. Having nothing to do but talk for the last three days, Kate learned more about Brandon. Their connection deepened and she realized how fate had worked overtime to bring them together. Yes, they belonged together. She felt it in her heart and realizing that, she was ready to take the next step. Brandon told her it wouldn't be his decision. He'd wait for her to make the first move.

Tonight would be her first move and she had no regrets about wanting to go through with making love to Brandon. It felt right…especially soothing the stress from his muscles. She knew her touches made him want *her* just as bad.

In order to reach his shoulders, she straddled higher on his hips and that only made things worse for her.

Brandon wiggled just enough that she had to tighten her thighs to keep from tipping off, which tightened other muscles in that area. She tried to keep her mind on the massage, but now she wanted one of her own.

In time, be patient.

Kate breathed in slow.

Her fingers pressed firmly along his shoulders and worked at the tight muscles. Making her way across his shoulder blades, again she kneaded up to his shoulders and down each bicep. Kate couldn't believe the great shape Brandon was in. His body was hard.

And it was *hers*.

She doubted she'd ever tire of having her hands on his body. In a few final strokes, she pressed up and down along his spine, working out the aches and pains for him. Groans of pleasure came from her patient, giving her satisfaction that she'd done a good job. Kate stretched out along Brandon's back and ran her fingers down his arms to entwine with his. The scent of Obsession filled her senses as Kate breathed it in. She pressed her hips against his ass, wanting him more than she could stand.

A groan satisfied her. "That was amazing, thank you."

Placing a kiss on his neck, she moved to lay beside him and admire his peaceful expression. "It's the least I could do with you doing all the driving."

He rolled to his side so he could see her better and his gaze moved lower. His finger traced over the curve of her breast as a hardened nipple puckered. *Does he know how his touch brands me?* She tried to breathe normally. Brandon taunted her, taking his time to tease her senses. When his fingers threaded through her hair, he pulled her close for a kiss that curled her toes. His tongue demanded a reaction as it swept the tender parts of her mouth. She swirled her tongue around his as his body pressed against hers. The hardened bulge between them rubbed her thigh before he raised above her.

"Now it's my turn to relax you. I hope there's more oil."

Kate held up the bottle and he swiped it from her hand, then rolled over her toward the edge of the bed. Getting on his knees at the side of the bed reminded her of a cougar preparing to take his mate. The graceful strength in his body tore at her wants and needs. He fanned his hand toward the center of the bed for her to take her place.

As she moved to lay before him on her stomach, he shook his head. "Off with the nightie. I'll allow you to cover that cute ass with the towel if you must."

Her cheeks heated as she rolled to sit on the edge with her back to him and pulled the silk nightie over her head. She grabbed her towel and wrapped it around her waist. When she turned back to him, Brandon's gaze moved to her chest and he drew in a deep breath. Her stomach flipped to know that she could affect him this way. Laying on her stomach, Kate twisted her hair out of the way and placed her hands out to the sides. Her nerve endings already sparked with sexual tension and he'd not even touched her yet.

Brandon straddled her hips and made her wait. "God, you're beautiful…and so perfect."

She could almost feel the path his gaze took over her shoulders and down her back. It

seemed like she'd lain there for several minutes. Perhaps this was his way of creating more mood for her.

Still, she waited.

Warm oil dropped onto her middle back, up her spine and over her shoulders. Strong hands fit her body like a mold, his thumbs moving over the muscles along her spine, back and forth, relaxing her as he massaged. His fingers worked the tender muscles along her ribs, then up over the sides of her breasts and she moaned as her nerve endings sparked beneath his touch. Taking a deep breath, Kate relaxed as though she floated while Brandon worked to release the tension from her body like a skilled masseuse. Each hand worked one of her arms, kneading over and over and she thought she'd drown in pleasure.

"God, you're good with your hands."

"I'm just getting started on you. Give me an hour."

Soon, Brandon scooted down her legs and before she realized it, her towel moved and her ass was bared for his viewing. She gasped and clenched the sheet in her fingers. Even though he couldn't see her blush, Kate's cheeks heated. Oil landed on her ass and then…seeped between her cheeks. Brandon cupped her ass in each of his hands and gently kneaded until she was almost dizzy. The oil worked between her cheeks each time he moved them.

"I feel like we've done this before, like Deja vu. It's as if I know your body as well as the back of my hand. Your body is putty in my fingers, to mold the way I want. I love touching you, white woman. You were made for me."

His voice soothed her emotions and paved the way for a sexually tension-filled night ahead. Kate was relieved to hear it wasn't just her imagination that all this seemed familiar. Loving

Brandon came easy to her and she wondered why she'd fought it since waking up in his home that morning. Visions of her and Taima together drifted through her mind when she realized it was her and Brandon.

"Turn onto your back. And don't argue with me."

"Yes, sir." She turned over as instructed. It's not like he'd never seen her naked breasts before, so why did this embarrass her when she wanted it so badly?

"Keep your eyes closed and your arms out to the side."

Again, he straddled her thighs…above her center and she couldn't help flexing her hips upward. Brandon started with her breasts, massaging, oiling, licking and sucking her nipples. She tried hard to keep her moans to herself but one or two slipped out. Then his hands massaged her ribs while his fingers reached her back and made their way down her sides to her hips. Brandon moved but she dared not open her eyes. When he separated her thighs and moved between them, Kate held her breath. Now she lay open to his inspection and she was glad for the dimly lit room.

A package tore open and her stomach twisted. She knew that sound, glad that he'd brought protection for them.

Again, she waited.

More movement.

Warm lips touched below her navel as Brandon slowly kissed his way up her body, his hands moving along the mattress. Anticipation stalked her, wanting him so bad she couldn't stand it. His lips lingered on one breast, then the other. Soon, the pressure of his body lay atop hers, his fingers fisting in her hair as his mouth devoured hers. Wrapping her arms around him, Kate held him tight as her fingers dug into his corded muscles. She loved that his kisses demanded a reaction from her, like she could refuse that. Every fiber in her body sparked like a snapping wire. Her hips flexed up again as she felt him at the entrance to her center and slowly, he eased forward, filling her as she'd dreamed he would.

When she tightened her inner muscles around him, Brandon broke the kiss and groaned against her shoulder. "Keep that up, woman, and this will be over before we both want it to be." He raised up on his elbows and looked at her as he slowly moved inside of her. "This is exactly how I imagined it would be."

Kate pulled her knees up and wrapped them around his hips.

"I warned you and again…mmmm…you didn't listen." He thrust and she pushed up, creating a rhythm that seemed to take her over the edge and back. Stars burst around her, or so it seemed. She kept pace with Brandon and when she sucked in a deep breath and felt herself nearly burst into flames, her release was more than she ever thought possible. He held her head and kissed her hard again, her tongue swirling with his as their sex heated another degree and tears pooled in her eyes.

Brandon shivered in her arms, his body taut as he peaked. Kate moved with him until he slowed and then rolled with her onto his side. "Did I hurt you? Why are you crying, babe?"

His thumb gently wiped her cheek. "There was no pain, but the passion between us is so tender, I couldn't help it." She touched her lips to his and looked at him through blurred vision.

"I can't explain what you just made me feel. I only know how beautiful it was."

He pulled her close against his chest with his chin on her head as she cuddled within his embrace. The beat of his heart matched hers that still seemed to race out of control. She took in slow deep breaths, loving the smell of his body. When fingers threaded through her hair and down her back, they touched her soul. The all-powerful cougar could be gentle when he made love and he'd taken her over the edge more than once. Happiness swelled to waves of joy as another tear blurred her vision.

Would he understand her emotions or think it silly that he'd made her cry?

A knuckle beneath her chin brought her face up to his. "I will cherish this night in my memory forever." Brandon kissed her nose. "I want nothing more than to spend the rest of my life being loved by you."

His deep whisper caressed her senses and Kate knew he was right. "I could say the same.

I think you made me see stars tonight." She touched her fingers to his lips as he smiled.

"I'm glad I could do that. You've exhausted me in a matter of minutes. Our connection is different than any I've ever experienced. It's just different…as you are different."

After a small breakfast the next morning, Kate looked forward to getting home. That would happen by late this afternoon. She was anxious to see Monica and her parents. They'd love Brandon like she did. Especially once they realized he was the answer to her dreams, but Monica is the only who'd truly understand.

Brandon reached for her hand and she entwined her fingers with his. "You're amazing, you know that, right?"

Even several hours after they'd driven today, Brandon still made her blush. She giggled.

"You've told me that at least five times already today, silly."

"I just want you to know that."

She shook her head and smiled. "I do. I'm glad we won't be going through Chicago at rush hour on this turnpike. It gets insane at five o'clock." Tractor trailers raced by like freight trains in the westbound lanes on their way to deliver goods from the east coast. *Would she miss this insanity?* No!

"Traffic gets worse than this? And those toll gates are nuts! I'm glad we don't have those out west."

"Somebody has to pay for the wear and tear this traffic causes on the roads." Kate helped Brandon navigate the roadway as they headed toward

Pittsburgh and thoughts filled her mind of what she'd tell her boss. She knew in her heart she wanted to move to Wyoming to be with Brandon. Her parents would think she wasn't being rational, but she didn't care. It was her life and she knew what she wanted. Last night made her realize that.

A few hours later, she had Brandon turned onto the Pittsburgh exit. "We're almost there. Are you ready to meet my parents?"

Brandon concentrated on the road as he answered her. "I am. I hope they like me, but if they don't…I guess we'll cross that bridge if it happens."

Kate's cell phone rang. "I knew Monica would be calling soon. Hey woman!"

"Where the hell are you? I'm tired of waiting to meet this Romeo of yours."

"We just turned off the exit and should be at my place in half an hour. Can you be there?"

"You bet your ass I'll be there. I'll bring the champagne. See you in a few.

I know you have me on speaker! Hi Brandon! Later chicky!"

Monica hung up. "I better call my parents so they can be at my place, too. I told mom last night that I'd call when we got close." She made the call short, knowing she'd have to give Brandon directions to the small home she rented in a quieter part of Pittsburgh.

As they turned into her driveway, Monica and her parents sat on the porch of her little bungalow. "This is pretty small compared to *your* home. I hope you're not claustrophobic. It works for me with living alone and I'm not here much except to sleep."

Brandon took in a deep breath as he shut off the car and waved at her parents. "I'll be fine." He squeezed her hand and winked. "Let's do this."

Monica met her at the bottom of the stairs, dressed in her straw cap with a black band and sunglasses, squealing and hugging her tight. When she turned to Brandon, Monica paused, removed her sunglasses to look him up and down while she covered her mouth. "Oh my god, you lucky shit." She paused again as she stared. "Turn around…come on, humor me." Kate laughed as Brandon slowly turned around for her.

"Do I pass inspection?" Brandon held out his arms.

Monica nodded slowly. "Yes…you…do. Come here so I can hug you."

Brandon had to bend down to greet Monica and she tried to wrap her fingers around his biceps, making Kate laugh. "He's not a piece of meat and you aren't an inspector."

"I am now!" Monica's gaze continued the head-to-toe once-over.

He stepped back. "It's nice to finally meet you. Kate's told me all about you. She's lucky to have such a precious friend." Brandon glanced toward the porch where her parents were and headed in their direction.

Kate watched him shake her mother's hand and her father's as he stood up.

Her dad wasn't quite as tall as Brandon. "Thank you for taking care of my daughter and for driving across the country with her. When she gets a wild hair, there's no controlling her. I tried to get her to fly out there, but she said she wasn't sure where she was stopping."

"She *does* have a mind of her own and quite a stubborn streak," said Brandon.

He appeared comfortable in meeting new people. Kate relaxed, glad that her parents seemed accepting so far. "Let's go in and decide if we're going out to supper or what." She smiled all the way to the kitchen where she grabbed a few glasses for champagne. Monica set a cooler on the counter and pulled out one of the bottles. Brandon did the uncorking and Monica filled the glasses, then offered a toast to new friendships. Watching the two interact with each other made her smile. Kate could stop worrying that Monica might not like her handsome warrior with the chiseled jawline and muscled body. She counted herself fortunate to have found her dream.

Wondering how everything had

worked out so well, Kate sat amazed to watch her parents and Monica welcome Brandon to their circle. He remained calm and answered all questions they threw at him.

An hour later, they headed to the local steakhouse to get better acquainted. Brandon reached for her hand beneath the table and gave it a squeeze. He leaned close to her. "I'm glad I'm here and things are going well so far."

Dinner went better than Kate could have planned and when they got home, her parents said goodbye. They told her again to guard her heart and be careful, Brandon seemed like a nice guy. Monica stayed to relax in the living room with her and Brandon. Kate leaned against him as he wrapped his arm around her shoulders while she filled in all the details she could remember. Monica, who never sat so long without speaking, listened intently and held back her questions.

Brandon was glad Kate had a bottle of Jack Daniels™. Champagne wasn't his favorite. A drink or two was all he could handle, but he didn't want to hurt Monica's feelings after just meeting her. Long, wavy auburn hair fell over one shoulder as she pulled it forward. She stood as tall as Kate but wasn't as thin, not that he thought she was overweight by any means. He considered her voluptuous and a woman any man would be happy to call his own. Especially the full cleavage that peeked above the V-neck top she wore. Her green eyes were more hazel today and she looked at him with more knowledge than he was comfortable with. Being psychic gave her insight normal people didn't have and he could tell she processed everything around her and then some.

Monica met his gaze. "When you were wearing Kate's ring around your neck all those years, what did you sense and feel?"

He watched her, trying to gauge exactly what she might be getting at. "The visions of Kate started almost as soon as my father passed on the ring to me when I was twenty-one. The images became more clear as the years went by until she was etched in my memory. Pieces of our past life together would come to me and I didn't understand them all until Kate and I talked about so many things these past two weeks. She filled in parts I didn't know. I filled in some she didn't know." Brandon looked at Kate and pulled her close. He kissed her hair and breathed in the scent of heaven, relieved that he'd finally found her.

"I can tell by watching both of you that you have a connection not many have. You have a *connected past* not many have. You know that, right?" Monica kicked off her sandals and stretched her legs up on the sofa. "People, and even pets around you, have souls that are from your past. They're here so they can continue to protect the love which grows stronger within your hearts. You are both lucky to have found a love that's traveled through time to reconnect. Don't abuse that."

Kate ran her hand down Brandon's

thigh as Monica spoke and he couldn't wait until they were alone again. When Kate looked at him, he couldn't help but smile. "We're learning how much we do have in common. It's eerie, but erotic at the same time."

Monica scrunched her nose. "What do you mean 'it's eerie'?"

"I feel like there are spirits around us at times. I have no idea who they might be or what they want."

"Both of you have spirits with you. Some good, some not. Don't be alarmed. You'll figure out how to deal with the bad spirits. Stay positive and keep your love vibrant. I feel a great-grandfather from your past is around you, Brandon. I'm not sure what he does but he's always with you when you're at home."

He looked at Kate. "Grandfather told us the same thing the other day. He said Smoke was from our past."

Kate's eyes widened. "When Smoke came into my room that first day, I sensed something familiar about him. And he hates that raven!"

About to take a sip of her champagne, Monica stopped. "What raven? I knew you weren't telling me everything."

9.

Brandon rubbed Kate's shoulder as she tried to explain the problem to Monica. The muscles there were tense and knotted so he made a mental note to check that area for her before they went to sleep later.

Kate talked with one hand, motioning to Monica as she held her champagne glass in the other hand. "While I was *dreaming*, a shape shifter threatened me because she wanted Taima, well, Brandon, all to herself and that I was a threat. She gave me a medicine bag to wear, telling me it'd keep me save from the evil spirits and that I should never take it off. I didn't know any better. In time, it allowed her to take over my soul and she nearly killed me to get me out of the way."

"She's the raven. I can see it." Monica nodded.

"What do we have to do? It follows us everywhere at Brandon's place. It sits in the trees, on the railing around his deck, in the mountains when we least expect to see it. The damn bird even attacks us, like the day it flew in and knocked a glass of water off the deck post. Glass shattered everywhere."

"And things are escalating, aren't they? What's happened recently out of the ordinary?" There was that frightened look in Kate's widened eyes again when she turned to him. Brandon didn't like rehashing all this, but Monica needed to know. "Tell her what happened at your grandfather's the other night as we left his place."

Brandon still couldn't believe what he'd seen that night, but gave Monica the details of the crazy woman who jumped onto the hood of his truck. "She climbed up onto the windshield like some psycho woman. Her hair was all matted and her eyes held so much hate that it even scared me."

"She knows Kate is taking more of your time and more of your emotions.

Who is this woman to you? Someone close?"

"No. She works at the local mercantile store. Her name is Shelly. She's never given me any indication that she's interested in me. We talk a little when I stop at the store, nothing more than that."

Monica raised a brow. "To *you* it may not seem like a big deal, but to her...*you* are why she goes to work every day. Just for the chance that you might stop in to see her. Be careful and don't go in there alone if you can help it. Does Smoke ever go with you when you visit this woman? If he does, watch his reaction to her. It might prove interesting."

He scanned his memory but didn't remember ever taking Smoke into the store. "I'll take him in with me next time I go into town at the store. She seems pretty harmless though."

Kate shook her head. "That's what Taima said about Mai, too, and look what almost happened."

Monica straightened out her legs in

front of her and put her feet back on the floor. "I'm glad you're back here where I know you're safe. I've missed talking to you and I worried too much. I have my own visions of you both, you know. What I saw worried me. I just didn't know how true the visions were. Now you've confirmed that what I saw was *indeed* true."

Monica's friendly smile seemed to relax Kate. Brandon was glad for that. The long drive had worn him out and Kate yawned. Lights came on in the living room and he saw they were plugged into timers. Smart idea while she was away. Her cozy house was just big enough for her or a starter home for a young couple, but he was glad he didn't have to call this home. He liked his open floor plan with lots of space.

"I should go. You two have had a long four-day drive and look exhausted. Sorry, but you do." Monica got up and took her wine glass into the kitchen. Kate followed and hugged her friend. "Call me tomorrow when you're rested and the three of us can go do lunch or something."

Kate locked the front door after Monica left. The house appeared secure with plenty of locks so that he wouldn't have to worry about her if he had to fly home alone for now. Brandon leaned against the kitchen doorway to admire Kate. She rubbed her shoulders and then rolled them several times as she walked toward him. He held out his arm and pulled her close. The smell of her hair would always stay with him as she lay her head against his chest. He loved how she fit perfectly within his embrace as his fingers caressed her warm skin. "God, I love holding you. I'm glad I came along for the ride." He kissed the top of her head.

"I don't think I realized how glad I am that you drove home with me. Thank you for that. Mom and dad seemed to like you, but I'm sure I'll hear more from them tomorrow." Kate looked up at him. "I'm exhausted and need a hot shower. I know you are, too."

Threading his fingers behind her

head, Brandon pulled her in for a kiss. Kate's lips opened when his tongue slipped between them. Her arms hugged him and his hands slid down to cup her ass. He pulled from the kiss before he carried her to the bedroom. "You make me crazy." He pressed his forehead to hers. "We'll sleep better after a hot shower. Show me around so I know where things are."

Brandon liked the way Kate had decorated with calming earth tones as he followed her through the hall to her room and master bath. Nothing appeared out of place, the dressers were clear, the bed perfectly made and throw pillows lay near the head of the bed. Everything looked as organized at Kate seemed to be.

"I know it isn't as large as you're used to, but I hope it works for you. Let's go back to the living room and I'll show you how to work the remote. You can watch television while I take a shower." She instructed him how her remote operated. "Help yourself to whatever you find in the kitchen. The

Jack is still on the counter. I won't be long and then you can get in."

"I can't join you?" He winked at her, waiting for a reaction.

She stopped in the hallway and glanced over her shoulder. "I'll leave that up to you." With a soft smile, she headed to the bathroom.

The gentle sway of her hips set off his sexual thoughts. Memories of last night came back to him as he relaxed in the chair and reflected on the last few days. Traveling with Kate and spending time with her had allowed them to become closer. No one in his life had ever had this effect on him. Even though they'd only met two weeks ago, she'd actually been in his head and dreams for years. To finally have found her had changed his life and he thought about settling down in the near future with the woman of his dreams. For now, his heart was happy and it kept a smile on his face. He just hoped her parents would bless their union; it would make life easier. Brandon swirled the ice in his empty glass. *Would they accept me as a half-breed? I can only hope.*

Brandon stood and strode to the kitchen. He splashed a quick shot of Jack into his glass and swallowed it down, loving the burn, but he wanted to pick up a fifth of Single Barrel™ tomorrow that had a smoother taste.

He made his way to the bedroom to get his things from the suitcase and surprise Kate in the shower. Her hair should be washed by now. Images of her naked body swam through his mind and he smiled at the unmistakable connection they had. Their future life would be good. He removed his clothes and quietly stepped into the bathroom.

The shower curtain had a clear top half so he couldn't surprise Kate. She placed her face near the curtain as her gaze moved up his body before making eye contact. He had to smile at her curiosity. "Now I know how women feel when men ogle them as they walk past a construction zone. You are so bad, woman!" He opened the far end of the curtain and stepped into the shower with her.

She wrapped her arms around his waist and he cupped her face for a kiss. "You make me crazy. You cloud my judgment and make me do things I shouldn't…like carry you soaking wet to the bedroom."

She slowly turned both of them so the water hit his back and soaked his hair. "I'd have a mess to clean up later if you did that."

Warm lips touch his neck and her tongue made tiny swirls over his chest with each kiss, sparking every nerve ending on the way to his already hardened penis. "That will get you into trouble if you keep that up, not that I'm complaining, mind you." Brandon flexed his hips forward as he gripped Kate's ass. Her cheeks filled his hands as he pulled her tight against him. He had no doubt that after he made love to her, they'd both sleep well tonight.

* * * * *

Kate awoke to warm sunshine through the window, with Brandon's arm draped over her waist and wondered how many women were as lucky as she was, to be sleeping with a man who'd stolen their heart away. Her clock read almost nine. She'd have to call her boss today but didn't want to think about that now. Turning slowly beneath Brandon's arm, the muscles in his biceps corded beneath his skin and veins protruded even as he slept. She trailed a nail over his chest and down his abs, watching his face for a reaction.

His eyes opened. "You looking for trouble again, gorgeous? Last night wasn't enough for you and you need more of me today?"

Brandon's deep, sexy voice was something she could get used to hearing every morning. "I'm always looking for trouble if you're involved. That's the best kind." She tweaked his hard nipple and he grasped her hand to kiss her fingers.

Brandon groaned. "That will start something we don't have time to finish this morning. And you're going to turn me into a lazy bastard if I keep living in this time zone. Good thing that isn't happening."

"It's already nine o'clock. This time change is kicking my ass and I'm *from* here! I'd *prefer* to live out there with you." Kate wanted to give him an answer on moving but knew her job came first now. "I just wish I could give you a date when that will happen."

He pulled her close and kissed her hair. His cologne clung to his skin and tempted her senses as he released her and met her gaze. "I'm not pressing you for a date that you plan to move. You have too many things going on here that you need to take care of. I'm a patient man. If I know I can talk to you every day and spend a weekend with you here or out there, I'm good with that."

"You're sure? That's asking a lot of you." She kissed his lips, loving how tender he was with her. "I don't deserve a man as patient as you are. Thank you for that." She rolled and sat on the edge of the bed. "I'll go make the coffee and call my boss to see what's happening at the museum."

Brandon stretched and felt the sore muscles in his back. He missed his own bed. Some of those hotel mattresses weren't fit to sleep on. Tugging on his jeans and t-shirt, he padded barefoot into the tiny ten by ten kitchen and looked around. Far smaller than he was used to. Kate deserved to live in a larger house and he knew just the place for her. She talked on the phone so he kept quiet and poured their coffee. In the fridge were a few necessities they picked up before reaching her home yesterday, half and half being the most important for their coffee. He added creamer to their two mugs and sat one in front of Kate.

"What do you mean something happened last night? I worked so hard to make that section of the Native American village." Kate threw up her free hand as she talked. "How could birds get into the museum? That doesn't make any sense."

Brandon sat down at the small table with her and his intuitions began to flutter through his mind. Birds at the museum? Just *maybe* it was a fluke and not what he first thought as he tasted his coffee. The brew wasn't half bad with creamy hints of cinnamon and hazelnut.

When he looked up at Kate, she shook her head and ended the call. She sipped at her steaming coffee as her finger tapped the back of her phone. "This is going to sound as crazy as the past two weeks have been. As you heard, Tom said birds broke a window and got into the museum. They pecked at all the straw I used on the teepees, scattered it over the section I painstakingly worked on, and shit all over my section! We'll have to tear it apart and rebuild most of it. I don't have time for that."

Brandon looked at her across the table, but didn't want to speak of what he thought.

Kate sat still, chewing on her lower lip. "You're thinking the same thing I am, I can see it in your eyes. She's followed us *here*, hasn't she? What the hell? How do I fight this, Brandon?" A tear slipped down her cheek and she swiped it away with her fingers. "I refuse to let her win."

He reached across the table and took her hand. There was nothing he could do to calm her and hated feeling helpless in all of this. *Why are these spirits haunting us from so long ago?* "Should you call Monica and have her meet us at the museum? I'm pulling at straws here, but maybe she has a better idea than we can come up with."

Kate's phone buzzed and she turned it over to answer Monica's call. "Hey."

"What's going on today? My visions are in over-drive and your name keeps coming to mind."

"I don't know how you do it. You know everything. I have to go down to the museum. Birds broke windows to get in and destroyed the teepee village I created. Can you meet us there in forty-five minutes? Great. See you then, hon." Kate laid down her phone and emptied her mug.

"One more cup of coffee and then I need to get over to the museum." She grabbed the coffee pot and cream to refill both mugs.

Brandon loved watching her. His heart swelled just knowing he'd finally found the woman he'd dreamed about for so long. He reached for Kate as she stepped back to the table after returning the coffee pot and pulled her to stand between his thighs, hugging her close. Her heart pounded against his ear.

When he looked up at her, she cupped his face and her warm angel lips met his for a moment. "You make my heart happy, Brandon. I'm glad you're here with me. I can't bear to think of you going back home, so I won't."

"I would prefer to hold you in my arms forever and keep you safe, but we can't do that either." He kissed her again. "One day at a time is all we can do right now. Let's finish our coffee and then head over to see the damage. I'll help you repair things as best we can." His hands moved over the swell of her ass and he couldn't resist a gentle squeeze before he released her. He could keep her safe from the real threats. It was the unseen spirits he felt around them that he was unsure of. An eerie sense of foreboding had been with him all morning that he couldn't shake. Maybe once they got out of the house, he'd feel better.

Kate put her ringer on loud and dropped her phone in her purse as she gave Brandon directions to the museum. Her eyes scanned the trees and rooftops they passed and different birds perched on wires, yet didn't see any ravens. That didn't mean she could relax. She couldn't put her finger on the feeling of gloom that seemed to surround them today. Perhaps it was just because of the damage at work and once they fixed it, she'd feel better.

The car stopped at a traffic light and a group of motorcycles pulled up behind them, the engines making her SUV vibrate. A shiver shot up her back. Kate glanced in the side mirror. All the riders wore helmets with face shields so she couldn't make out who they might be. When she glanced at Brandon, his gaze was locked on the rearview mirror and when the light turned green, he slowly pulled ahead through the intersection.

"There's the museum, hon. We need to turn left up there." After Brandon turned into the parking lot, Kate watched as the motorcycles drove down the street. She couldn't make out the license plates. Brandon parked and she got out as three of the motorcycles stopped at the curb down from the parking lot. Thinking nothing of it, she headed toward the entrance of the museum. Kate opened the door and noticed that Brandon wasn't right behind her, but instead, stood a few feet away staring at the men on the motorcycles.

He glanced toward her and then back at the riders. When he took a step toward them, they raced off down the street. Brandon shook his head and rubbed his jaw as he walked toward her. He looked behind himself one more time, then turned toward her. "Let's go inside and survey the damage. I'm curious about this." He held the door and she entered, but turned to be sure he followed. The riders had given her an eerie feeling.

She took Brandon's hand for comfort as she led him through the halls toward her section. Today the building felt different than before she'd left. Now more shadows hung in the corners and even though she knew the cameras were there for security, something else watched her back. Kate turned to look behind her down the hall. She blinked and stared again at what seemed to be a dark form before it dissipated.

A chill crept down her arms and she squeezed Brandon's hand before stepping into the large room that held her creations. She smiled with pride as Brandon slowed to look at the figures and read a few of the information boards.

"Everything in this room is what I've put together so others can learn about the different tribes in the area when the white man stepped foot on their land." Kate turned to survey each setting carefully until she saw the figures of Iroquois Indians laying on the floor, their teepees shredded by claws. She let go of Brandon's hand to hurry over to the fallen figure, the colorful hair pieces she'd worked so hard to put together now torn to bits. Hair and beads lay strewn over the floor among the straw and tall grasses she'd glued into place. All of her hard work had been shredded in one night. She knelt to pick up one of the damaged head dressings she'd made and beside it lay a long black feather.

Shock widened her eyes

Kate picked up the feather and turned it over.

Blue-black in color.

A raven cawed outside the window, knotting every muscle in Kate's body. She glanced over her shoulder at Brandon just as he looked up toward the broken window. "I'll be right back!" he called as he ran out the door.

The village scene before her blurred as she sat back on her feet and pounded her fists on her thighs. Warm tears streaked her cheeks. "You can't be here! Leave us alone. Haven't you done enough damage?"

A woman's faint laughter came from outside the window, and Kate's blood nearly froze in her veins.

Fingers gripped her upper arms from behind and Kate lunged forward to fight off her attacker and spun around, ready to pounce. She crouched on all fours facing him.

Tom jumped back and held up his hands. "Kate, hey, it's okay, hon. I was hoping I could have met you at the door before you saw all of this damage."

Still on all fours in front of Tom, Kate let out a breath, but her heart still pounded like a drum. When she stood up, he held out his arms to her and she stepped into his embrace, hoping for a small dose of protection at this point. She hugged him tight, but his comforting support couldn't stop the tears that pooled in her eyes. Too much had happened today. Her strength began to seep from her body as though the raven outside had some kind of control over her mood.

Tom held her tight as his hands rubbed down her back. "Shhh, we can fix this."

Kate hated that her emotions got the best of her and that Tom caught her crying. *I'm stronger than this, damnit.* She stepped away from him and wiped her eyes, her heart feeling as though she'd been stabbed. "I put so much work into this display."

He shook his head.

Kate shook her fist. "Well, what I don't understand is how the bird even lived after breaking the glass. That would have killed a normal bird, Tom!"

Brandon strode back into the room with Monica at his side. Kate saw his tense jaw and narrowed eyes. "This damage wasn't done by a normal bird. We need to board up the window. There's a raven still in the tree just outside. Whether it's the same bird that did all this, I can't say."

Monica came to hug Kate and whisper in her ear. "We need to talk, but not in front of Tom."

10.

"Thanks for coming, Monica. What a mess." Kate met Brandon's gaze and he nodded. She fisted her hands. Her worst fears were coming true and she didn't know how to stop them. All she wanted was to be happy with Brandon, yet these spirits insisted on interfering. Kate searched Brandon's eyes for answers and guidance, yet somehow, she already knew the truth. "She couldn't possibly have followed us?" A quick glance at Monica told her differently and confirmed her worst fears.

Brandon shrugged a shoulder and shook his head. "Anything is possible at this point."

Tom's brows knitted together. "What are you talking about? You know how this happened or who may have done this?" He looked from Brandon to Kate.

Kate sighed. "Not actually. We're just guessing. As strange as it sounds, we had problems with a raven in Wyoming at Brandon's place. It's a long story." Kate pressed on her forehead between her brows, wishing the pain would leave. "I'm sorry, Tom. This is Brandon Wakiza. The reason I went out west in the first place."

Brandon stepped forward to shake hands with Tom and then turned toward the damage. "I'll help you clean this up and repair what we can. Tell me where to start." Brandon stood up one of the Iroquois figures, carefully placing it back on the rod that held it upright.

"I'll see what I can do about boarding up the window until the repair company can get new glass for us." Tom headed toward his office.

Kate picked up the headpiece for the Iroquois and sat it back on top of the figure. *All of my work has been destroyed and now I have to start over!* Her emotions balanced on the edge. "I'll need to grab the glue gun so I can fix all this." Again, her senses overwhelmed her. She covered her mouth, but couldn't stop the hiccup sob that slipped from her throat. Brandon pulled her into his arms, and for a moment, she knew she was safe. Monica took her hand and squeezed it. Kate hugged Brandon tight, breathed in the scent of Obsession and closed her eyes. If only for a moment, she blocked out everything but Brandon's protection. "Why can't we be left alone to be happy? What does all this have to do with us?"

"I don't know, babe. We'll figure something out." He held her head in one hand and kissed her hair. "I've no idea how Shelly got here. I'm sure she's the shapeshifter, but the motorcycle guys have me worried, too."

Monica moved into their little circle. "What guys? That might explain some of the visions I had this morning."

Kate leaned back so she could see Brandon's face. "I saw you watching them. I guess I didn't want to think the worst, so I tried to ignore them. He wouldn't have followed us all the way here, would he? Do you think *he* brought Shelly?" Kate shook off those thoughts and moved away from Brandon. "Okay, now *I'm* sounding crazy. I'll go get the glue gun so I can get this stuff fixed. Thanks for helping, babe." She stepped off the display floor and turned to Monica. "I'll be right back. Thanks for coming to help us." Kate strode to her workroom for the glue, but an evil foreboding wouldn't leave. The walls of the museum seemed to be closing in around her. As she gathered the items she needed, she gasped and jumped back.

Not another one?

Another raven feather.

She looked over her shoulder to each corner of the shadowed room. No one else was there, but the eerie feeling of being watched consumed her and made her paranoid. The floor appeared clear of feathers. Only the one on her bench haunted her. Afraid of what would happen if she left the feather there, she grabbed it, along with the repair items she needed, and went back to Brandon. The clean-up would take a few days, without a guarantee it wouldn't happen again.

Back with Brandon and Monica, Kate set down her supplies and then held out the feather. She watched their reaction before saying a word. "This…was on my workbench." The feather shook in her fingers. "She's been in there!"

Monica snatched the feather from her grip. "I don't want you touching any more of these. The raven gathers strength each time you touch one. Call me and I'll come get them. The feathers need to be burned, but not by either of you." She took one of the small bags Kate had brought out and stuffed all the feathers into it that she'd picked up from the damaged village, and then sealed the bag. "I'll take them home with me and do what needs to be done. We've got a lot of work to do *here* yet."

Hours later, Brandon gently pried the glue gun from Kate's small hand. He rubbed her fingers, knowing her joints must ache. "Hon, we've been here all day. Let's go. We've done all we can do tonight." He hoped she would listen. With a knuckle beneath her chin, he lifted her face and wiped a smudge of dirt from her cheek. Even hot and dirty, she looked beautiful to him.

"It's warm in here and we could all use a beer and a shower, not to mention something to eat."

Monica stretched from side to side, reaching over her head each time. She let out an exhausted breath. "I'll agree there, but it stops at the shower thing. I'm not joining you for that."

Kate kissed Brandon. "I suppose you're both right. I'm hungry and a cold beer sounds great."

"Dinner's on me. I can already taste a good, juicy burger. Then we can discuss my visions I had this morning and why some things didn't make sense at all, but I'm sure one of you can fill me in." Monica led the way to the door.

Brandon waited for Kate to go ahead of him or she'd try to stay and work. Once outside, as Kate locked the door, motorcycle engines sounded in the distance. A rumble Brandon didn't want to hear, and his gaze scanned their surroundings. While he could hear them, he couldn't see them as he climbed into the car and they followed Monica to the restaurant.

Inside the bar-restaurant, Brandon led the way to a table in the corner and he sat facing the door. He never sat where he couldn't see who might be coming toward him. His grandfather taught him to never let fate get the upper hand. *Always know what you're up against and tune into the vibrations around you.*

The waiter brought their beers and Brandon savored the dark stout. It'd been a long afternoon. He'd not drank enough water and the beer went down too well. A hunger pang stabbed his stomach as it growled. Breakfast had been several hours ago and they'd worked through lunch.

He reached his hand across the table and opened his palm. Kate placed her hand in his and he closed his fingers.

She looked at him with so much love that his thoughts went to what he wanted to do to her when they got home. Kate truly was an angel in his life. Today she'd been so busy and worried about repairing the set that the two of them didn't even talk much. "It's been a long day. You need to eat something."

Her sensuous gaze told him her thoughts ran along the same line as his and had nothing to do with food.

"Like I said, I'm buying tonight. Get whatever you want, but the burgers are their specialty here." Monica held up her glass for a toast. "Here's to a long friendship and finding answers."

"No shit. I hope you have some for us." Kate tapped her beer glass with both of theirs.

"After we order, I want to hear about the visions you were having this morning."

The waiter took their orders and Brandon also got a burger with onion rings. He wanted to know what Monica had seen in her vision this morning, too. Could she shed a bit of light onto this whole mess for them and give them a rational explanation? He glanced at her as she leaned toward them.

"So…I'm interested to hear about this motorcycle gang or whatever symbolism that might be to you two because it made no sense to me at all. I *did* see one of them with a scar down the front of his face. It seemed to have missed his eye as it went down his forehead onto his cheek. What the hell?"

Kate's pulse throbbed at her temple when she glanced at Brandon. Her eyes held the same knowing look he felt in his heart. She raised her brows. "You tell her."

Monica tipped her head and narrowed her gaze. "He's here. I can feel it. He rides one of the motorcycles. Who *is* he to you?"

Brandon shifted in his chair wondering how much he actually needed to tell her that she didn't already know. He rubbed his damp palms on his jeans. "We knew each other in high school. He'd always been a bully, on the football field and off. Once he came at me with his fists, looking for a fight. I'd been woodworking that day and had a knife in my hand. He swung, I swung, and my blade made contact. That was it. He's had a grudge to get even ever since."

"His spirit comes from your past life. The two of you have battled before, and he didn't win then, either." Monica drank her beer, but Brandon wouldn't release her gaze.

"He won't win now." Brandon could see she contemplated her thoughts and debated on how to pick her next words.

"The spirit of the raven is also from your past. These I see around both of you, past and present, as though to haunt and threaten you. The raven does *not* represent anything good. It's a shapeshifter. I'm guessing once she broke the window and got in to do the damage, she shifted into the raven again, dropped feathers all over, and left through the window. She could have come with your high school enemy or she flew here, but there's no doubt that *she's* here. My visions are making more sense now that all this is falling into place."

Kate rubbed her face with both hands and then slammed them onto the table. "I don't want to deal with the damned bird here."

Monica laid her fingers over Kate's forearm. "Give me a few more days and maybe I can figure something out. I need to concentrate on those feathers. There have to be answers there."

Brandon heard the rumble of engines and glanced out the window. His jaw clenched and so did his fingers. "Son of a bitch." He took another drink of his beer, hoping the three of them wouldn't be noticed by the group when they came in. Maybe now he could get a better look at them without helmets. The door swung open and Brandon's breath caught as the band of nerves tightened around his chest. Memories of his high school fight flashed to the forefront.

The last biker through the door stopped and stared in Brandon's direction with tightened brows. The biker's lip lifted in anger and wrinkled the scar on his cheek. He rolled a shoulder as though warding off the temptation to head toward Brandon. When he turned to follow his group, Brandon took a deep breath as he watched where the bikers took over two tables on the far side of the crowded bar area.

Monica turned as they came in and she studied each one in the group as they took a seat. She turned back toward Brandon. "He's followed you across the country to settle an old score from hundreds of years ago. His anger runs deep, my friend."

Kate leaned in closer. "What else did your vision show you?"

"Gray clouds follow both of you and I don't see a change. The next few weeks won't be easy for you here. I felt a foreboding where scarface is concerned, but I couldn't see the trouble he causes. Be on guard at all times."

Brandon rubbed his jaw. "I hate this. It all needs to go away. The past shouldn't be in my life now, yet every time I turn around, there's something else I have to deal with. Finding Kate is the only good to come out of all of this." He took Kate's hand in his. Being able to feel her warm energy calmed him right now. Drinking the last of his beer, he set the mug at the edge of the table so the waiter could bring him another.

When their food arrived, Kate hadn't realized how long it had been since she last ate. Repairing her setting at the museum had kept her busy all day with no break for lunch. Her burger came wrapped so it didn't drip over her fingers and it ended up being a good thing. She loved a juicy burger with all the topping and took another bite. The broiled flavor of the meat woke up her taste buds as she savored the mustard and relish, so different than savoring the happenings around her.

If only life could be as calm as she was at the moment, with friends and lovers. That's all she wanted, to be happy and not constantly on edge waiting for something else to go wrong.

Kate knew their problems weren't over, however, and she hated that each day would present a new problem that would no doubt involve the raven or scarface.

How can we be prepared for the unknown?

She glanced up to meet Monica's gaze. "You'll never know when one of them will strike. Nothing will be certain for either of you until they are dead. That's all I can tell you right now."

Kate swallowed a drink of beer, wishing fate hadn't chosen them to go through all this. She tried to think of a solution over the next half hour as they quietly ate, each of them lost in their own thoughts of how to solve this dilemma. The beer would only calm her for a short while, and tomorrow they would be facing more problems.

Right now, her problem was her bladder. The motorcycle guys sat between her and the only way to the restroom. Back in Dubois, at lunch one day, scarface confronted her about leaving Brandon and allowing him to show her what a good ride *really* was. *Can I ignore him today and walk past him fast enough on my way to the bathroom?* She'd still have to pass him on her way back to the table.

Damnit!

I hate this!

She leaned toward Brandon. "I'll be right back. I need to use the restroom." His stern gaze connected with hers. "I'll be fine."

"Do *not* stop to talk with him, no matter what."

Monica stood up. "I have to go, too. Come on."

"This is ridiculous. We're giving him more power than he has." Kate shook her head but allowed Monica to follow her. The closer she got to scarface, the more her stomach knotted. Her palms began to sweat as she remembered their last conversation. Refusing to look directly at him, Kate scurried past and made it to the bathroom door. When she looked back, he had detained Monica by standing in her way.

Kate gripped the door handle as she watched words being exchanged before her friend stepped around him. She held the door for Monica and closed it behind them, barely able to contain her curiosity. "What did he want with *you*?"

Monica stared wide-eyed at her. "I truly didn't want to believe he actually had something to do with your past but…he does, damnit. He said to tell you he's not giving up on taking you away from Brandon."

"What an ass!" Kate turned to use a stall, her temper boiling over as she contemplated on a come-back when she got back out there to his table.

From the other stall, Monica whispered to her. "You can't confront him. Don't give him the upper hand. Ignore him and go back to our table."

"You're right. I would just get pissed and say something I shouldn't. But the bastard is so irritating!"

Monica waited near the door for her to dry her hands and they walked out, Kate leading the way. As much as she wanted to put him in his place, she walked by the guys, but that didn't stop him. When Monica passed scarface, he called out to her.

"Did you tell your friend the offer still stands for a better ride?"

Kate's temper boiled hotter and her cheeks burned as she sat down next to Brandon. He waited for an explanation and for the moment, she ignored his silent question. She wanted to deal with this alone but knew Brandon had to be involved in any decisions.

"What is he shouting about?" Brandon asked.

Monica leaned in close. "He wanted me to be sure Kate knew that the offer still stands if she wants to leave you for a better ride."

Brandon shot his chair back and Kate reached out for his thigh to stop him from going over to the gang. "That's exactly what he hopes you'll do so he can call you out in front of everyone. We don't need a brawl inside the bar. We *do* need to leave before they do or they might wait for us outside in the dark. I don't want that."

"I know. We can only hope he screws up enough that the cops have to arrest him. I'm ready if you two are. Let's go home. Monica, we'd love to have you over." Brandon stood as she and Kate walked in front of him.

Kate tried hard not to glance at the gang, though she could feel their eyes on her. Wolf whistles echoed in the bar as they strode out the door. She hurried to her car and waited for Brandon to unlock the door. "Monica, follow us home. We'll see you there." Brandon hit the remote on the doors and Kate jumped in and relocked it. Her gaze stayed on the bar door, hoping the gang wouldn't come out until they were long gone.

"I'd like to know how he finds us when we go somewhere," Brandon commented as he reached over and took her hand.

The firmness of his touch gave her renewed strength that she felt seeping from her bones. "It's getting scary to know they'll eventually show up every time. Brandon, I don't get it." Kate's cell phone buzzed and she grabbed her purse. Her mom had texted her a message: *Hope you and Brandon are getting along well. We really liked him. Love you.* She texted back to let her mom know all was fine, but glad they were concerned.

"That was just my mom. She hoped we were getting along and they like you." Kate put her phone away and looked toward the door to the bar to be sure no one else had left as Brandon pulled from the parking lot. The more she thought about the motorcycle gang following them, the more her gut wrenched at her insides. There was no way she could tell her parents about any of this.

Their unnecessary worry couldn't fix anything.

Brandon glanced in the rearview mirror. "Monica is still following us. She's pretty interesting to talk with. I like her."

"I'm glad. We've been friends forever. She's helped me with so many things in the past." Kate guided him to her house and hurried inside with Monica and Brandon. She loved that he'd come home with her and still couldn't believe how well they got along. He dropped her keys on the counter and she watched as he sauntered into the living room, mentally stripping the skin-tight tee shirt from his broad shoulders. Kate couldn't wait until bedtime, cuddled within his embrace.

Memories drifted through her mind of making love with Taima and passionate feelings of a shared love wrapped around her. Fate had delivered her into the arms of a man who loved her unconditionally, based on his family legends.

Can I live up to all he hopes for between us?

Monica stepped close to whisper in her ear as she dropped her purse on the counter. "Stop staring. It's not fair. Hey, maybe he's open to a three-some? He's such a hunk...you lucky shit." Monica sighed.

"I know, and *no*, I don't share...with anyone!" Kate looked to see if he'd sat down yet. "His mannerisms are so like Taima's that I have to remind myself sometimes that he isn't. What if this doesn't work out?"

Monica rolled her eyes. "Stop it! I would have foreseen that by now and I haven't. I've seen the two of you together in the future, enjoying life." Monica hugged her and Kate pulled her close. "I'm glad you're finally happy."

"We are, really. We just need to get better acquainted. He's relying on his dreams and visions of us and is sure we're supposed to be together. But it feels like pieces are missing for me." Kate reached for three beers from the fridge, grabbing Brandon a dark one. She opened them, handed one to Monica and took two glasses from the freezer door. "He makes me feel protected and safe. With everything that's happened lately, I need that right now."

"The way you both look at each other, I'm going to guess that you're sleeping well, too!" Monica poured her beer into the frosty glass and followed.

Kate headed toward the living room to Brandon but commented over her shoulder in a whisper. "Better than I *ever* have." She sat next to the handsome man on her sofa and handed him his dark beer, then looked around for her phone. "Shit, I left my purse in the car. I'll be right back. Find us a movie or something." Kate scurried into the kitchen, grabbed the keys from the counter, and headed out the back door. The big garage light lit the whole yard and driveway. She stepped around to the passenger side, hit the remote to unlock her door and opened it. Happy her purse still sat on the floor, she grabbed it, stepped back and closed the door. After hitting the remote to lock it, she turned toward the house to go around the SUV and something hit her in the face, knocking her to the ground.

When her head and back hit the grass, it stunned her. She blinked to clear her head and lay there for a moment. Kate assessed her body for injuries and refilled her lungs. Nothing felt broken and she still held both her purse and keys.

What the hell hit me?

Before she could get to her feet, fingers wrapped around her ankles and began dragging her toward the garage.

11.

Kate screamed as loud as she could, hoping one of her windows were open and Brandon would hear. At the same time, she kicked her attacker, whose face was shadowed, but the ratty hair reminded her of someone and the stench nearly made her throw up the burger she'd eaten earlier. Her body gathered mud and grass as her backside skidded along. Kate held tight to her purse and tried to tug her feet from her captor's strong fingers.

Her attacker hissed like a snake. "You don't belong with him and he doesn't belong to you. He's mine and I'm making sure of that. You'll not see another sunrise."

Familiarity with the voice rattled her mind. She screamed again as loud as she could and then heard the back-door slam. Kate tried to flip herself over to escape the bony grasp on her ankles as her free hand clawed at the ground to get free. Thinking that Brandon must not have heard her scream, Kate screamed again.

"Kate! Where are you?"

Renewed adrenaline propelled Kate to fight harder at hearing Brandon's voice.

From the shadows of the floodlight, she saw him rush forward. He stood twice the size of her attacker. Brandon wrestled an arm around the waist of whoever it might be and yanked them backward, far enough that Kate could scramble to her feet. Anger propelled her forward as she gripped her purse tight, swung it back and hit the stranger across the face with such force that Brandon lost his hold as the thin stranger struggled loose to run behind the garage.

Kate yelled out while her attacker ran through the yards. "You'll be dead if you come back here again, trust me, you little bitch!"

Brandon's fingers gripped her

shoulders. "Hon, what happened? I knew I should have come out here to get your purse for you."

"This is normally a safe neighborhood. I don't get it." Kate scrunched her nose. "God, they stunk. Can you smell that stench?"

Brandon pulled her closer to connect with his gaze. "Are you hurt?"

"No, just my pride that I didn't sense someone nearby. My clothes are filthy now, damn it." She brushed at the grass and dirt on her clothes while she looked for signs of the stranger's return.

Brandon tugged on her arm as he glanced around the yard. "Let's get inside."

Under the light near the porch, Kate had Brandon brush the mud from her back and jeans so it didn't get dragged into the house. His strong large hands worked diligently to clean her up and then he paused, causing her to turn around. She followed his wide-eyed angry gaze to the driveway...*littered with black raven feathers.*

Kate growled under her breath and

looked at Brandon. His eye twitched at the corner, but she spoke first. "That's it. I've had it with her. If I would have had my gun with me just now, she'd be laying there instead of just feathers!"

"Let's get you into the house and lock the doors. We'll both be walking Monica to her car tonight when she leaves."

Once inside, Kate dropped her purse on the couch and stormed through the living room toward her bedroom. "I'll be right back, Monica. I need to change." She slipped into comfortable sweats and dropped the dirty clothes into the hamper, ran a brush through her hair, then gazed at her reflection. Kate nearly scared herself. Seeing her nails in the mirror, mud had caked beneath them and she scrubbed her fingertips with her nail brush until she was satisfied they were clean enough.

A shudder ran down her back when she thought about all that could have happened tonight. Shaking her head, she flipped off the light and returned to the living room to sit by Brandon.

He held her as close as he could, kissed her cheek, and handed her a beer. "You probably need a few shots of Jack instead of this right now."

"This will do, but I'm sure I'll go through a few. The nerve of whoever had the guts to come into my yard and do that. What the hell? Did you tell Monica what was out there?"

"I'm not sure if it was male or female, but I had them around the waist until my little ninja swung her purse full force across their face. I lost my grip on them. They got away and then I glanced down at the driveway…" Brandon waved his hand.

Kate watched Monica's wide-eyed reaction as she relived it again at Brandon's telling.

"Raven feathers lay scattered all over out there," he continued.

Monica's mouth dropped open. "Oh my god! Not again." She leaned toward Kate. "You're not to touch those feathers in the driveway. I'll come by tomorrow, collect them all and burn them. Like I said before, neither of you can touch them."

Kate covered her nose. "Okay, fine. The smell out there would have knocked me over if she hadn't."

"Some spirits have a putrid odor. It's part of the evil that hangs around them. For sure, this one is among the devil's doing. Do you have sage here? If you do, I'd suggest lighting some tonight and walking the house with it. It works on cleansing most spirits, but…" Monica shrugged a shoulder before she continued. "I can't promise it'll work with this one. At least it was just outside. That's a good sign."

Kate rubbed Brandon's thigh, feeling his strength as she squeezed her fingers. "I can only hope she doesn't find her way into the house. I'm not sure I'll sleep tonight now. And we're walking you to your car when you leave. She could still be lurking outside."

"I'll help you sleep tonight, baby," Brandon said.

Heat flooded Kate's cheeks as she

thought of all the ways he could make that happen.

Monica looked from her to Brandon and back. "We need to figure out how to fight this shapeshifter, but we can discuss that tomorrow. I'm heading home." She took her empty glass into the kitchen and grabbed her purse.

Kate followed her to the kitchen. "I'm taking a flashlight with us but the street lights will help, too. We'll walk you out." She hugged Monica tight, hoping she'd be safe when she got home. "Thank you for being here with us. We'll see you tomorrow and decide how to fix this shapeshifter thing. Call me when you get home and inside." She led the way to the front door and unlocked it. Kate stepped outside with Brandon and watched Monica get safely to her car, then pull away.

Brandon looked around before going in the house with Kate. She watched as he locked the door and leaned against it. His arms opened and she couldn't resist stepping into his embrace as he wrapped her in security. "We're going to make it through this. I promise." His deep voice caressed her ear and sent sexual thoughts through every nerve in her body. She put her arms around his waist while she placed her head on his chest, breathing in the scent of him. "As long as you're here with me, I will believe that."

He cupped her face and the pad of his thumb lightly skimmed over her lips. The near-electrical charge brought them to life and set her body on fire with need. When she met his gaze, his mouth covered hers as his fingers cradled her head. His kisses took her breath away and she closed her eyes as his tongue found hers. His hand moved down her back and cupped her ass with a gentle squeeze before he pulled from their kiss. Brandon searched her eyes and took in a deep breath. "I still can't believe I can actually kiss you in person after dreaming about you for so many years. It feels so *right* to be with you."

Kate saw the hunger swimming in his eyes. "It does. I don't understand it, but it's like we've known each other forever." She hugged him and his cologne filled her senses as her fingers moved over the warm muscles of his back. Kate wanted to stay locked like this forever.

He kissed the top of her head. "Let's turn out the lights as soon as we hear from Monica. I just want to hold you, to fall asleep with you in my arms, always."

Kate stepped away, but took his hand so he'd follow her into the kitchen. She had to return the flashlight to the drawer and turn out the kitchen light. "Let me grab my phone so I don't miss her call, then we'll get ready for bed."

"I'll go wash up and brush my teeth. Don't be too long or I'll come find you." Brandon winked and went into the bathroom.

Kate turned out the light while the night light set off a dim glow. Shadows in her own living room created a haunted feeling that she wasn't comfortable with. She hated that she felt so afraid, but with all that had happened lately, she also doubted she'd sleep tonight. Thankfully Brandon would be cuddled next to her the entire evening and she smiled. No one else she knew could be as happy as her heartfelt since she'd found Brandon. Perhaps fate truly *did* have a part in souls reconnecting.

Her phone vibrated in her hand when Monica texted that she'd arrived home, locked inside and safe for the night. She breathed a sigh of relief. At least she could stop worrying about her best friend tonight. Kate walked in to set her phone on the nightstand beside her bed and then leaned against the bathroom doorway to admire her soul mate. His broad shoulders narrowed at the waist of his jeans.

When she glanced up at the mirror, his sultry gaze captured hers and she all but surrendered to him where she stood. Her cheeks heated to think he'd caught her admiring him. She loved the chiseled cut of his cheekbones and jawline. They made something tug in the pit of stomach, creating a need only he could satisfy as she shifted her weight from one foot to the other. No man had ever made her think of sex so often.

"You make it hard for me to keep my mind out of the gutter, you know," she commented. Memories of the way his tongue had touched her skin so many times in the middle of the night made her want him *now* as she stepped forward to watch her hands embrace his waist in their reflection of the mirror. She splayed her fingers over his firm abs and pressed her hips against his ass.

"Get your clothes off, woman, or you'll find them ripped from your body." He winked and gave her a lopsided grin. He turned within her embrace and cupped her face. "I'll be waiting for you, naked and hungry. Don't be long, white woman."

His mouth took hers in a kiss that sparked every nerve ending in her body. Her lungs struggled for air. His thumbs caressed her cheeks and then he pulled from the kiss. "Take too long in joining me and you may find yourself over my knee."

Brandon slapped her ass and left her standing alone in the bathroom having to grab the counter for support. She needed to learn more control over her rubber knees where thoughts of him were concerned. The man knew how to make her feel wanted and she loved it. Their short relationship didn't seem new at all, but rather as though they had loved before. Actually, they both had relived the visions of their past lives.

She turned on the water and held her hot hands beneath the faucet, hoping to cool off her thoughts so she could finish getting ready for bed. *Bed…cool sheets, hot bodies, passionate love-making with a man who looked like model–material. Damn, I'm a lucky woman.*

Brandon tossed his jeans on the end of the dresser and folded back the comforter. He slid beneath the sheet, fluffed his pillow and stretched out on his back to wait for the woman of his dreams. All the times he'd prayed for this moment came back to him. To be with her now nearly overwhelmed his senses and fogged his mind at times. He'd waited a lifetime to touch her face and kiss the lips he'd dreamt about and here he was. She was everything he thought she would be and more. Other women in his life had come and went, none of them meeting the expectations of his visions of Kate.

Is that really the reason I couldn't commit to any of them?

Shelley had tried to get his attention for several years. Each time he visited the Mercantile Store in town, she would engage him in conversation, find some reason she needed his assistance at the store, or get him to meet her for lunch. He'd met her a few times, and for him, it was nothing more than a friendly lunch. *Was I so naive not to see she had feelings for me?* Brandon blinked away the memories. She was the last person he wanted to think about tonight as he watched the doorway of the bedroom, hoping to see Kate. Shelley seeped into both of their thoughts and he knew that's how shapeshifters obtained more strength, so he immediately thought of holding Kate in his arms, feeling the softness of her body.

A shadow stood in the doorway, silhouetted by the bathroom night light. The sexy shape of Kate's shadow as she stood naked before him sent blood rushing to the lower part of his body, making him hard with a need only she could satisfy. He breathed in deep to get more oxygen, as though all of it had suddenly been sucked from the room. She sauntered over to her side of the bed and he tossed back the sheet. Her perfume followed to assault his senses, to entice him to take her, to send her over the edge of passion. Kate rolled toward him to cuddle against his chest and he cupped her ass, fitting so well within his grasp.

"I didn't want to end up over your knee, although that could be fun." Her voice taunted him to take her.

"I know I would have enjoyed it, but I enjoy holding you in any position." He moved his hand over the curve of her hip to her lower back, and rolled onto his back, adjusting her weight on top of him. Kate braced her hands on the bed above his shoulders and her hair brushed over his chest as she bent to bite his nipple. Teeth tenderly tugged on it and it puckered at her bite.

His fingers dug into her hips when her thighs straddle him.

"Keep that up and you'll get more than you planned on." He rubbed the length of himself up against Kate, feeling her silky heat. Tonight would be another special one they wouldn't soon forget as he thought about hearing her cry out for release later.

Her eyes narrowed. "Bring it on, babe. I can handle whatever you have in mind for us. I might even surprise you with a few tricks of my own." She giggled before touching her lips to his and turning his world into an ocean of ecstasy.

Brandon woke the next morning with Kate spooned in front of him, still sound asleep and a breast cupped in his hand. Joy flowed through his blood when he woke each day like this. He buried his face in her dark hair and breathed in her scent, never wanting to forget it. Tasting the skin on her shoulder, he kissed a path to her neck and she rolled onto her back, the sheet still at her waist. The perfect body exposed to his view only added to the images she'd already endowed him with. He cupped her breast and kissed the tip, watching for those emerald eyes to open, but instead, a soft moan escaped her lips as her fingers clutched at the sheet.

"Now this is a perfect way to wake up each day." Kate met his gaze but then leaned up on her elbow. "What's that on the sheet down there?"

Brandon reached for the object and shook his head as he smiled at Kate. He turned the long feather in his fingers. "This is an eagle feather and represents blessing and protection."

Kate narrowed her eyes and looked from him to the feather and back. He could tell she remembered something. "In my dreams, while I was at your place, Taima had been badly injured and near death with a high fever. We awoke one morning to find an eagle feather on his body and Ahanu said the same thing. It was for protection…but he still died in the end."

"This is meant to be a good thing for us. I have no idea how it got it here. We don't question *how* at times like this. Our union has been blessed by the Great Spirit and those who watch over us."

Kate leaned over to her side of the bed to check the floor. "I'm looking for raven feathers."

"This didn't come from the raven. The two are not connected, babe. Trust me. This is the best way to start another beautiful day. Let's enjoy that."

Later that week, Brandon walked into the museum with Kate and Monica for the meeting with Tom and men from the Iroquois nation. He looked forward to talking with them to learn some of their customs and hoped that's what this would accomplish.

"Thanks for letting me tag along, guys. I'm already sensing things that surround this meeting. I promise I'll keep quiet until you're done. I've got my notepad so I don't interrupt the conversation."

Glad that Monica had wanted to join them, Brandon felt that she might be able to give them some insight that he and Kate wouldn't know about. Thoughts of impending danger had tugged at his mind since yesterday, but he couldn't nail down exactly why. The past few days had been uneventful considering all the commotion of last week with the attack in the driveway.

Tom led them to his office and introduced him to two of the tribal elders. When Brandon shook each of their hands, he felt a connection with them, especially the frail hand of the eldest.

He sat down, ready to listen as to why they wanted to meet with him.

One of the elders appeared to be in his late seventies and reminded Brandon of his grandfather because they both wore their hair in a single braid. His head shook slightly as he concentrated and he glanced at Monica several times. "Kate, it is always good to see you;

something that doesn't happen often enough. You've done a great deal of work on the Native American section and we thank you for that. We were sorry to hear of so much damage." He paused to breathe before continuing. "I've had visions of a faraway visitor and when Tom told me of you being here, I understood my dream. You are a connection for us, though I don't understand how yet, but I will, soon enough."

The younger man shifted in his chair. "My father was outside in our yard a few weeks ago when he saw a raven several days in a row. He would tell me of the angst this bird made him experience by staring at him and it made me uncomfortable, thinking the bird meant danger somehow. The raven also tried to attack him one day as he sat on the deck. Shortly after that, we heard of the damage done here, probably by the same raven."

Kate nodded. "I would guess it was the same one, too. Brandon and Monica helped me get everything cleaned up. There were feathers everywhere."

The old man looked at Monica and then reached over to rest his hand on her forearm. "Keep them safe. You alone can do this." He pulled his wrinkled hand back to the arm of his chair but kept his gaze on Monica. "You didn't allow her to touch the feathers, did you? That would make the danger worse."

Monica glanced at Brandon, then back to the elder. "Yes, I was the only one who cleaned up the feathers and I burned them."

"Good." He slowly shook a finger at Kate. "You must never touch the feathers."

Again, Kate nodded. "I understand."

The younger man shook his head. "My father has had too many visions that have come true and he sees a warrior with a scar where Brandon is concerned. Be careful. We saw this man riding a motorcycle when he tried to torment a group of us at the longhouse last week. We meet there often with other tribal members. His gang rode in a circle around the lodge and he tried to run two of us down. We ended up calling the police and he disappeared before they arrived. My father has had nightmares after seeing that and somehow, the raven is connected to the man with the scar."

Monica gasped at his comment.

The older man gazed long and hard at her. "You, too, know of this menace."

"I do. Evil surrounds him. I'm not sure how to protect these two from him and the raven."

The old man pounded his finger into the palm of his other hand. "You must sprinkle sage over the feathers before you burn them. This will give added protection against the evil they bring here."

Monica scribbled a few notes as she listened.

"My father insisted on this meeting to give both of you his warning so you will be more careful."

Brandon sat amazed at the visions the elder man had passed on. "We appreciate that. Both of us are always keeping an eye out for danger. Too many things have happened since I've been here and it's only been a short time."

The old man gazed at Kate. "You belong wherever he goes. Your souls journey together and that will *never* be broken, no matter how many lifetimes."

Goosebumps broke out on Brandon's arms and legs. Kate reached toward him and he took her hand in his. "I've told her as much. I hope one day she'll join me back in Wyoming."

"She must. That is the only way to put an end to the evil that follows both of you. It cannot be accomplished here where the sun rises. It must be back where the sun sets, to close the door of evil forever." The old man nodded as he paused to breathe and now stared at Kate. "You *must* go. Waiting will only prolong the danger. He will know what must be done when he speaks to the elders of his tribe again."

Kate squeezed Brandon's hand tight and then looked at Tom. "How can

I leave the work I've started here? We've put so much time into this. No one else will take over when I go."

"I will worry about that. We can find someone with the same passion that you have. The danger that surrounds you now is not worth staying here. You two need to decide what's best. Just keep me posted on your plans. In the meantime, I'll begin my search."

The old man stood and shuffled to the door. "My job is done. Peace be with you, my friends."

"Thank you for allowing my father the time to relay this information to you. His mind is clear now and perhaps he can rest. I wish you the best in dealing with the dangers in our universe."

12.

Brandon shook both of their hands before they left, and he sat back down. He stroked his jaw as he thought about the warnings that were only reiterated from his grandfathers before he and Kate drove back here. The elders were all aware of their soul journey and the dangers that followed them from past lives into the present.

Tom leaned on his desk and steepled his fingers. "You have a tough decision to make. You know I hate to lose someone with your passion for history, but you have to live your life and do what's best for you two. Personally, I think there are many things in Wyoming that you'll find to keep your passion alive."

Relief spread over Kate's face as she looked at the man behind the desk. "Tom, thanks for understanding. This has been a hard month for me with all that's happened. I appreciate you agreeing to this. I'm not sure my parents will be. I'm their only child and if I move across the country, what are they going to do?" Kate laughed at herself and looked at Brandon.

He hated seeing her so torn up inside with decisions to make. "I'm not pressuring you to move, babe. This has to happen only when you're ready. You understand that, right?"

"Of course, I do."

Brandon pulled out his phone vibrating in his pocket. "Shit." He looked at Kate.

"What? Who is it?"

"My producer. Let me take this. I'll be right back." Brandon answered the call but didn't speak until he closed the door and stood in the hall outside Tom's office. "Cody, what's up?" Brandon's stomach knotted even though he had no idea why Cody would call him. Deep down, he guessed he might be afraid he'd have to fly home for something and leave Kate alone.

"Brandon, I've just received some great news. The investors only want *you* in the sequel and they want to meet with you next week in LA. We've also set the film release date for 60 days out and we have the promo to do. I've got dates setup and am going to need you on-sight for these. Tell me your thoughts."

He leaned against the wall and stared at the ceiling with the phone at his ear. Recognition is not what he wanted and now Cody wanted him in the limelight, which meant leaving Pittsburgh. Traveling around the country wasn't something he'd ever planned on. Crowds made him uncomfortable.

"Dude! You still there? Hello?"

"Yeah, yeah. Guess I'm a little shell-shocked at all this. The movie was fun, but I certainly didn't expect anything to happen after that." Brandon laughed at Cody and himself for being so naive.

"The previews are getting rave reviews, man. Come on. Step into the game and let's make this happen. They love you."

"Let me talk this over with Kate and get her thoughts on all this."

"Shit, pack her up and bring her out here. I can't wait to meet her. I'll wine and dine her so she'll make you do this."

"I'll call you back, Cody. I'm glad this is taking off, I guess. Talk to you later, man."

Brandon put his phone into his back pocket and pushed away from the wall. He had to admit that he might be a little excited after all. The movie busted his ass, and maybe now it would pay off a little. A few extra bucks in his pocket wouldn't hurt either. He pulled open the door to Tom's office and rejoined everyone.

"So, I hear you're a movie star."

Brandon rolled his eyes and laughed. "Not quite." He took Kate's hand. "They've set the movie release for two months from now. Cody wants me in LA next week."

"You'll be there. You're not refusing to go like you said before."

Kate's eyes lit up like a Christmas tree, only brighter.

He shrugged and raised a brow. "Cody wants me to bring you along, too. He thinks if he wines and dines you, I can't refuse to be his puppet."

Monica flipped her hair backward off her shoulder. "I knew it! Now it all makes sense. Don't even ask how I know this. I'll make sure she's packed. Neither of you is going to miss any of this."

Kate covered her mouth and stared at Tom. "How can I leave? I have a job."

"Not anymore you don't." Tom shook his head. "I'm not standing in the way of progress. Go enjoy the excitement. You deserve this. Both of you."

The expressions on Kate's face made Brandon happy. To be able to share this with her would be something he hadn't expected. First, her eyes went wide, then her brows knitted together and then she'd drop her jaw as thoughts went through her mind. She appeared so easy to read. He loved it and wanted to pick her up and spin her around, but this wasn't the place. "I'll call to make plane reservations when we get home. We need to let your parents know, eventually."

"Shit, yes. I'll call them later. We can go out for supper tonight and celebrate. Oh my god! Monica! You're coming home with us. Better yet, you're coming to LA with us! We have to make plans. Tom, thank you for everything. You're the best."

Tom came around his desk to hug Kate. He appeared genuinely sorry to be losing her as an employee. "You deserve it. I'll deposit your last check in the bank for you. No worries. Thank *you* for all you've given to us. Don't forget to stay in touch."

Back at home, Kate sat at the table with Monica and had talked her into flying out to LA with them. Brandon called the airline for reservations while Kate invited her parents to dinner with them. She then wrote out a list of things to do before they left. *How could all of this be possible?* She looked at Monica and covered her mouth as she smiled, thinking her heart would beat out of her chest at any minute. So much excitement bubbled up inside of her that she thought it would bubble out. "Who would ever think this kind of thing would happen to *me*? LA? Really? Oh my god, girlfriend." She kept her voice low while Brandon got the tickets done.

Monica took her hand. "This *so* explains things for me. I knew something good was going to happen and at first, I thought it was Brandon finding you, but something else kept nagging at me. I couldn't put my finger on it, but it's going to explode for both of you. Not that Brandon doesn't make you explode. Ooops! Shit, that's none of my business!" She raised her wine glass and chimed against Kate's. "Your parents are going to be happy for you once they stop to think about this. Are you just going to surprise them at supper? No warning?"

"Yes. I want to tell them in person, not on the phone and I want all of us there, to celebrate as a family." Kate leaned back in her chair to take a breath and just shook her head at how fast all of this was coming together. "This is ridiculous." She looked at Brandon as he put down his phone. The blue plaid unbuttoned shirt he wore over his light blue tee shirt made his eyes so sexy set against his darker complexion. She was proud of his heritage. *And he's all mine.* "I'm so proud of you, babe. You're in a movie and they love you. I can't wait for it to go public so we can read what they think. It'll be fun."

Brandon held out his tumbler of Jack Daniels™. "Only if I can share it with someone I love. That's my only stipulation for continuing with this. I want *you* with me."

Kate touched her glass to Brandon's tumbler. "I'm ready for the next step in our journey. I don't care if others say I haven't known you long enough, because I'm sure that's exactly what my parents are going to say, but too bad. Only the three of us truly understand what our relationship is all about. Friends and family here in

Pittsburgh have no idea who you are, but they'll just have to trust in my judgment. My *heart* knows what I want." She loved that Brandon's emotions were easily read in his eyes and his love touched her each time he looked at her.

"We fly back in three days and then head to LA two days later. I love living in Dubois, but flying out of Jackson Hole is going to get old. That drive takes well over an hour. I might have to consider an apartment there if we end up doing much flying."

Monica perked up. "I can't believe I'm going with you. There has to be a *single* cowboy there somewhere." She glanced toward Brandon, who tipped his head, contemplated a moment and then smiled that sexy way he does.

Kate knew he had something up his sleeve.

"Cody is single. A little busy, which would explain *why* he's single."

"Hmmmm….and he lives in LA. What could be better?"

"I'm thinking the two of you might

get along well." Brandon laughed and finished his drink. "I need to freshen up if I'm meeting your parents again." He stood next to Kate and lifted her face up. "You're so cute." He bent to kiss her and headed to the kitchen with his glass, then on to the bathroom.

Kate enjoyed her wine as she waited until he'd left the room. She leaned over to Monica giggling so hard she about wet her pants. Obviously, she'd already had too much wine in celebration, but what the hell. Then she followed Monica's gaze. "Were you just watching his ass?"

"God he's so hot."

The hunger in Monica's eyes made Kate smile. "You're so bad! Good thing I love you, too. I wouldn't want to share this experience with anyone but you. Monica, his home is huge. I about got lost in it."

She curled her fingers over Kate's forearm. "I'm so happy for you that all of this is happening. It makes all the evil not seem so bad right now. We need to concentrate on the happiness. Brandon is so good to you."

Kate thought of how happy Brandon made her when they spent time together. Not many people could say they were actually happy. Her parents were, that much she knew. The kind of marriage they had is what Kate wished for herself and Brandon. They did everything together as best friends. Even as a child, she remembered them holding hands no matter where they went.

Her father loved her mom and now she had a man just like that.

She sipped her wine and enjoyed the time she and Monica spent together. "I really am a
lucky shit, huh?" More giggles and Monica joined.

Brandon couldn't help but listen in on Kate and Monica as he was about to return to the dining room. He smiled as Kate's laughter floated down the hall toward him. An angel had landed in his life and he would never jeopardize losing her now that he'd found her.

Monica seemed like a great friend, someone perhaps Cody would find interesting. She'd be a nice surprise for Cody. As he stepped into the room from the hall, Kate's gaze caught his as he raised a brow, but couldn't keep the smile from his lips. "Did you two finish all that wine?"

"We did. But we're starting on a fresh one at the restaurant." She went to the kitchen to toss the bottle and Brandon's attention landed on the curve of her hip as she sauntered, albeit a bit tipsy, into the kitchen.

Monica cleared her throat and he glanced her way. "I do love the way you pay attention to her. I had my doubts about you when she called me from Wyoming, but you've changed my mind. You're good for her. Thank you."

"She's my other half. I'd die for her." Brandon's comment surprised even him, although he knew he meant it. And his heart would certainly die if he ever lost her.

"Let's hope it doesn't come to that. She's already lost a soul mate once."

Monica headed to the back door and Brandon followed the women to the car for a night of celebration. He still wasn't sure this was happening. It had all come together in a rush today, or so it seemed. Kate's parents might not be as delighted.

Brandon's stomach knotted as he opened the door to the restaurant and looked straight into the eyes of her father. Had Keith not smiled right away, Brandon wasn't sure what he would have done. Instead, he shook the firm hand Keith held out to him and then hugged the beautiful green-eyed woman at his side. Kate was the spitting image of her mother, just a bit taller as she hugged both of her parents.

"Monica, I'm glad you're joining us," Micki said as they hugged.

Kate talked with the hostess, who led them to a table near a window looking out at the parking lot. Brandon caught himself searching for parked motorcycles as he took a seat across from her dad.

The waitress took their drink orders

and Brandon crooked a finger for her to come closer. "This will all be on one tab, please." He caught the wide-eyed look from her father and Brandon shook his head. "Tonight is on me."

"Dad, we're here to celebrate good news tonight and happy that both of you are here. Brandon got a call from his film producer today. They want him in LA next week." Kate stopped to gauge their reaction.

Brandon looked from her dad to her mom, who had reached for Keith's forearm and curled her fingers over it. *Would they try to tell Kate she couldn't go? Non-sense.* He didn't think she took orders from them anymore.

Silence.

He tried to gauge their reaction, as they looked at each other as if to ask whether they should agree. Kate's fingers slipped into Brandon's hand under the table as they waited for her parents to absorb what she'd said.

Keith's eyes narrowed at Kate as he pursed his lips. "Are you going with him?" He looked at Brandon and back at Kate.

She squeezed Brandon's hand. "I am. Monica has also agreed to go with us so that I have someone to hang with while Brandon is with his producer. We're leaving in three days. Mom, the movie comes out at theaters in two months. This is so exciting. We wanted to tell you in person. I've got Tom's blessing at the museum and he'll find someone to replace me. He said I better jump at this to help Brandon. The producer wants him out there for promotions and to discuss the sequel."

The wide-eyed expression on Micki's face made Brandon's cheeks heat. "We're going to have a movie star in the family! Of course, you need to be there."

"I'm not so sure that's a good idea. All this is too quick. You just got back home."

"Dad, I knew you would feel that way, but I'm fine with this. Brandon and I have gotten to know each other pretty well."

"In two months? Aren't you jumping into this?" Keith crunched his brows together as he looked over at Brandon. A muscle twitched across his jaw. "If anything happens to her, I *will* hunt you down."

"Dad!"

Brandon took in a deep breath and then her father laughed out loud as the drinks arrived. He wasn't sure how to take her father for a minute there. He meant business. Being the retired marine he was, Brandon had no doubt he'd come find them. Now that her parents seemed to be onboard with Kate traveling to LA with him, Brandon tried to relax, but that killer-look Keith had shot him still messed with his nerves.

Kate squeezed his hand again beneath the table. "He likes you. Don't worry, babe."

Once they all had their glasses, Monica held hers toward the center of the table. "Cheers to new beginnings. I see only happiness in their future."

Brandon lifted his glass to join in the cheer and tapped the others. "Thank you for allowing me to take your daughter along for support. The two of us share something special and I want to pursue what might be between us that many don't share."

Her father caught Brandon's gaze. "I'm trusting her to your care. Don't disappoint us, son. Enjoy Los Angeles and good luck with the film career."

"Thank you, sir. That means a lot to me. Kate and I have a connection that I've never had with anyone. Neither of us can explain it, but when both of us met, it was something we each felt immediately."

"Hang on to it then. That's what I felt with her mother when we met. Every year goes by faster. Cherish the time you have." Keith lifted his glass for a drink as he looked in Kate's direction and listened to her and Monica carry on about traveling.

Brandon could now relax more than he had since arriving in Pittsburgh. He'd not spent much time with Kate's parents. The destruction at the museum had consumed her time and kept her and her parents apart. He knew she wanted more time with them and now he was whisking her away. *Is this a good idea? I'm taking her away and being selfish.*

As if she'd read his thoughts, Kate reached over to place her hand on his thigh and looked at him with those emerald eyes and a full smile. She beamed with happiness. "You know I want to go with you. My parents are fine with this. What is it?"

He covered her hand with his, astonished that their thoughts were parallel so often. "I know. I just hoped I could have spent more time with them before we go."

"We'll work it out. Maybe we can spend tomorrow with them and pack the next day."

Kate leaned over for a kiss and Brandon appeased her, hoping her parents wouldn't think he was being inappropriate.

The conversation moved to getting Monica to Los Angeles to meet some single guys and Brandon laughed with Keith as they teased her for still being single. It was easy to see that Kate's family had included Monica long ago. Their friendship sounded like it went back several years. Her ability to see into the *other world* astounded him and he wanted to ask her several questions but held back. Although, when he arrived here, she had asked many of her own questions and knew more about him than he was comfortable with. Like Monica, his elders had the ability to see visions of what would come to be. Brandon would actually like her to meet them. Perhaps one day that would come to be.

The roar of distant motorcycles drew his attention to the parking lot outside. He waited as a tingle slithered up his spine and hoped Kate was too busy talking to notice the sound of the engines. He clenched his jaw as eight cycles slowly rode through, careful of the pedestrians walking to their cars. When they glanced in Brandon's direction, he hoped they couldn't see inside the restaurant. Luckily, they didn't circle back around and drove off down the road. While Kate chatted with her mother across the table, he glanced at Monica. She'd seen them, too, but turned her attention to Micki's question.

Brandon didn't look back at the parking lot, but his hearing had been piqued and he stayed alert. His internal anger tightened his insides like the string of a bow, ready to release if provoked. *How do they know every single place we go?* He couldn't put his finger on it. A tracking device? That'd be a bit far-fetched! Then again, all of this was a bit far-fetched. His visions, his grandfathers' visions, finding Kate, Monica knowing and seeing so much, the raven's destruction…none of it made sense.

He thought about the real possibility of a tracking device. It would have to be somewhere on Kate's vehicle. If they took it in for an oil change, maybe he could ask the attendant to scan underneath to see if he could find anything without alerting Kate. Tomorrow might be a good time for that and he made a mental note.

"Brandon?"

Keith called his name again. He didn't think he had spaced out so much that he didn't hear the conversations but he had. "I'm sorry, Keith. Just mentally checking off things I need to do before we go. I want to make sure we get the oil changed in Kate's car after driving it across the country. Then we won't have to worry about it while we're gone."

Glad that the meal had been uneventful, Brandon's tension didn't release until he and Kate were back at home, locked inside. She cuddled next to him on the couch, her legs across his, as they watched the news before going to bed. As he rested his hand on her thigh, he thanked the Great Spirit for bringing them together after so many years of hoping. Holding her close felt good, her head resting on his shoulder. He'd waited what seemed a lifetime to do this, to take care of the woman of his dreams. Their feelings for each other grew stronger each day and Brandon looked forward to a future with Kate.

When she looked up at him, her

mouth drew his attention. The softness of her kisses was like silk and his thumb reached up to caress her lower lip. The heat of her tongue touched his thumb and sparked through to his heart.

She smiled. "I think I'm falling in love with you. My mind never lets go of the memories we've already shared."

"I've been in love since the first vision I had of you after I tethered your ring around my neck so many years ago. Finding you has been a dream come true. I pray daily that our love grows stronger."

Her finger touched the side of his neck and trailed down to the hollow at his throat. "Your heart beats as fast as mine does."

Brandon laced his fingers behind her neck, his thumb touching her cheek as he pulled her close and took her mouth in a kiss that heated him to his toes. Kate's fingers went over his forearm as a moan slipped from her throat and her tongue tangle with his. Kissing her could not be compared to any other woman he'd *ever* kissed.

Their souls were bound and their spirits connected.

Love was in everything she did to him.

13.

When Brandon pulled from the kiss, he touched his forehead to hers and reveled in their closeness. To actually hold the woman from his visions in his arms felt amazing. His heart nearly beat out of control. Breathing in her scent cooled his blood and calmed his senses. No other man could possibly find a woman as good as he'd found. "God, I love you."

The warmth of Kate's fingers cupped his cheek as she lifted her face to look into his eyes. "I wasn't sure my feelings could be so strong this soon, but we can't question what *is*."

He admired her soft features, the smooth skin of her cheeks, and the tenderness in her eyes. "No, we can't. The Great Spirit is guiding us and I trust in the visions I've been shown. What is meant to be is happening and I don't want to question *why*. We must follow our hearts and surrender in the magic of fate. I'm just glad we're following together." Her gaze snared his emotions like a dream catcher and he allowed himself to become tangled in the web of her affection.

Her shyness attracted his attention as she spoke. "Our children will have the best father a child could ask for. I know they will learn the ways of your people and be wise in choosing their life path."

Brandon loved the thought of children with Kate and he easily envisioned them playing in the backyard. "I can't wait to raise our family with you. I hope they all have the heart that you do." He hugged her close and threaded his fingers in the silkiness of her hair.

Nails trailed over his shoulders and her breath heated his neck. "I love how protected I feel wrapped in your arms. You block out all the bad in the world for me and make each day a happy one…even when trouble walks through our life. We *will* win." Kate reached for the remote and turned off the television. "Take me to bed and make me forget about the bad things."

Brandon scooped Kate from his lap as he stood and she wrapped her arms around his neck. "Your wish is my command, white woman." He loved using the expression she said Taima used to use with her. It seemed appropriate. He carried her toward the bedroom. "I'll make you forget *all* of the bad stuff and only remember *my* touch. I'll make you beg for more of what your body craves." Her eyes told him everything he needed to know as her tongue moistened her lips.

The next day Brandon made sure Kate's car got the oil change it needed. While she sat inside the dealership waiting, he talked with the service guy. "Before you finish and let the car down, can you look around the undercarriage for a tracking device? I don't want to sound crazy, but I think she's being followed."

"Yes, sir, I can do that for you. I'll let you know when we're done."

Brandon joined Kate inside where he grabbed a cup of coffee for both of them and handed one to Kate. "I'll feel better knowing this is done after driving back here from Wyoming. I'm sure the oil needed changing."

"Thank you for caring so much." Kate smiled and placed her hand on his thigh.

Heat from her hand penetrated his jeans as her fingers inched their way toward his knee and she squeezed his leg. Her touch electrified every nerve in his body. If Kate only knew what she made him feel each time she touched him, she'd probably laugh. He covered her hand with his and rubbed the length of her nails…remembering what they'd done to parts of his body last night tightened his groin. This woman ignited a fire in his blood that he never wanted to be extinguished. Brandon curled his fingers into her palm as he looked into her eyes. "I enjoy taking care of you."

Half an hour later, the service tech

drew his attention at the front desk and nodded for Brandon to come out to the car. "I'll go take care of the bill. Sit tight." Brandon followed the tech out to the car that still sat up on the hydraulics.

"This was stuck up beneath the driver's seat of the undercarriage." The tech dropped a small black box into Brandon's hand and he looked it over. The antenna was about two inches long. "That son of a bitch! Have a hammer I can use?"

"Yes, sir." He pulled a hammer from his toolbox and took Brandon over to a workbench.

Brandon wrapped the box in a grease cloth, laid it on the bench and hit it at least five times, wishing it were the head of his enemy instead of a mechanical device. He shook the grease rag over the trash barrel to be rid of it all and narrowed his gaze at the tech. "This is just between the two of us."

"You got it. Let's settle the bill and you're on your way."

He returned to the waiting room and Kate joined him at the register where she opened her purse to look for money. "Everything okay?"

Brandon pulled her in for a hug and kissed the top of her head, thankful Scarface wouldn't be tracking her anymore. "It is now. I got this. All the fluids are topped off and ready to go when we get back from Los Angeles." He paid the charges and drove away with Kate, scanning the area for the sound of motorcycles or any sitting around nearby. His anger at finding the black box had infuriated him. He was glad Kate didn't find out about it. That would have made her worry even more and right now, she worried about enough shit.

He couldn't wait to get back home and out of all the traffic. Then he remembered Los Angeles. Fat chance of getting out of congestion. At least Cody would be doing the driving there. He and Kate could relax and enjoy the area if they could get some free time away from the promos. Cody didn't go into much detail about how busy the promo schedule would be so time would tell.

Glancing over at Kate, she seemed to be deep in thought and he hoped she wasn't having second thoughts. "Did you want to spend the day with your parents?"

Her green eyes widened and she smiled. "You're okay with that? I don't want you to be bored."

He reached over to squeeze her thigh. "They need to get to know me better and to feel comfortable with me taking you across the country again. Tell me the way."

"Thank you, babe. I think they really like you. Dad will be glad to get to know you better." She texted her mom to let them know they'd be there soon.

Brandon followed her directions as he prayed her parents truly were alright with Kate being with him. He wanted them to know he could afford to take care of their only child in the way she was accustomed to. Kate would be an asset to him in many ways when he considered her offer to help with the computer site for his furniture. He didn't want her to be bored back home in Dubois and if she wanted to look for work, she could, but she didn't need to work. Money wasn't an issue and he needed to make sure she knew that.

Kate's parents lived in a large home. Brandon pulled into the driveway and he followed her into the house. At the back entrance, he saw their beautiful sitting area beneath a covered patio with a firepit and hot tub nearby. Would they ever travel west to see where Kate would be living?

Keith and Micki greeted them with hugs. "Let's go sit outside. It's a beautiful day."

Her dad opened the refrigerator and handed Kate a beer. "Brandon? What can I get you? I have regular or dark beer?"

He laughed. "A man after my own heart. I'll take a dark beer. Thanks." Although he preferred Jack Daniel's™, having it this early in the day was never a good idea.

Keith handed him a beer, took one for himself and Micki, and they all made their way outside. The cushioned chairs and table created a cozy area out here in the shade and Brandon made a mental note to make a few changes to his deck area when he got back home with Kate.

This was good for him to see where she was raised.

Her mom reached over and took Kate's hand and glanced at Brandon. "Kate's told us a bit of your background. We're happy that you both seem to get along. We're a little protective of our baby, but we know we can't keep her at home forever. So, tell us a bit of what you have planned for our little girl."

Brandon truly enjoyed her parents and understood their concern. "We're going to move slow with our relationship to get to know each other better. I'm not sure how familiar you are with Native American culture, but I've had visions of your daughter for years. The emerald ring she wears has been passed down through our family for generations. I know this might be hard to understand for those who don't believe in fate, but my grandfathers are visionaries and have also seen Kate in my *future*." He paused long enough for her parents to take in what he'd just told them before he continued. Micki raised an eyebrow and glanced at Keith, who looked back at Brandon. "We believe in soul reincarnation and Kate's soul has traveled back in time, part of the dreams she's had. My grandfathers think both of us have lived before and that our souls connected long ago."

Micki gave a short gasp and looked at Kate. "I had no idea."

"Monica knows the whole story, mom. All of this *is* possible. It sounds silly, but we feel like we've known each other before."

Brandon rolled his beer bottle between his fingers as he looked from Keith to Micki. "Her ring was passed down in our family through the years to the oldest son of each generation, believing that one day the woman it belonged to would reclaim it…and now she has."

Micki rubbed her arms. "That story gives me goosebumps!"

Kate blushed as she smiled at her parents. "I know, right? Who would ever have thought *this* was even possible?" She reached over for Brandon's hand and rubbed her thumb over the back of it. "We've talked of nothing else for the past few months. Our destiny seems so normal."

She looked back at her parents. "I hope both of you are okay with us together. He's amazing and I want you to know him like I do."

Keith held up his beer. "Thank you for making our daughter happy. It's easy to see she is. Just be careful in LA. Things happen out there and you're taking her pretty far away from us."

"I promise she'll keep in touch so you know what's happening. I'm pretty amazed myself. This isn't what I'd planned when my friend asked if I wanted to be a part of his project." Brandon laughed and shook his head as he tapped his bottle to Keith's. Neither of them had any idea of the supernatural things that had followed them through time and all the way to Pittsburgh. He could do without informing them of that stuff tonight, but he'd follow whatever Kate intended to tell them and leave that all up to her.

"Brandon also makes lodgepole furniture for a living. His pieces are beautiful. He's made beds, nightstands, dressers, and armoires. Mom, you'd love them. He even sells them online."

"The email orders have been crazy lately and those alone keep me busy. Now my friend wants to do a sequel to this movie thing. I don't know." Brandon hadn't really thought about all he had going on to realize his future might be very busy.

"Hon, we can do it together. I'll help where I can. I promise." Kate squeezed his hand.

Micki pursed her lips as she gazed at her daughter. Brandon could see her heart breaking already. "That would mean you have future plans to move out west. I would hate to lose you, but I knew we couldn't keep you here forever. We just want to know you're happy, Katie."

She hugged her mom tight. "I can't begin to tell you how happy I really am, mom. So much has happened since I've met Brandon and my dreams make sense to me now. You know how bad some of my dreams affected me. I had to find answers and I think I have now." Kate let go of her mom and relaxed back in her chair. "We want you to come visit. His log home is huge and has extra bedrooms for you to stay for a while."

Keith raised an eyebrow and appeared to take on a new liking to Brandon that he felt across the table. "A log home is quite an investment, son."

"I followed my heart when I had it built, yet didn't know whether I'd ever find the woman of my dreams to share it with. I was beginning to think I'd spend my life alone until I saw Kate in town during her visit. Our connection was immediate and I felt as though I'd known her all my life. It was as though she was plucked from my dreams and came to life the day I saw her."

Tears came to Micki's eyes. "To think someone has had feelings their entire life that were meant only for my daughter makes me happy. Thank you, Brandon." She wiped a tear from her cheek. "This is too much like a fairy tale."

"Mom, we truly *are* happy. Brandon's life could change so much after we get to LA. Who's lucky enough to have this happen to them? I promise I'll call as soon as we land there and call every day so you know what's happening. Monica is driving to the airport in the morning. That way, her car is there when she returns."

"Then we only have celebrating to do, I guess."

Brandon enjoyed spending the rest of the afternoon with Kate's parents, who seemed genuinely happy that their daughter had found someone who loved her. Time would tell if they continued to feel that way, but he'd do his best to meet their standards. Before he and Kate left, they both hugged her parents and reassured them Kate was in capable hands.

"I know you have packing to do

so we won't keep you any longer. Call when you get there." Keith shook Brandon's hand. "She's made a good choice. Good luck on the movie deals."

On the way home, Brandon held Kate's hand and she could feel his love through his touch. Their connection still amazed her as she enjoyed the drive home, knowing she might not be back to Pittsburgh for a while. She hoped her parents wouldn't worry too much about her safety. Calling them daily would help them with her absence and reassure them she'd be fine.

Brandon squeezed her hand. "Changing your mind about traveling?"

She turned toward him and her throat tightened as she thought of the love shared between them. "Don't you *even* think that way. I was just thinking about how long it might be before I see Pittsburgh again, but I'm so excited to begin this journey with you. Thank you for choosing me."

"I'm glad the Great Spirit picked you for me. Fate is amazing sometimes.

I couldn't have chosen a better partner, babe. We can help each other."

Kate smiled so big her cheeks hurt. She couldn't remember the last time she was this happy. "We should be able to get our packing done in time to get to bed early. This will be fun for us. And I'm excited that Monica is going with us. She and I will have a blast. While you're with your producer, she'll keep me busy." She directed him home and once in the house, she scurried around to pack. The laundry got finished last night so all they had to do was throw things into the luggage.

Brandon set both bags by the front door and turned toward her as she handed him her carryon bag. He set it on top of the suitcases. "You're sure this is what you want?"

She took a step toward him and reached up to cup his face. The tenderness in his eyes wrapped her in a love that she'd felt only one other time in her life…with Taima. "How can you even think I wouldn't want to share the future with you when you could have picked any woman to take my place?"

His arms pulled her against him and he stared into her eyes. She held her breath and placed her palms on his chest, hoping he'd never change his mind as he stared at her. Then his lips parted and she still couldn't breathe. "You were chosen for me long ago, white woman. No other female has come close to getting near my heart the way you have. Not long ago, I thought I would spend my life alone because the woman of my dreams hadn't appeared, even when I dreamt of her so often. I just assumed I would live in that huge home alone forever."

Brandon's warm fingers threaded through her hair, his thumbs caressing her cheeks as he bent to kiss her. She slid her hands around his waist and met his kiss as though it were their first. He sucked the air from her lungs and their tongues teased one another while their bodies melded together. Kate loved being in his embrace and it was a good thing for as weak as he made her knees.

He pulled from the kiss to gaze at her. She looked back at him, searching his eyes with only one thought on her mind...wishing he'd carry her to bed. "You take my breath away each time you kiss me and I hope that never changes." She hugged him close, kissed his neck and tasted his skin.

Soon warm fingers made their way beneath her tank top and up her back. "I'd like to do more than take your breath away." Brandon peeled her top over her head and cupped her breasts as he shook his head. "You are so perfect for me."

"Take me to bed, handsome." Kate's fingers worked at the buckle of his belt.

"You've become an addiction for me. You have no idea how much I need and crave your nearness." Brandon picked her up and carried her off to bed.

* * * * *

Kate gazed out the window of the plane as they came in for landing at the airport in Jackson Hole. Her stomach flipped with butterflies at the thought of showing Monica her new home and hoped she'd visit more in the future once all of this movie excitement had died down. She reached over the seat in front of her and rubbed Monica's shoulder. "I'm so glad you came with us. I hope you love it out here."

"The snow-covered mountains are beautiful, but the snow should be gone by now, right?"

"No, the upper elevations have snow all year round. Even in August, when the temperatures climb at ground level, the snow is still there because the elevation reaches over thirteen thousand feet out here in the Rockies. And it's not humid here!"

Monica turned around in her seat to talk with Brandon. "Thank you for letting me tag along. I can't wait to see everything out here."

Kate rubbed Brandon's thigh and then tightened her fingers as the plane landed. Her time with Brandon had become a necessity the longer they were together and she knew, at some point, she and Monica would be flying home without him when his time would be spent working on the movie sequel. She smiled at him, knowing that event might be a month away yet.

He leaned toward her as the passengers began to stand for departure. "I'll grab us a rental car after we get the bags and we can head over to Dubois. Come on."

Inside at baggage claim, Kate nudged Brandon as she watched Monica stare at the cowboys grabbing luggage from the carousel and hoisting them over their shoulder. Kate put her arm around Monica and leaned closer. "Kinda makes you want to learn how to ride horses, doesn't it?"

Monica's gazed followed more than a few of the men as they made their way out. "I'd let any one of them teach me."

Kate laughed. "We'll find you a cowboy to ride. Come on." Brandon had pulled their bags from the carousel and she grabbed her bag and followed Brandon to the rental area, all the while watching Monica admire the scenery.

Kate waited with her as Brandon secured the car for them.

He soon joined them. "Wait here while I go get the car. I'll pick you up at the door over there in a few minutes. I'm also going to call Dan to let him know I'm home and see how Smoke is doing." Brandon pulled her bag with his as he made his way through the crowd and disappeared through the door and out to the rental lot.

Monica shook her head as she looked up at the huge log beams inside the airport. "I love the architecture out here. This is beautiful. I'm glad I decided to come out here with you."

"Wait until you see Brandon's place. He drew the plans and helped build it. It's huge and has room enough for several guests. Let's head out to wait for Brandon. He said the ride over to Dubois takes about an hour. We'll be back here in two days to fly to LA. It's going to be busy for a week, that's for sure."

14.

An hour later, Brandon pulled into his driveway and breathed a sigh of relief to be home. Dan and his wife were there as Smoke ran around the yard. The wolf jumped into Brandon's arms when he walked around the rented SUV and Brandon hugged him tight. He'd missed Smoke more than he realized he would and thanked Dan for taking care of Smoke. "I have to leave again in two days for a trip to LA. Are you two fine with watching out for him for another week?"

They agreed as Dan shook hands with Brandon, hugged him and wished him luck. "It's been a long day and we're ready to put our feet up for a while. Thanks again." Brandon pulled out their suitcases from the SUV, unlocked the front door and Smoke beat them inside.

"Brandon, this is a beautiful home! It's huge and you live here alone?"

"Not for much longer…I hope." He winked at Kate and held the door open while Monica pulled her luggage behind her. He loved her reactions as she looked up at the second-floor walkway. He was proud of his home and enjoyed sharing and showing it off. "There are several guest rooms upstairs. Feel free to pick which one you want."

"I feel like I'm in the log home of somebody rich and famous. It's breathtaking, really. The lodgepole design is like something from a magazine." Monica held her hand over her heart as she admired the log-railed staircase to the second floor. "I'm going to sleep well tonight. Thank you."

Brandon's pride bubbled to the surface as Monica's wide eyes looked around. "Get comfortable in your room and I'll get us a few beers once we unpack for tonight." He went to his room and Kate went to her room. He hoped soon she would join him. Sleeping together at her place had been nice and he didn't look forward to sleeping alone tonight. He placed his suitcase on his bed and unpacked so he could repack in a day for LA.

As he turned to open a dresser drawer, he saw Kate leaning against his doorframe looking so sexy with her head tilted against the frame. "I'm not unpacking much, but I'm sure you need to repack other clothes for LA."

"I suppose. I doubt the investors want to see me in jeans." He laughed at that image.

"I'm glad you'll be there to meet them. You deserve this, you know. And I can't wait to see the premiere."

"It will only be more fun because I know you'll be at my side the whole time." He put the clothes in the drawer, pushed it shut, and stared back at Kate as his heart swelled with appreciation that she cared enough to go with him. "I hope *tonight* you'll be by my side also." Brandon held his breath as he waited for her answer.

"I thought you'd never ask." Her green eyes pleaded for a hug.

"I wasn't sure you'd want to with Monica upstairs." He moved close enough to kiss her, their first after such a long day, and then pulled her against him. Her body felt so tiny within his embrace, but he loved that the top of her head was the right height to tuck her beneath his chin. "I didn't want to start assuming things between us. That's not good." Brandon breathed in her scent and then released her enough to lightly run his finger down the bridge of her nose. Being this close to her made the blood rush through more than just his veins.

"Monica would be disappointed if I let you sleep alone tonight. She already assumes what is happening." A rosy blush covered her cheeks as she looked up at him.

Footsteps came down the stairway and a faint 'hello' called out to them.

Brandon lovingly swatted Kate's ass, wishing he could take her to bed right this minute. "There are beers in the fridge or Jack in the cupboard. I'll take a Jack, if you would, and I'll be right out."

Monica and Smoke were getting acquainted when Kate stepped into the room. "Did you find a room to suit you? I think all of them are great up there. Are you wanting a beer or Jack on the rocks? I don't think he has any wine here yet. We'll have to remedy that soon."

"I'll do a beer for now. Smoke is quite the pet. He's a wolf, isn't he?"

Kate filled two tumblers with ice and poured the amber liquid in. "Yes, he is, but I have to tell you, something about him makes me think he's more than just a wolf. The Native Americans are close to them and this one almost seems to be human to me or had been in a prior life. Does that even make sense to you?"

"How far back in time are you thinking?" Monica pulled out a bar stool at the island and made herself comfortable as Kate poured her beer into a frosty glass from the freezer.

"I think he is Taima's father, Sakima, whom I met when I traveled back in time in my dreams. He was the medicine man for their tribe. I find him watching me at times, as though he knows who I was and where I've been. It's a good thing you believe in all this because anyone else would think I was nuts."

Monica looked at Smoke who stood nearby. "Should your name be Sakima and not Smoke?"

Smoke barked and tipped his head to the side as he looked at Monica.

Kate watched their interaction with interest.

Then his tail wagged as Brandon entered the room. "Easy, boy. Are these women getting *you* all riled up, too?"

Monica reached out to Smoke and he stepped closer so she could pat his head. When her fingers scratched behind his ears and rubbed his head, she gasped and glanced at Kate. "You aren't going to believe the visions I just got from him." She met Smoke's gaze and the two stared at each other.

For several minutes, it seemed as though Monica had a silent conversation with the wolf. Kate knew something else was transpiring between her best friend and Brandon's. Smoke whined and sat at attention before Monica as his tail dusted the floor. Then he barked again and placed his paw on Monica's knee. She patted his head again and looked from Kate to Brandon.

"You had no idea of the spirit that has lived with you all this time?"

Kate turned to Brandon as he sipped his drink, looking from Monica to Smoke. "I know he's special to me and keeps an eye on the place. How do you know of Taima's father, Sakima?"

"I have abilities that allow that. Your souls have traveled side by side through many life cycles. You've been together for a long time, Brandon…or should I call you Taima?"

Smoke barked again and walked over for Brandon to scratch his ears. When he reached down for the small interaction, Smoke rubbed against his thigh and sat down.

"There are other souls that follow both of you and we know who they are. It will be Smoke who will put an end to them both. How or when, none of us knows, but he showed me who they were."

"Let's get comfortable over here." Brandon set his glass on a coaster on the end table next to the leather sofa and sat down. Kate joined him and Monica sat in the recliner and put her feet up. Smoke curled up on his huge pillow bed near Brandon. "This is a lot to take in when I was hoping it would end. So, it really isn't over, is it? The raven and Scar Face won't stay back east, will they?"

Kate gripped her glass tight as her breath caught, fearing what she already knew to be true.

Monica shook her head. "Not from the visions Smoke just shared with me. You've named him wrong, too. He is Sakima."

"My great, great grandfather."

"Yes." Monica took a drink. "This is all pretty crazy for me. I've had visions before, and when Kate first came out here, I had more visions. When I didn't hear from her for a few days, I panicked, but couldn't get through to her on the phone and I had no other way of reaching her." Monica looked at Kate. "I saw the dangerous bird and a crazy woman, but couldn't make sense of what I saw."

"Do you ever see visions of how you are tied into all of this with us? Because I don't have a clue." Kate swirled her glass so the ice mixed around her drink.

"I have no idea. Maybe something in LA will give me more of a clue. It'll be interesting. Right now, I'm exhausted from flying today and it feels good just to put my feet up. The drive over here from Jackson Hole was gorgeous. Do you ever get tired of the beauty out there?"

"I don't. There's a different view around every bend in the road. To be able to look down on the wildlife feeding in the valleys here is truly a gift." Brandon hugged Kate. "I'm thankful for many things right now."

She snuggled against the man who had become her rock, reminding her so much of Taima that it made her memories come alive. Or was it just because the setting sun was darkening the room? She glanced at Smoke as he rested on his bed, but kept his head up and ears alert. His eyes stared into hers as though he understood everything being said. When he suddenly snapped his head around to look out the sliding glass door, Kate's stomach knotted as his ears twitched.

Smoke scrambled over to the door and scanned the backyard.

When Monica looked at Kate, her brows scrunched in question. "Is he always that alert? I didn't hear anything." A moment later, she pressed the foot of her recliner down and sat forward in her chair. "Don't get up or go near the window."

Goosebumps covered Kate's arms and Brandon pulled her close.

Monica set her beer on the end table and walked over to rub Smoke's head. Now they both gazed out the window. "She's out there, isn't she, boy."

The wolf growled and stood on his

hind feet, placing his paws high on the glass. He looked at Brandon, jumped down and paced in circles to be let out. Monica called him to her side. "That's not such a good idea right now, my friend. That's exactly what she wants."

Monica pulled on the door handle to be sure it was locked, and Kate relaxed a bit. This isn't how she envisioned their evening going. As she rubbed Brandon's thigh, she knew he'd tensed up when Smoke wanted out and now, she looked into his eyes. "Monica can read the spirit world. She knows what's happening and she knew Smoke's spirit and where he came from."

"I think we should close the drapes." When Monica turned for approval, Kate nodded and Monica pulled them across the doorway.

Brandon touched a lamp next to him to turn on the light. "The darkness isn't as welcoming as it used to be." He turned his glass as it sat on the coaster. "I can't say I felt uneasy here until I brought Kate home the day she fell on the rocks in Whiskey Basin. Ever since then, I've seen shadows and felt a presence around me."

As Monica returned to her chair, she pushed back and sipped her beer again. "Has Smoke appeared more watchful since that time, too?"

Brandon nodded. "He has. I catch him watching the treetops and his ears are always up." Smoke walked over and rested his head on Brandon's knee, begging for a touch.

Kate watched Monica, who watched Smoke as Brandon stroked his head. Since the two had been friends for so long, she knew when Monica was seeing visions and right now she was. Dare she ask what Monica saw? Was she as aware of the past as Kate? She wondered how much Monica knew of all that she'd experienced when she traveled back in time.

"Brandon, how much do you want to know of your past lives?" Monica spoke softly but waited for him to consider her question.

He looked at Kate. "You already

know what she is about to tell us, don't you?"

Pausing, Kate debated, but then chose to let Monica relay what she saw. "I do, but she may tell us something I didn't perceive about our situation." Looking back to Monica, Kate took a long drink before the words came out.

Monica looked from her to Brandon and took time to choose her words. "Smoke shows me visions of his village when he walked the earth as a man." Monica looked at Kate. "Taima could easily have been his father. The resemblance is astounding."

Chills ran down Kate's back. "The blue eyes come from Taima's mother, who had been captured by Sakima's men. She chose to continue her life as Sakima's wife and Taima was an only child. His son, Kelee, also had blue eyes." Kate's vision blurred as she remembered the young boy and how they'd become so close while she'd been there with them.

"There was another couple that I see around Taima. Best friends maybe,

I'm not sure." Monica appeared to be sorting through what was being shown to her and then her eyes rounded. "Oh my god!" She gasped and set down her glass as she stared at Kate. Pushing down the footrest, Monica sat forward and then put her face in her hands as if to concentrate more.

This made Kate sit on the edge of the sofa, still with her hand on Brandon's thigh.

"Monica…what?"

She slowly glanced up and stared at Kate. "It makes so much sense now…why we're best friends." She held out her arms and Kate saw the goose bumps on her arms. "Was her name Aiyana?"

At hearing that name aloud, Kate nearly dropped her glass and decided to set it on the coffee table. "You're right. I didn't put that together but yes, Aiyana and I had become very close in just a short time." She looked at Brandon. "Taima's best friend was Ahanu, whose wife was Aiyana. Taima and Ahanu were nearly inseparable and because of that, Aiyana and I grew closer." Kate shook her head. "I can't believe how the past plays into our future lives."

"That's how reincarnation happens and our souls normally stay close to one another through time and many life journeys. It's very rare that we're allowed to realize just how close souls travel with each other and for the four of us, Smoke included, to be here, now, is amazing.

We don't always come back as humans, especially the Native Americans." Monica finished her beer and then ran her fingers through her auburn hair. "Smoke is here as a protector to Brandon, the same as he protected and guided Taima as his father, Sakima. I do have to warn you again…the evil from back then has also traveled through time to follow both of you. That is the uneasiness that you feel around you now."

Kate lifted her glass and emptied it. "Scar Face and Mai are the two troublemakers. Neither of them would stop bothering Taima and me. They hated when life went smooth and Taima's people were happy." Again, she remembered so much of her time travel, the nights around the campfire as his people danced in celebration. "How can we put an end to this so that those two stop traveling and following our souls?"

"For that, I don't have the answers. Wow, tonight has been quite a journey for me, guys. Life makes more sense and tells me why I am within your circle of life. It's going to be interesting. When I met Dan and his wife this afternoon, I didn't receive any special signs or visions around them. My guess is that they're just souls connecting with you here and now." Monica stood to walk around a bit.

Kate held out her hand for Brandon's glass. "I know you need a refill as much as I do. Monica, how about you?"

"Hell yes, I need another beer. I'll be right back."

Brandon followed Kate into the kitchen and opened the Jack Daniels™ as she filled each glass with more ice.

She watched as he poured the amber liquid to melt some of the cubes and she got lost in thoughts of how life melts together sometimes. Her gaze moved up to Brandon's and before she realized, his lips touched hers as his fingers threaded through her hair and pulled her closer.

He released her from the kiss and stared into her eyes. "I just needed to make sure you were still real and that I'm not dreaming." His tongue wet his lips and her thoughts drifted to places they shouldn't.

"I'm here…and feel like this is where I belong. That's so strange."

Monica screamed and Smoke howled at the same time a thud hit the house near the sliding door. Kate followed Brandon into the living room. As he tore open the drapes and flipped on the porch light, all of them screamed when they saw a crazed woman raise her arms in the air as if to attack. Right before their eyes, she shifted into a raven and flew from the deck off into the trees.

Smoke dug at the door wanting out,

then barked and paced before the window.

Kate and Brandon turned toward Monica, her eyes nearly as wide as Kate's felt.

Monica touched her chest. "Tell me you saw that woman!"

"Brandon, she was the same woman who jumped on the hood of your car that night."

"So you've seen her before this?"

"Yes!" Kate turned to try and calm Smoke, but he wanted outside. "Brandon, look at the feathers all over the deck. Damnit! Not now!"

Brandon opened the slider and Smoke darted out the door and dove off the deck into the darkness. He relocked the door. "He has to find out for himself that the raven is no longer in the yard." Brandon stared up at the rafters. "I don't know about the two of you, but I need that drink. This is a lot to take in for one night." He turned on the lights over the kitchen island and Kate sat in a chair next to Monica.

Brandon set down their drinks on

the island, emptied his and refilled his glass. "I can't say that I've dreamt of any of this stuff happening. Kate I've dreamed of for years, but nothing after that. This shit is crazy."

Kate sipped her whiskey in silence as she thought back to her time with Taima and all the problems Mai had caused for them. The woman had nearly taken her soul when she had entered Kate's body and that still knotted her stomach to even think back on that time. "The evil surrounding that woman can seep right through us. I hate this."

Monica leaned over and hugged her. "I wish I had answers for you. I do know that it is now between the spirits of Sakima and Mai. He has tried to destroy her spirit for centuries."

The howls of a wolf eerily came through the windows of Brandon's home and they each looked at the other. Brandon led the way to the sliding door and opened it to wait for Smoke's return.

Kate stood with them and peered out into the darkness, praying that

Smoke was safe. Waiting, watching, praying for Smoke, a band around her heart tightened. She knew Brandon worried.

Another two howls drifted on the breeze that came through the door. Kate tried to make out shapes at the back of Brandon's property.

She blinked twice.

Then there was no doubt.

A warrior dressed in deerskin shifted into a wolf and sat in the shadows at the edge of woods.

Kate spun around to Monica, her face void of color. "Tell me you saw *that*!"

Monica nodded, her face drained of color. "I did. That's exactly how I see Smoke when I look into his eyes. Was that how you remember Sakima, the warrior?"

Kate rubbed her forehead, then looked at Brandon. "Did you see him shift? I take it you've never seen him do that?"

"Never. I've always known there was something special about him, but that's it." Brandon stepped out on the deck and called for Smoke.

Kate waited beside him. Smoke disappeared into the shadows but soon came running toward the house. "What is he carrying in his mouth?"

Smoke scurried onto the deck, dropped a dead bird along with a piece of dirty material and stepped back. The raven's neck had been broken and the head had flopped forward to lay in front of the bird's chest.

15.

Kate stepped closer for a better look at what Smoke had dropped onto the deck, but a hand on her shoulder pulled her back. A stench surrounded the dead bird

"Don't go near that." Monica took over and splayed her arm out so Brandon would move backward also.

Smoke barked, as if he were asking for approval in killing the raven.

Monica crouched next to the wolf and gently took his head between her hands, her thumbs stroking his cheeks. Kate watched, amazed at the tender touch her friend bestowed on Smoke, then she noticed the blood on one of his ears. There had to have been a fight between Mai and Sakima.

"Good boy. You can be proud that you've put an end to a centuries-old evil spirit and many can now rest. Thank you, Sakima, for protecting Brandon and Kate." Monica touched her forehead to Smoke's forehead and Kate watched as the two shared a special moment between them. When Monica stood, she took a deep breath and looked at Brandon. "He said you will have to deal with Scar Face. I have no idea when or how that will come to happen, but Sakima has done what he was here for. He said the rest is in your hands, but he'll be here when you need him again." She paused to watch Brandon. "He's the biker that came into the bar that day, isn't he?"

Brandon didn't answer right away, but didn't look away from her gaze. "Yes. I don't think he's a shifter though. So his travel is the same as ours. I can feel when he's near though." Brandon glanced at Kate. "When we had your oil changed, the service guy showed me a tracking device that had been put beneath your car. That's how he knew where to find us all the time."

Kate gasped at the audacity of their intruder who seemed to follow no matter where they were. "I just don't believe how far he goes. Will he ever stop?"

"He won't. Sakima said it's an old wound between those two and you. How it can be resolved is anyone's guess." Monica looked at all the feathers still on the deck. "I will need a shovel and we need to start a fire out here to burn the carcass and piece of material. Neither of you can touch anything. While you start a fire, Brandon, I will sweep up these feathers. They must also be burned."

Kate hugged her best friend, thankful that she was here when this happened so they could better understand the past and present. "Thank you so much. I'm glad you're here. I'll get the broom."

Brandon headed down the steps into the dark in search of firewood.

When Kate returned, Monica was talking to Smoke as though he were a person that everyone talked with. She stood at the slider, not wanting to interrupt their special moment. Her friend had connected on another level with the spirits around her. Smiling, Kate was glad that she could be a part of all of this. Now to put an end to some of the evil surrounding her and Brandon. Yet, they still had to deal with Scar Face, or Bear, as Brandon had called him. Did the man even understand why he followed her and Brandon all the way to Pittsburgh? She wasn't sure she even understood it all.

If he and Brandon had gone to school together, was their heated hatred something that had always been there between them? If she could get Brandon to discuss it more, maybe Monica would know how to deal with him. Brandon had brought up the shovel and was now starting a fire out back in the fire pit.

"Hon? What are you so deep in thought about?" Monica tipped her head and held out her hand for the broom.

Kate shook her head. "I guess I'm still in shock that so much has happened tonight after all the time we've dealt with watching over our shoulder. Remember all the trouble she caused us back home? Is *her* part in this really over? How do we know it is really Mai?"

Taking the broom, Monica swept the dead bird and feathers into the shovel. "Yes, it is. Sakima showed me their battle and her death. It is done." Monica paused to look at Kate. "Although, I'm not as confident about the biker. I haven't seen what he's up to or even where he might be right now. If he can't track the two of you, he might think you're still in Pittsburgh."

Kate closed the slider. "Let's get her down to the fire and watch her burn in hell."

"Take Smoke with you and pull me a few sprigs of fresh sage to throw on the fire when we're done."

Brandon watched Monica carry the shovel and dead bird toward him. He prayed this would be the end of Mai, or…would she find some way to come back to haunt them? Would he and Kate ever be free of her? Even though Kate had told him repeatedly what Mai had put her through, he wasn't sure Kate would believe she could be free of Mai. "Where is Kate going?"

"I need fresh sage to throw on the fire once the carcass has burned for 30 minutes. I'm glad you have chairs out here. It's a beautiful evening to celebrate freedom from evil spirits." Monica sat down with her shovel near the fire. "Before Kate gets back here, I want to say how happy I am for both of you. She's dreamt of you for years without understanding what you were all about or why she had the dreams. That is how spirits work to bring people together, even when they have no idea who the other person might be or their purpose in our lives. You both belong together, so it's wonderful to see her this happy."

"My dreams of her have also gone on for years, never knowing when I would find her. The day I saw her in town was amazing. I felt her nearby. Then in the store that day, I don't know, I just can't explain it or how it came to be. She was there when I turned around and we stared at each other. Then I waited for her outside the store."

When Kate approached the fire pit, Brandon held out his arms to her. She sat on his knee and snuggled close. He caressed her backside as he admired the angel in his arms. "I nearly had to beg in order to show her around town that day. Now I don't ever want her to leave my side."

She kissed his nose. "Are we ready to put this evil behind us? I hope this works."

Monica stood. "Both of you hold hands. I have no idea how this will happen, but I'm hoping it just burns to dust."

Brandon held tight to Kate and took her hand, feeling her tremble as they waited. He loved the smell of a campfire, but tonight might change that. Monica tossed the shovel full of bird and feathers into the fire. Bits of burning material floated up into the night sky as Brandon prayed to the Great Spirit that the evil would end.

The awful smell got worse as the flames surrounded the carcass.

It took a moment for the oily

feathers to take on the flame. When they did, a raven caw sounded all around them, the wind picked up and suddenly the eyes of the raven widened and stared directly at Brandon and Kate through the flames. The mouth opened and another raven cry could be heard through the backyard all the way to the woods.

A woman's scream sounded in the distance.

Smoke barked and howled, as if to say good riddance.

Kate buried her face against Brandon's neck and her entire body shook as she cried.

He held her tight, knowing how tormented she had been all this time.

Monica stepped closer and took Kate's hand. "Hon, you have to watch so you know that it's over. She's gone for good. I promise. Watch the remains shrivel and disintegrate."

Kate turned toward the fire and she trembled in his arms, but didn't look away from the flames. "We are free of her and she can no longer hurt you, babe." He kissed her cheek and watched the orange flames lick around the wood, consuming the bones and feathers of their enemy. Monica used a stick to stir the fire and it reached higher into the sky.

Brandon continued to pray as he sat with Kate. "Let this be the end of her reign. Send her to hell for all time." He sat back in the large Adirondack chair and Kate snuggled as they watched for another twenty minutes. Crickets in the distance began to chirp and Smoke even relaxed enough to lay down between Brandon and Monica.

"Kate, you are the one who must place the sage branches on the fire to purify the flames and surroundings of her evil. Are you ready for that?"

"I am." Kate bent to pick up the tiny branches and held them to her nose to breath in the scent. She glanced back at Brandon and then tossed them into the fire, one at a time until six had been placed on the wood. Brandon breathed in the aroma and watched as the embers floated into the air as a blessing. A heaviness lifted from his heart and at the same moment, Kate turned toward him again. "You felt that too, didn't you? She *is* gone."

Smoke sat up and barked.

"You felt it also, didn't you, boy? I think I will call you Sakima from now on." Brandon rubbed his head and hugged his wolf.

Another bark and a tail wag told Brandon he agreed.

After an hour, the fire had died down and Brandon realized that he no longer felt the lurking evil presence. His eyes scanned the hills around him and the mountain peaks pointed toward the moon. He loved living out west versus the bustling cities back east. Those people had no idea what peacefulness truly was, because now, *he* was also at peace, with the angel of his dreams. He trailed his fingers through Kate's hair. "I'm ready for another drink and celebrate that we are free. How about you?"

"I second that. Monica, thank you for being out here with us. Let's go in and find something to eat before we head to bed."

Brandon took her hand as they walked toward the house. *Sakima* played with Monica as they chased each other around the yard before going in. Brandon laughed to see his wolf this happy. "I think he likes his new name better. It fits him. Look how happy he is now. There *has* been a change!"

Hours later, Kate stood before one of the sinks in Brandon's bathroom and he had to stop just to admire how good she looked sharing his home. Hopefully, soon enough, she would be here to stay and they could concentrate on their relationship more. Tomorrow they would relax, but the next day he'd be driving them back over the pass to Jackson Hole to begin their journey to LA for the premiere of Cody's movie.

Clothing hit the floor in the bathroom and Brandon's gaze admired slender thighs, a rounded bottom, curves at her waist and then…Kate turned toward him. Full breasts begged for his attention, hard pink nubs begged for him to taste them and his breath caught in his throat. He knew he couldn't take a step forward yet, so he met her gaze and stared. Could she out stare him?

He doubted that. The longer he stared, the more she begged.

Her eyes pleaded for him to come closer.

Her lips parted.

Slowly her tongue moved over her lip and she tipped her head in that sexy way she had.

Standing barefoot, the tiles of the bedroom floor did nothing to cool his blood.

Control over his emotions was something he'd mastered years ago, but he'd waited all day to be alone with her, caress her skin, feel the beat of her heart beneath his touch. Brandon peeled his tee shirt up and over his head, tossing it on the chair in the corner.

Her gaze moved to the button on his jeans and he waited for her to meet his gaze. "Turn on the shower, White Woman. Your night has only just begun."

Kate opened the glass door to the shower.

Water sprinkled onto the stone floor as Brandon undid his jeans and stepped out of them on his way toward Kate. Wrapping his arms around her before she could turn around, he pulled her back against his chest. A breast filled one hand while his other slipped down past her waist. As she tipped her head, his tongue tasted her skin and a whimper slipped from her throat.

"Hang on to me because my knees are going to give out if you keep this up."

Brandon took in a deep breath of her scented hair. "Step into the shower and under that hot water. I'm sure it's cooler than how hot you've made my body." Without letting go of her, they stepped together into the body jets and overhead rain shower.

Kate turned in his arms and moved her hands around to his back. The water ran over her face as she stood with her eyes closed. He could watch her all night like this. Images of her were already burned into his memory. Brandon's fingers fisted in her hair and tipped her face up for a kiss he'd not soon forget.

Wet, naked skin melded together, hot against the other. They were meant to be joined.

Her tongue played over his as he lifted her, her legs went around his waist as her arms moved around his neck, holding tight. "I can't wait any longer, woman, you make me crazy."

Barking woke Kate from a sound sleep, but she lay cuddled in the arms of her lover, not wanting to stir him awake just yet. His skin was warm against hers, his breathing slow as he slept. Memories of last night were still fresh on her tongue, her lips still swollen from his kisses. God, she loved this man. Their souls had been bound through time, much like their fingers were woven together now, in sleep and while awake. A woman shouldn't be this happy when her family lived so far away, but she knew she was loved by the warrior beside her. He would forever protect her heart.

"It's about time you woke up. Your man needs coffee, White Woman." He moved her hair with his chin and tenderly kissed her neck, making her arch her back against him as they spooned.

"Be careful or I'll roll you over and neither of us will get coffee."

"Hey cow hands, you're burning daylight!"

Kate giggled. Monica had beat them to the kitchen. "We'll be right out." She rolled over to look at Brandon, still not believing that he belonged to her, heart and soul. He was beautiful to look at and memories of Taima drifted in. So much the same it was uncanny.

The smell of coffee drifted through the hall as Brandon made his way toward the kitchen, still pulling on his tee shirt.

"I didn't think you'd mind if I made a pot of coffee. By the way, your beds upstairs are like sleeping on a cloud."

"I'm glad you slept well. Thanks for the coffee."

Kate stepped next to him, stood on her toes and he kissed her, feeling as though it were as normal as getting his coffee. "Morning, baby," she said.

He gave her a wink and light pat on her behind. The joy in Brandon's heart couldn't be compared to anything in his past. Kate certainly filled the void in his life and he looked forward to their future. He poured her a cup of coffee as well and then opened the refrigerator to get the half and half for her that they grabbed before leaving Jackson yesterday.

"Thank you for remembering that I need my creamer, babe. God, I'm a lucky woman."

"Yes, you are. I think he spoils you quite a bit. It's so good to see both of you happy. It'll make life easier when I have to return home and leave you out here with him. But that's a week or two away. I don't want to dwell on that."

"Let's enjoy this out on the deck and plan for tomorrow. I can't wait to get to LA." Kate grabbed her coffee and headed that way, followed by Monica.

Brandon hung back for a moment, admiring Monica. Beautiful would top the list. Not as gorgeous as he found Kate, but close. Close enough for Cody. They could both be lucky if he played his cards right and wasn't an asshole. Brandon wasn't normally a match maker, but since she was joining them in LA and…Cody was still single, maybe there was just a chance. He chuckled to himself and then joined the two outside with Sakima, already basking in the sun. The new name fit him better than 'Smoke'. The Adirondack chairs were comfortable and made sitting outside nice. He'd made them several years ago from the extra lodge pole he had and they turned out pretty well.

The women chatted as he enjoyed the views of snow on the mountaintops. Fall would soon be here and the snow was already piling up in the high altitude. Work on the second film would be starting soon and he'd still not checked his website for furniture orders.

Kate had mentioned an interest in helping with the website orders. Maybe it was time to expand that and hire an employee who could help build with him. Dan lived next door, or rather, down the road, and he enjoyed building furniture, too. Not to the extent Brandon did, but perhaps he could talk him into it. He'd have to consider that if the movie deal took off.

Those were interesting options for a future as long as he and Kate were in the planning stages. She would be a great help and he could quit worrying about that end of the business. That just might be a plan, he thought, as he emptied his mug. "I need a refill. How about you two? I can bring them back out after I make another pot."

Brandon split out the remaining coffee, got another pot made and whitened Kate's coffee just the way she liked it. He set their mugs on a tray, grabbed a few food bars, his cell phone and strode back out to the deck.

"Brandon, thank you. What a

sweetheart. Maybe I'll steal you away when I go back to Pittsburgh."

"I'm not cut out for big city living, sorry, hon. LA is going to be a stretch for me. Been there, done that. My home is here for a reason."

Kate laughed. "It's nice to know not just anyone can use a pickup line on you!"

Brandon's cell rang. "Hhmm…it's Cody." He glanced at Kate. "Hey, dude, what's up? You change your mind and you're coming *here* instead of me having to come out there?"

"You wish! I have too much planned for you next week for that to happen. I felt vibes from you so thought I better give you a jingle to make sure you haven't changed *your* mind. Still bringing that hot little number with you?"

"Yes, Kate is joining me and so is one of her friends. Mainly to keep her company while I'm busy with you. Hope that's okay."

"Sure, sure. You're stilling arriving

at the same time? I've got the limo scheduled in case I need to change it."

"No, same arrival time. A limo eh? The ladies will love that." Brandon smiled at Kate as she listened with interest.

"Her friend wouldn't happen to be a red-head, would she?"

"I'm not going to tell you what she looks like. Would it matter?" Brandon watched Monica, knowing she listened.

Monica pulled one sexy foot up onto the edge of her seat and hugged her knee as she kept an eye on Brandon. He winked at her just to get her curiosity up and it worked.

"Of course, it doesn't matter. Just a vision or two that I've had recently. Kind of strange because I normally don't get these kinds of daydreams. They've even moved into my dreams at night, so I'm curious as to who you're bringing with you."

"Well, let me just say…I don't think you'll be disappointed. She'll be more than a handful for you, dude, and she might be a little bossy and outspoken. A nice distraction for a while. Not that I'm playing matchmaker, but you could both use some new company I think and some downtime. You can't stay a bachelor forever. See you tomorrow, Cody."

Brandon ended the call and set the phone on the side table, grinning at Monica. "Sorry, had to humor him. He gets too tied up in his work. You could be just the distraction he needs for a few days. It'll be fun, if nothing else. He's picking up the tab for it all, so enjoy yourself."

"Wow. You could be movie-star-status in no time. Thanks for letting me tag along. Being the producer's date doesn't hurt either. You're sure he doesn't have a girlfriend?"

"Positive. I'd be the first one to know." He savored the rest of his coffee as the sun warmed his jeans and bare feet. This quiet life is what he craved and didn't look forward to the fast pace of LA at all. Too much traffic, too many people. Kate liked it quiet, too. They would do well in their life together. So far, life was perfect…now that Mai had been destroyed. Kate hadn't mentioned any nightmares so he hoped there wouldn't be any issues for her.

Somewhere, one day, they'd have to deal with Bear. Him showing up was not an *if*, but a *when* and Brandon wanted to be ready. *Could we work out whatever issue Bear has with me?* It couldn't possibly be something centuries old. Perhaps Bear didn't even know that he resembled Scar Face from two hundred years back in Kate's past. Hopefully, he and Bear would get an opportunity to put an end to the hatred.

For the rest of today, he would relax and enjoy the peace and quiet. Tomorrow night would be a rowdy difference once they arrived in LA with the glitz and glamour Cody had planned.

16.

Kate leaned forward and peered out the window as the plane flew over LA. She rubbed Brandon's thigh for comfort, loving the feel of his heat on her palm. That he would ask her to accompany him to this event left her speechless. The thought of being on the arm of an upcoming movie star was an honor and she held that in her heart.

Excitement swirled through her head like the clouds outside the window as she thought about the parties and the producers she might get to meet. Then again, the meetings could happen behind closed doors, meant only for those behind the scenes. At least Monica would keep her company so that she wouldn't be left alone if Cody pulled Brandon off with the other producers.

Today, she'd worn a silk top, a light

sweater, and dress pants with medium heels. The airports were hard to maneuver in high heels, so those got packed for later. This week would be fun and perhaps she and Monica could get in some time for the pool, or better yet, the spa.

She'd never been to LA and now she would be at a movie premiere…with the hero and star of the show, no less. Kate had to force herself to breathe and with that thought, Brandon's warm hand rubbed her back to calm her. She met his gaze and smiled as she felt his reassurance. All of this was a lot to take in, yet he acted like it was just another day. He hated being in the limelight. That much she had already learned about him. Leaning back in her seat for landing, she squeezed Brandon's thigh.

He tipped his head against hers and whispered in her ear, "Please don't stress about this, babe. They are going to love you."

Kate breathed in his cologne and wished they were going straight to their room. "I'm so proud of you, just so you know." His eyes gave a tender wink and she felt the love he was sending her. "I love you, you know that."

"I do. Are you ready? The limo should have champagne to calm you. This will be fun." Brandon stood and pulled their bags from the overhead and she stepped in front of him and off the plane.

Monica grabbed her hand and gave a huge smile. Kate loved the look of her hat and sunglasses. "We are going to have a blast this week. Relax and enjoy."

"I will. I'm glad you're with us. You look *hot* today, girlfriend. I love your hat. Brandon will pull our bags at the claim area and then we can find our driver."

At baggage claim, an attendant held a sign with Brandon's name on it. When he greeted the attendant, he made Brandon point out their bags so he could grab them. "Your car awaits, sir. One moment, please."

Kate stood aside with Monica and waited. "I'm not sure that I'm ready to be waited on hand and foot. It's going to be strange."

"We deserve this, and anyway, they're used to treating the rich and famous like royalty. If Brandon's movie takes off, you better get used to this, hon. You were made to be treated this way. God, I'm so happy for you." Monica hugged her and she pulled Monica close. Their friendship was closer than normal and she would never jeopardize it. They could have been sisters in another life.

Brandon approached, held out an arm for each of them and Kate hooked her hand over his arm with pride, looking forward to the premiere. They followed the attendant to the limo as the warm breeze greeted them. He loaded the car while another held their door open. "Sir, as soon as things are ready to depart, we'll be heading to the Ritz-Carlton. Please enjoy the ride."

Inside the plush white leather interior, string lighting lit the floor and the ceiling. Two bottles of champagne sat in ice buckets with towels for serving. A covered meat and cheese tray completed the refreshments. The bottle had been opened for them and Brandon filled their glasses. "Ladies, this amazing journey would not be as much fun if I were doing this alone. Thank you to both of you for joining me. Cheers and may you enjoy the evening. It's only just begun."

Thankful for meat and cheese, Kate tried to look around as they rode to the hotel. They didn't get to open the second bottle, but the meat and cheese hit the spot and would hold her until dinner. At the hotel, luggage was unloaded. "Mr. Wakiza, I've been told to send this bottle of champagne up to your room. It'll be iced and waiting for you."

Brandon tipped both men and strode to the front desk. Before long, they arrived in their two-bedroom suite and Kate chattered at Monica as they looked around the rooms. Kate returned for a warm hug from Brandon, feeling as though she were dreaming. "I hope when I wake up from all this, that you're still beside me. This is almost too much to take in." She stood on her toes to kiss him, his lips warm and inviting. "Is this truly real?"

"It is and I'm glad I get to share this with you." He kissed her nose.

Monica cleared her throat when she joined them in the main living room and soon the luggage and more champagne arrived. "Let's have another toast and sit a bit before we unpack."

Brandon did the honors and then sat on the sofa next to Kate as she enjoyed the glass of bubbly. To actually be in LA was a bit overwhelming for her, but so exciting.

"So tell me a bit about my producer-date? I'm curious." Monica crossed her legs, her nylon-stocking feet now void of heels.

Her eyes appeared more green than hazel when she was curious and sexy. When she got concerned and worried, they seemed to be more brown. Kate loved her auburn hair as it lay over her shoulder. Kate tipped her head, waiting for Brandon to tell her about Cody.

"Hhmm, describing Cody isn't easy. He's quiet because he's constantly watching people and their reactions to their surroundings. Generosity is a good word that fits him. I could tell you he's a short stocky man with a temper, but no, that's not Cody. He's my height, wears a beard or five o'clock shadow most of the time. His emotions are in his eyes and his heart on his sleeve. That's probably something I shouldn't tell you. He expects his people to do as he tells them when he's paying for their service. He surrounds himself with a knowledgeable staff so they can make him look efficient, not that he isn't himself. Don't take that the wrong way. He loves watching people, as I've said, to see how they react. I think he secretly measures their talents and abilities as his way of a try-out for placement in an upcoming script or something." Brandon watched Monica's reaction, but she only tipped her head to the side. "I think after a bit of back and forth, the two of you will find a common ground and interests."

Brandon's phone rang. "Hey, Cody. Yes, we're in our rooms. Thank you. They're beautiful." He listened and Kate winked at Monica. "We'll meet you in the bar downstairs. See you then." After ending the call, he laughed and looked at Kate. "So how long before you two can be ready? Cody said he'd be down there in thirty minutes."

"I'm ready now. Monica?"

She quickly stood up and headed toward her room. "I need to primp if I'm meeting Mr. Wonderful for the first time. Give me five minutes!"

Kate watched her close the door and then shook her head. "Are those two even going to get along? I'm not sure if this is a good idea."

"I guess we'll have to wait and see. If nothing else, it'll be an interesting week. Nothing says they have to move beyond that." Brandon put his arm around Kate and scooped her close. "I'm glad we decided to move forward. I wouldn't want it any other way. I waited too long to find you."

"I'm happy we did, too." The blue

of his eyes narrowed as his pupils grew larger. It seemed to happen when he was happy. Kate admired him and thought about the movie. For the first time, she found herself curious about the woman in the female lead of the project. Brandon had never even mentioned her, yet there had to be one. She'd keep silent about that until the time came for her to meet this woman. After all, if the sequel happened, Brandon would be working more often with that woman and she'd have to be okay with it. Pettiness wasn't in her makeup and she'd prided herself on that.

Brandon leaned back to look at her and he smiled. "I think I'd like you two to sit together and I'll sit alone until Cody arrives. That way he'll have to guess which one of you is Monica."

"But didn't you already tell him she had auburn hair?

"True, I suppose I did. Still, it will give him an opportunity to let me know his thoughts on meeting Monica. We can compare notes later tonight." He gave her a full smile.

"I think that's a great idea. We'll wait for you to let us know where dinner will be." Kate finished her champagne and stood to return her glass to the table. Tonight, Brandon had chosen to leave his dark hair loose, which he didn't do often. The length hit just past his shoulder blades. His tanned features made his blue eyes pop, in turn, making Kate forget her words.

Brandon sat sipping Gentleman Jack Daniel's™ as he waited for Cody to enter the hotel lobby bar. He'd chosen a seating area around a small table and winked at Kate across the bar where she and Monica sat facing him so they could also know when Cody arrived. He wondered what Kate's thoughts would be on the movie when she viewed it for the first time. She'd not asked any questions and he'd not said a word about any of the other actors in the movie. Would she be jealous of the love scenes? He wondered, because at the time, finding her was all he'd thought about and the movie had helped take his mind off wondering exactly when he would find Kate.

"You're such a deep thinker, man."

Brandon glanced up at the near whisper to stare into a pair of eyes that looked more green than hazel today. Cody's shoulder-length hair was brushed back and he'd not shaven in at least two weeks, although he had shaven beneath his chin to give him a groomed appearance. He looked well rested. His white shirt was unbuttoned at the neck and the green of his suit jacket helped tone his eyes. Brandon had missed his good friend. They shared more than an actor-producer relationship. It was hard to explain, more like knowing someone for a lifetime or more.

Cody sat in the chair next to him and Brandon shook his hand with a firm grip. "It's nice to see you. I thought the girls came with you."

"They did, they'll be around later."

The barmaid appeared and placed a hand on Cody's shoulder. "Your usual, babe?"

"That'd be great, Stacy. I can't let

this guy get ahead of me." Cody waited for the waitress to step away. "So how are things going since you've found this woman of yours?"

"Life has been wonderful. I'm not sure how to even describe it, other than to say I've never been happier. She's everything I dreamed of and more."

"I wasn't sure you'd come back home last time we talked. You had me worried because I have people wanting a sequel to this thing. They love you. Of course, having a top lead female doesn't hurt either. I hope your woman is good with all this." Cody accepted his whiskey and took a long pull of the amber liquid. "Damn that shit tastes better some days than others. Today's a great day."

"Kate is fine with it all and is anxious to see the film. She also knows that there may be times this week when I'll have to meet with you and leave her on her own. She's good with it." Brandon watched his friend and admired his laid-back attitude with all the commitments he had on his shoulders. "I hope life hasn't kept *you* too busy."

Cody raked his fingers through his hair to push a strand off his forehead. "I just have to make time for myself and without a woman to distract me, I guess I let work have more of my time. Then again, I've not met a woman yet who interests me that much."

Brandon laughed. "When you aren't looking, it's easy not to get distracted. So, tell me about these dreams you've been having."

Cody glanced around the crowded bar area and Brandon noticed he paused in Kate's direction for a moment or two. After Cody shook his head, he turned back to Brandon. "Take that woman at the bar for instance…she could distract me, I'm sure of it."

He stared at Cody. "You can tell that from clear over here?"

"Just something about her." He looked again, then took a swallow of whiskey. The waitress brought them both another drink and Cody picked up his glass. "She could easily be the woman I've seen. That is just too damn strange. The hair, the way she holds her head. Pretty familiar, yet she's a total stranger."

When Brandon turned, he caught Kate's attention and lifted his chin. She bumped Monica's shoulder and soon both women walked in their direction. Kate could even stir his emotions from across the room. She moved like an elegant cat in the dusky lighting. He turned his eyes to Cody to gauge his interest in Monica.

"Now those two are gorgeous. Damn auburn hair gets me in trouble every time. They're coming over here." Cody glanced at him. "Do you know who they are?"

"I do." Brandon couldn't prevent his smile.

Then Cody stood. "You lucky bastard."

Kate walked behind Brandon's chair and he took her hand. She leaned down to kiss him and Brandon felt the silky tendrils of her hair caress the back of his hand. "Mind if we join you, handsome?" She looked at Cody as he smiled from ear to ear. Kate reached out to shake his hand. "You must be Cody. I'm Kate. Nice to finally meet you. This is my friend, Monica."

He shook Kate's hand. "No wonder I couldn't get him to make a decision to come back here once he'd found you. You would have made a great lead across from Brandon in the filming."

Cody shook Monica's hand as well and sat once the ladies were comfortable. Cody couldn't take his gaze off Monica. Brandon watched him and had to admit, he'd not seen Cody this off balance before so he had a little fun with him. Brandon leaned closer to Kate. "Beautiful women always make him want to request an audition."

Monica gave Cody a once over and then Brandon could see her wheels turning. "I doubt I would pass an audition. I don't take orders well…from anyone."

"Not even for good money?" Cody narrowed his gaze.

"I guess that would depend on what

the audition was for, but I don't see acting in my future."

Their little banter back and forth amused Brandon as the two bated each other.

"You can see into the future?" Cody asked.

Monica tipped her head a bit. "And into the past…but I'll leave it at that. So, what's a woman to do here in LA when it's her first time?"

Cody watched her close as he thought for a moment, as though he were imagining her for a movie part. "Considering you've traveled all day, a leisurely dinner would probably be a great place to start, nothing real fancy. The hotel has a great restaurant up on the 24th floor. You'll enjoy the city view from there at night. They're known for their Asian menu. You won't be disappointed. We can try Wolfgang's other restaurant tomorrow after you've had time to rest up."

"That sounds like a nice way to spend the evening." Monica watched

Cody over the rim of her glass as she sipped her gin and tonic.

Brandon saw Monica raise a brow at Kate, who smiled and shook her head.

Cody didn't miss their interaction. "Is that secret language there? Do I pass as an escort for dinner?" Cody smoothed his short beard.

"The night is young. Time will tell. So, does your job take up all of your time?" Monica tapped a nail on the rich leather of her armchair.

"I've not yet found anyone to pull my interests in another direction…so far."

The banter between these two amused Brandon and he reached for Kate's hand, loving the feel of her warm slender fingers. Her nails lightly scratched his palm and he met her gaze. Not sure how he could possibly have gotten so lucky, he dwelled on what might happen between them later tonight.

Monica cleared her throat and Brandon looked in her direction. She pointed at them. "You two aren't allowed to do that yet. The night is only just beginning. You'll have time for that later." She turned her attention back to Cody. "So, tell me what it was like working with Brandon. Does he take direction well?"

He laughed. "As an actor, yes. The movie will easily show he's a natural. As a friend, he's been distracted for years, but…I think that may have come to an end. Or rather, perhaps is now only just beginning. I had to beg him to come back out here to discuss a sequel."

Brandon just shook his head. "I think we need to make our way up to the restaurant and at least grab some appetizers. Your whiskey is affecting your judgment." He stood and helped Kate to her feet and they followed Cody to the elevators. The elegance of the hotel suited Kate and he liked seeing her in this environment. She fit in. He still thought she was the most beautiful woman he'd ever laid eyes on.

The elevator doors opened into the lobby of the restaurant and Kate could see the lights of the city sparkle around her. Before they got seated, she needed to use the restroom and tugged on Monica. "We'll be right back, hon." She couldn't wait to get Monica alone. It would also give Brandon time to quiz Cody.

Once in the bathroom, she had to ask what Monica thought of Cody. She was dying to know. "I think he's pretty handsome."

Monica shrugged a shoulder. "I guess. Yeah, he's not bad looking. I think I could run my fingers through his hair while we watched movies. I like his confidence. I find that sexy in a man. Not cocky, there's a difference."

"As a producer, he would have to be or the actors wouldn't do what they're supposed to."

"True."

Kate finished her business and touched up her make-up as Monica did the same. "I'm hungry now that I think about it. It's been a long day. We're going to enjoy the night ahead." Monica laughed. "I doubt I'll be having as much fun as you will be later."

"Hey, you never know!"

"Stop it!"

Kate led the way back to the guys, who had already been seated. The lush red leather seating formed a semi-circle facing the windows. The bamboo decor was woven throughout the restaurant. Cody stood up so they could be seated. She scooted in next to Brandon. The guys had ordered drinks for all of them and she stirred the ice in her glass of Jack. The lighted skyline of the city drew her attention. Pittsburgh was pretty at night, too, but here, one might see movie stars if they watched the people around them.

Then she looked at Brandon and realized that she was already with a movie star of her very own. She rubbed his thigh as he leaned over with a menu. She waited for him to look up at her. "I love you. Thank you for bringing me along."

He kissed her nose. "You'll never leave my side, ever."

"I should feel guilty for being this happy," she whispered to him.

"Never feel guilty for being happy. We all make our own happiness. If people are unhappy, it's their own fault."

Monica chimed into their conversation. "I have to agree with you, Brandon. People have to love themselves and be confident in who they are. One can't depend on others to make them happy, but when that *does* happen, the world becomes a beautiful place. The two of you have found that dimension. Some never do."

Cody held up his glass. "A toast to both of you and your future."

Kate's cheeks heated. She had to agree with Monica. She and Brandon had found happiness. "Thank you, Cody."

He smiled. "My pleasure. Everything on the menu is top notch, so order whatever you want."

Kate liked Cody. She wasn't sure what she had expected, but he seemed genuine and truly appeared to be a good friend to Brandon. The food order was taken and Monica began quizzing Cody.

How much of his life could Monica read? Kate watched them with interest, how long their eye contact lasted and the number of times they each reached out to touch the other's forearm. Cody soon had Monica laughing as she let herself relax. Whether these two had a future or not was a moot point. The next few days would be fun for them all.

After dinner, and another round of drinks ordered, Cody gave them directions for the next day and what would be happening. In the afternoon, Cody and Brandon would be meeting with the promo crew for interviews.

"You ladies are welcome to join us. I'll send over a limo at three o'clock. The promo gig will be at five down the street at LA Live, dinner at six thirty upstairs at Wolfgang's and the premiere starts at nine back at LA Live. This will include all interested advertisers and investors."

"I'm looking forward to meeting each of them." Brandon looked at Kate. "Are you ready to head to our room, babe?"

Kate thought he'd never ask. She didn't think she could keep her eyes open much longer. "I am. It's been a long day and tomorrow sounds like another one." She finished her drink and scooted out of the booth when Cody and Monica stood up. Kate hugged Monica. "Have a nice evening. I'll see you in the morning, hon."

"I'll try not to wake you when I come in."

Brandon put his arm around Kate and his warm fingers spread over her lower back as they left the restaurant. Her stomach fluttered with excitement as she thought about Monica. "I'm glad she's staying to talk with Cody."

Brandon raised a brow. "He said she intrigued him when you two went to the restroom. He's been having dreams about an auburn-haired woman, so he was quite surprised at her hair color tonight."

Kate loved Brandon's expressions. Reading his thoughts had gotten easier for her these past few months and they got along better with each day. She met his smoldering gaze as the elevator opened and instantly knew what their night ahead would entail.

God, she loved this sexy man.

17.

Monica watched Brandon and Kate leave the restaurant, hoping one day she would find her own man who would care for her as much as Brandon showed that he loved her best friend. Now she looked forward to quiet time with her producer-date in hopes of learning more of what made this workaholic ignore enjoying life.

Cody slid into the booth across the table from Monica and gazed at her before speaking. She liked the way he slightly tipped his head as though trying to gauge her thoughts as the lights twinkled in his green eyes. "I don't bite in case you're worried about that. Perhaps we should move to a smaller table in case they need this one for a larger party." Cody reached for his glass as he waited for an answer.

"That would be best, I suppose."

Monica picked up her drink and Cody led the way to a vacant table for two. This handsome, hard-working man interested her and she wanted to know how he had escaped the clutches of another woman this long. With his gorgeous hazel, sometimes green eyes, it seemed as though he could read her thoughts, and she turned her attention to the squeezed lime floating in her drink. The first date was too early to ask about the spirits surrounding him who tried to reach out and connect with her. *Why does one, in particular, seem familiar?*

"I wish you wouldn't look away. Your eyes intrigue me the way they change color with the lighting."

Monica slowly glanced up to meet his gaze as heat covered her cheeks. Cody's eyes seemed to reach out and touch her soul. She'd have to be careful around this man who knew all too well how to get others to do as he wanted.

"I noticed you earlier as you and Kate sat at the bar. I can't put my finger on it yet, but something is familiar about you. Maybe it's your hair color that attracts me." Cody watched her as he took a drink. "I've met a lot of women, but I can't say I've ever felt a connection with any of them."

This man could be dangerous for her single lifestyle she'd grown accustomed to if she wasn't careful about what she shared of herself. Too many drinks would pose a problem, also and she would refuse his offer for another if it came to that. This was her last one.

He smoothed his neatly trimmed beard, still not letting her gaze wander. "You stated you can see into the future *and* the past. I'm curious about that. I don't know any psychics. Is this a talent you learned?"

She took her straw from her glass and put it into her mouth, knowing men loved watching a woman do that. Cody's gaze moved to her lips as her tongue slid over the straw. Monica chewed the end as she debated how much to tell him. "Psychics are *born* with the talent. What they must learn is how to interpret what they channel.

Brandon and Kate are a good example. Their souls have traveled together through time. Sometimes souls reconnect hundreds of years later, as in their case."

Again, there was that sexy tilt of his head. "And you can see that?"

Monica stared at him, watching him wonder how she knew all this. "I can. I've been able to help them understand the other souls involved in their current life who are from their past."

"The movie Brandon's in for me deals with exactly that aspect." Cody paused but didn't look away.

She couldn't resist pushing the fact that he brought up spirits. "And do you think it's just a coincidence that the two of you have crossed paths in *this* life?"

"I hadn't thought of it that way. Do you see it differently?" His eyes narrowed as he waited for her answer.

"People don't always believe in what we see. With you, I don't feel that. You have a genuine interest in people. You're open, but careful with what you share of yourself." Monica watched him as she chewed the end of her straw, then traced the edge of her drink coaster with it while she let him considered what she'd said. The dark corner of the bar gave them a bit of privacy. She glanced up at Cody in the dim light. "You and Brandon have a connection that also includes Kate, and…the two of you were best friends in a past life. Souls *do* stay connected through all of our life journeys."

Cody stared at her for several moments and she held the gaze. His lips parted to speak, yet he paused. "So how are the two of *us* connected? Because I *do* feel it. Can I share something with you?"

Monica nodded, curious at what he would say. He'd surprised her at being so tuned in with his sense of the spirit world.

"I've had visions, or dreams, of you yet…we've never met."

"Really? Now you sound like Brandon. Have the two of you spoken about this?"

Lifting his glass, he drank before

continuing. "I mentioned it before all of you came out here. That's it. We haven't discussed anything. When I told him about an auburn-haired woman, he refused to tell me what you looked like."

"I'm glad they suggested I come with them to keep Kate company while you and Brandon do business." Monica glanced at her watch and her eyes widened. "Where has the time gone?"

Cody glanced at his Rolex. "Holy shit! You've put a spell on me, I'm sure of it. Let's get you to your room. I have to be up early." He finished his drink and led the way out.

He walked her to the room and a veil of sadness came over her as her room key clicked open the door. There was more to this man than she first thought. Monica had expected him to be a cocky director-type personality and things couldn't be further from the truth. A strand of hair had fallen over his forehead, giving him a sexy appearance, not that he needed help in that category. This man had all of those bases covered. "Thank you for walking with me."

"I'll sleep better knowing you got to your room safely. Thank you for an entertaining evening." He paused as he watched her. "Are you coming along with Brandon and Kate tomorrow?"

The sadness disappeared as she nodded. Monica couldn't hide her smile and it produced one across Cody's bearded face.

"Good. The limo will arrive out front at three.

He said goodnight and she watched him stroll toward the elevator. Monica stepped into the room and leaned against the door, unsure of what she felt at the moment. Butterflies fluttered in her stomach as though she were a teenager. She'd not expected to feel anything with Cody. Stepping away from the door, she saw the door closed to Kate's room and prayed they enjoyed their time alone.

The next day, Kate enjoyed the time she had spent at the pool with Monica while Brandon worked out at the gym. Now they each waited in the elegant lobby for their ride. The limo arrived on time. Kate couldn't keep her toes still during the short ride to LA Live down the street. Camera crews unloaded cases and equipment as they rode up to the main entrance. Several suits waited to open the car door and usher them inside. She spotted Cody as he talked with a group of men and one beautiful Native America woman with sleek black hair that hung to her waist. Her delicate features accented her cheekbones.

Kate's stomach twisted at the thought of her being Brandon's leading lady as visions of possible movie scenes came to mind. She took in a slow deep breath to ward off the slight jealousy.

A warm hand tenderly grasped hers.

She met Brandon's gaze. "There is no emotional connection for me where she is concerned …just so you know." A knuckle beneath her chin lifted her face to his and soft lips touched hers. "Please do not entertain those thoughts of her and me or be concerned. I see them swirling through your mind. She is just a fellow actor. My connection is *only* with the woman I love."

She lifted her hand and cupped his cheek. "I promise not to. You do what is required today without worries of me. I know what we have is unique and genuine. I love you, babe."

"Thank you." Brandon squeezed her hand as the limo door opened.

After stepping out, he offered his hand and Kate got out with Monica. Kate admired Brandon as his eyes sparkled against the light blue of his sweater. He took her hand to follow Cody inside and Kate turned to be sure Monica was still with them.

Cameras flashed and the crowd closed in as Brandon let go of her hand to stand with Cody and his leading lady. Kate covered her mouth to ward off the tears of pride she felt building. He looked as gorgeous as his partner as they posed for several photos.

Monica put her arm around Kate's shoulders. "You lucky shit! He is so handsome and he's all yours. That was sweet of him to reassure you as soon as you laid eyes on her. His feelings for you go deeper than you can imagine. So, don't stress about the sequel anymore, hon. You're solid. Let's enjoy the day."

Kate had expected a roller coaster of emotions today, but Brandon's reassurance had put all that to rest. Prayers for a successful premiere replaced her worries and she looked forward to tonight. Kate found herself excited to meet the woman who would occupy much of his time and her anxiety lessened.

A young man with a press pass stepped toward her and Monica. "Ladies, Cody asked that I escort you to the visitor's viewing area where there is seating, a big screen set up to watch the promos and a full bar at your service. Please enjoy." The man disappeared and Kate ordered a Jack and Coke for her and a Mojito for Monica. Others already sat at several tables. A large screen allowed them to watch the crew being photographed and interviewed. As she took her seat, a nearby man with broad shoulders and dark hair brushed away from his sculpted jawline drew her attention. For a moment, she admired him and wondered why he wasn't part of the interview. He appeared too gorgeous not to be.

Monica sat down across from her and Brandon stayed in her line of vision. It looked as though the group was being interviewed and Cody did most of the talking as they sat at the table in front of a camera crew. Kate glanced at the screen then back toward the group.

She saw that Cody kept an eye on Monica at the same time and that made Kate smile. "I'm glad you and Cody had time to talk alone last night. He seems like a nice guy. A workaholic, but nice!"

Monica watched the interview. "The conversation was smooth and easy, time passed quickly and he asked if I'd be here today." Her gaze met Kate's and knew her wheels turned. "The three of you have a past life connection, that's why he and Brandon get along so well. I'm not sure where I fit into the past-life scheme, but I'll figure it out."

Placing her fingers over Monica's forearm, Kate leaned in close. "How do you get all of this info?"

"I have spirit guides that have been with me throughout my whole life. I've learned to trust what they show me." She paused, but didn't look away. "I love the future they've shown me for both of you and that's all I'm saying." Monica gave her a wink and looked back toward Cody.

"Do you ever see glimpses of your own future?" Hope for Monica bubbled inside of Kate.

Without looking at Kate, she replied, "No, I never have, but I'm fine with that."

Cody glanced in Monica's direction and she smiled back. Kate wondered what the future held for those two and if it involved the four of them. She hoped so.

When Kate caught Brandon's gaze, he was already watching her. His eyes contrasted too damn well with his dark skin tone and blue sweater. He was so attractive. Yes, her heart was open to whatever he had in mind for them. No matter what it might be. She already knew it would be the *final surrender of her heart* to any man.

* * * * *

Excitement lifted Brandon's mood as he followed Cody toward the girls in the waiting area. The first promo went faster and better than he thought it would and couldn't wait to see the film in full. The correlation between the film and his life with Kate was uncanny. He wondered how long it would take Kate tonight before she figured it out while viewing the premiere.

Filming the sequel would begin in two months. Kate made him promise to accept if the opportunity came up. Fortunately, filming would begin in the Teton Foothills outside of Jackson, Wyoming. The film company wanted him for the sequel so bad, they told Cody to double what he'd been paid for filming the original. He wasn't sure how Kate would feel about Krystal turning down the lead female role unless Brandon signed on to do it as well.

Kate wore a sage green, sleeveless top with a low-cut cowl neckline that draped below a full cleavage despite her small frame. He loved her in heels whether she wore slacks or a skirt. Today she wore black leggings and carried a black hip-length sweater in case the weather changed. This beautiful angel belonged to him and he thanked the Great Spirit daily for bringing them together.

Playing his part opposite Krystal made the filming easy because she and Kate had a close resemblance. Kate wasn't Native American, but they were about the same otherwise. Krystal had followed him and Cody back here, and the two walked over to where Krystal's husband waited, not far from Kate and Monica.

Kate watched Krystal, which allowed Brandon to approach Kate from behind. He cupped her face and tipped it up so he could kiss her. Her fingers curled around his forearms as he lifted from the kiss to gaze into her eyes.

God, he was a lucky man. "Hey, beautiful!"

The crowd around them cheered as a deep blush covered her face and crept up her neck.

He leaned close to her ear. "I'd like you to meet someone."

Brandon held out his hand to help her up as she glanced over to see Krystal approaching with her husband! *It was him!* The same handsome man she'd admired earlier. They made a beautiful couple. Visions of Brandon holding this woman in his arms for the movie seeped back into her mind like a mysterious fog that crept through the mountains after a rainy day. She refused to let it be an omen and knew she would see how it actually played out when they viewed the premiere later. Of course, they would have to act out the love scenes, but Brandon's heart was hers for all time. She knew that and it brightened her mood.

Krystal gave Kate a huge smile and held out her hand. "It's a pleasure to meet the woman who finally captured the heart of this wild warrior. You complement each other well."

"Thank you, but you two are a beautiful couple, too."

Introductions continued and Cody soon came over to tell Brandon the limos were ready to take them to dinner. To Brandon's surprise, Cody's arm went around Monica's shoulders, he whispered in her ear, gave her a wink and off he went.

Monica stepped over to Brandon and leaned toward him. "I'm supposed to wait in the limo with you and Cody will join us before we leave."

"Stay close then. We'll be meeting up front soon." Brandon took Kate's warm hand in his and gave it a squeeze. She looked up at him to admire his smile.

Along with Krystal and her husband, they headed toward the main entrance to the waiting limos. Kate stepped in after Krystal. Monica slid onto the seat last to wait for Cody. He had to make sure the drivers had directions back to the Ritz for dinner.

Kate adjusted her purse and sweater on her lap, glad that she had worn her dressy top and slacks. This event seemed elegant and she felt comfortable around the others. Excitement seemed to surround all of them today.

Krystal smiled at Kate when she met her gaze and leaned across to touch Kate's knee.

"You and Brandon make a very sexy couple. I'm glad you made the trip so we could meet."

Kate relaxed some now that she'd met Krystal and her husband. The two appeared happily married and in love. She dismissed the idea of this leading lady having any interest in Brandon, other than for the movie, and would *never* voice her opinion to that effect.

When Brandon's hand scooped hers into his, Kate looked at him. She couldn't ignore the love that filled his eyes. "What Brandon and I have is certainly special." He kissed the back of her hand and was surprised at how easy a simple gesture fluttered her heart. Kate looked back at Krystal and her husband, clearly seeing the love they shared. Both of them were beautiful people.

Her husband caressed Krystal's thigh. "I was fortunate enough to attend some of the filmings to see the chemistry she and Brandon have on-screen. Hopefully, the public will love it and want more."

Kate met Monica's gaze and instantly knew the woman bubbled with visions of their future and she couldn't hold back. Monica looked from Krystal to her husband. "I feel the public is going to go crazy and we've not even seen it yet. It's just a feeling I have."

The limo door opened and Cody slid in next to Monica. A relief to Kate as she knew Monica didn't want to make the evening about anything she envisioned. That information was between the four of them.

The attendant closed the door. "Dinner shouldn't be more than two hours. Afterward, the limos will take us across the street to LA Live for the premiere. It's great to have all of us together for this. Thank you for making the trip."

The look he gave Monica let Kate realize that Cody, at least, held a bit of interest in her. She hoped so. Monica didn't have a special person in her life either. She had spent the past month doing readings at several seminars around the country. If a relationship began for them, Monica could do her seminars from any location. Perhaps things would work out. Time would tell. Kate didn't understand why Monica couldn't see indications of her own future, yet see so much for others.

The limo ride took mere minutes and soon they were back at the Ritz-Carlton. Cody and Monica lead the group. Kate smiled at the way he made sure Monica was around him. He seemed to be an attentive individual.

At the restaurant, Cody followed the manager toward a large room set up with round tables for thirty people and a bar set up in the corner. Cody had spared no expense to show his stars a wonderful evening so far. Investors and producers milled among the crowd and wait staff stood ready to help along the side. One held a tray of champagne glasses and offered them to the ladies. Kate took one along with Monica and Krystal, each tapping their glass with the other. Brandon and Cody soon had their whiskey in hand.

Brandon had met a few of these people at the promo interview and several unfamiliar faces now joined them. He kept Kate close, scooped against his side, as he was introduced to new people praising him for agreeing to the sequel. Never once did he leave her side or turn his back on her to talk with someone. She heard snippets of conversation as the investors mentioned the film clips they viewed and were anxious to see the entire movie.

When Kate caressed his fingers at her waist on the left, he looked down at her. "I'm so glad you finally gave Cody the answer he wanted about doing the sequel."

"Me, too. We have several decisions to make when we get home.

Our future is going to be very busy." Brandon kissed the top of her head as he pulled her closer. "All of this is a bit overwhelming."

She leaned closer. "You can do this."

The manager whispered something to Cody and soon all were being seated. Kate hung her sweater on the back of her chair and sat down. In front of each setting were slips of colored paper with dinner choices of rib steak, shrimp or chicken. The waiters collected a slip from everyone and soon salads were served and drinks refilled.

Monica held up her glass. "I'd like to toast to a very successful opening week when it happens. I see a chart topper and wish you success on the sequel as well."

Cody leaned close to her, but spoke loud enough for Kate to hear. "I may have to keep you around to be sure I know what my future holds." He laughed as he carefully tapped his glass against hers.

"We can discuss that later. It could

be interesting." Monica gave him a wink.

Dinner was served, discussions done while they ate and Kate listened. After dinner, Cody took Brandon and Krystal to meet several people at other tables. Kate talked with Monica and Krystal's husband. Soon afterward, Cody said the limos were waiting downstairs.

As they drove up to the theaters at the LA Live complex, crowds had gathered outside the theater. Cameras flashed as soon as Brandon and Krystal stepped from the limo. Cody stood with both of them for photos, while several were taken with the stars together. Pride swelled in Kate's heart as she watched the man she loved enjoy being in the spotlight. If the movie did become a chart-topper as Monica stated, their privacy could be in jeopardy. Was she ready for that? He would be spotted everywhere they would travel.

His eyes sparkled among the flashes as the blue of his sweater accented his eyes. Brandon searched the crowd behind him until their gazes locked and Kate touched her lips to send him a kiss. It was as though they were the only two outside and no one else mattered.

Monica nudged her and laughed. "You two are so cute together. I love it."

"Me, too. He's such a special guy. I've not met anyone like him. Oh, here they come. Cody is walking straight toward you. Enjoy tonight!"

Brandon took her hand and they followed Cody into the theater lobby. They ordered drinks and took them in to be seated. Kate could hardly stand the excitement of finally watching the movie she'd heard so much about. In a matter of minutes, the movie ads popped on the screen and Kate couldn't believe how many big brands endorsed the film.

Brandon put his arm around her and she nuzzled close. "This is going to be strange watching myself on screen. Please keep in mind that what you see is all for the movie, babe. You are who

I envisioned being with in every scene I did with Krystal."

She touched her heart as it nearly beat out of her chest. The movie started with aerial views of the craggy Teton mountain range and zoomed in on a Native American settlement along the winding river.

Flashbacks of her and Taima infused her memory hard.

18.

When the on-screen camera landed on Brandon as he turned to talk with a medicine man, Kate's stomach dropped. She gasped aloud before she realized it and covered her mouth. "Oh my god, Brandon!"

Goosebumps covered her entire body.

He looked identical to Taima.

Kate closed her eyes and pressed on her temples, unable to believe the movie could mimic their past. When she opened her eyes, warriors raided a wagon caravan of white settlers and a white woman was scooped up just in time to save her from nearly being killed. The warrior and his other braves rode off in another direction from those who began the attack.

Kate widened her eyes, not believing how close this movie ran to her encounter with Taima. Now she understood what Brandon has said about the upcoming scenes. Kate knew the passion that would be portrayed between him and Krystal. She gripped the arm of her seat as she watched intently. Her past played out before her eyes and when the love scene began, Brandon leaned close. "I love *you* so much. I hope you know that. You are all I thought about during the filming and now you are truly with me."

She gazed up to see the lights sparkle in his eyes and she saw Taima, both one in the same in her heart. Kate reached for his hand that draped over her shoulder and held tight to it through the rest of the movie. The two actors had touched everyone in the theater. Kate tried to keep the jealousy at bay as she watched Brandon kiss Krystal with a passion she knew all too well. Krystal's hands trailed over Brandon's chest and soon they were both naked, yet tastefully done on-screen.

She squeezed Brandon's fingers, but couldn't take her eyes from the couple in front of her. Brandon had made love to her just like that so many times at his home and as they traveled east, but to see this…she could only take in a deep breath and tell herself it was for the public to enjoy. *Nothing more.*

As the film came to a close, Monica's hand touched Kate's thigh as she leaned toward Kate. "You are one lucky woman and don't you *ever* forget that. If you get tired of that hunk in your bed, call me! Damnit he's good."

Kate could only laugh and was thankful Monica had made her smile. Yes, she had made a *final surrender* of her heart and it would be forever. A knuckle beneath her chin turned her face toward Brandon for a kiss in front of all who now stood to exit the seating. The crowd around them cheered, but Kate only felt the nearness she shared with the man of her dreams.

"I love you, White Woman. I can't wait to get you alone tonight." Brandon helped her up and the cheering didn't stop. The crowd now chanted 'more,

more, more' and Kate hugged Brandon before turning to leave their row.

She knew the public was going to enjoy the love story as much as she did. Brandon held her hand as they walked out among the congratulatory comments and handshakes from all around them. Her man would be a recognized celebrity in no time.

As they exited the theater, more photographers waited outside to capture the first reactions to the movie, while short interviews were taken from each star and producer. When Brandon pulled Kate close, photos were taken of her and Brandon together. His arm around her back comforted her as his fingers held on at her waist. He allowed a few more photos and then noticed Cody stood waiting at the limo for them. An attendant pushed the photographers away and ushered Kate and Brandon to the car.

She couldn't wait to get away from the cameras and commotion. She wanted time alone with Brandon, or at least the four of them. Monica sat alone and she took the seat across from her, followed by Brandon and Cody. Kate assumed the six of them would be riding, yet they were the only four inside.

When the vehicle pulled away from the theater, Cody relaxed back against the seat and raked his fingers through his hair to get it off of his forehead. He appeared relieved that the event was over. "Krystal and her husband took the other limo. They're headed to a night on the town together. I didn't think you wanted to be in the limelight any longer. The bar at the Ritz will have a quiet corner for us up there." He watched Brandon for a reaction but got none. "Today went well. The film opens at theaters nationwide in two weeks."

Brandon placed his hand on Kate's thigh and the heat of his palm penetrated her slacks. "A quiet corner would be nice. I have to admit…the excitement today was a little overwhelming."

Cody chuckled. "Then you might not like the idea of being a guest on a few late-night talk shows, but I think it'll be good exposure for the film."

Monica reacted with wide eyes. "Brandon, you can't turn that down!"

He looked at Kate and she sensed his hesitation. She had to go along with whatever Cody had planned. Far be it for her to stand in the way of Brandon getting famous. She smiled at him, wanting all of his dreams to come true. "The choices are yours to make, hon. I'm here for you, no matter what or where we have to go."

"Then considered it done," Cody said as a smile showed perfect teeth.

Brandon glanced at Cody and the grin on his face. "When are the appearances scheduled?"

"Is Friday night and Saturday morning too soon? They had cancellations and called me this afternoon." Cody chuckled.

Brandon looked at Kate and back at Cody. "That's in three days!"

"I can make a phone call and take care of getting your return flight extended." Cody turned toward Monica.

"That would give me more time to get to know *you* better. Of course, if you can't stay longer, I'll try to be understanding."

Monica looked at Kate.

"We could spend more time at the pool," Kate said.

"I don't have any appointments pressing for a few weeks." Monica gazed at Cody and teasingly looked him up and down. "I'm game for the extension. This will be interesting."

Kate took Brandon's open hand and he squeezed it for reassurance. "Are you sure?" he asked.

His concern melted her heart. "Of course, I am. Right now, we need to do whatever is necessary."

"Let's book it. Tell me when and where. I'll be there."

They arrived at the hotel and walked into the lobby toward the elevators. "Hey Cody, we've had a great time today, but I don't think I'm ready for any more to drink tonight. Kate and I are going up to the room. You two have a good time. Call me tomorrow with the details for Friday and Saturday tapings."

"I understand. I'll take care of things in the morning and be in touch. Get some sleep, man!"

Kate was glad Brandon told Cody they were tired and they stepped off the elevator on their floor. Brandon held the door for a moment as he stared at Cody and then nodded toward Monica. "Make sure she gets back to our room safe and sound, old man!"

Cody laughed as the door closed. Kate loved the concern he showed for her best friend and hoped Cody would watch out for her well-being. Brandon turned to Kate before heading down the hall and bent to kiss her. His lips lingered on hers before he stepped away. "You were amazing tonight. Everyone loved meeting you, but I'm tired of sharing you. Tonight, you are all mine."

Without another word, he led the way to their room, opened the door for her and Kate walked in as she removed her sweater. "I still can't believe that was you in the movie. Hon, you're beautiful and every woman who watches the movie is going to wish they were Krystal. And best of all, I get you whenever I want."

Brandon wrapped his arms around her and pressed her hips against his. She grasped his hard biceps, knowing what lay ahead. He touched his forehead to hers. "I hope you want me tonight, because watching that with you has gotten me pretty aroused. Now I can relive those scenes with the woman of my dreams. Get out of those clothes…now, before I tear them from your body."

"At least let me take a quick shower. It's been a long day." She turned at their bedroom door. "I'll wait for you in the shower. Don't be long." Kate pulled her blouse over her head, kicked off her shoes, and removed her slacks to hang them up. There couldn't be a better place on earth that she'd rather be than right here with Brandon and the beginning of a new career for him. She pinned up her hair and turned on the shower, happy to see the body showers that went down the wall. Those were the best.

Brandon stepped behind her, already naked and pressed himself against her ass. His hands cupped her breasts as his hardness sent her mind on a colorful trail of what would happen both in and out of the shower.

* * * * *

Cody's hand pressed against Monica's lower back as they followed the hostess to a quiet corner booth where they sat across from each other. Getting to know Cody on her own would be easier without others around, not that Kate would interfere, but Monica was more comfortable alone with him right now. Peace and quiet at last. They'd all had a long day. She was curious about Cody. He'd made sure she was aware of his presence all day, no matter where he was. His eyes had sought her out in a crowd, he whispered in her ear to wait for him in the limos, and now she wanted to get to know him as a man, not as a director.

As they waited for their drinks, Cody leaned on the table and crossed his arms in front of him as he watched her. Questions shown in his eyes and she knew he had several. She had her own list of items she needed to check out, but would wait for him to ask first.

He moistened his lips and tipped his head slightly and she tried to listen rather than watching his tongue move over his lips. "You're a beautiful woman. Why are you still single? Do you spend all of your time working as hard as I do? That's why I'm still single."

Monica moved her gaze to his eyes and his smile reached there, too. "Thank you. You've been very generous to us since we've arrived. I appreciate that. I *do* work a lot. I guess I don't think of it as work though. Reading the future, the past and reconnecting people with loved ones who have passed is never work."

"If you do that often, may I ask where and when?"

The waiter delivered her drink and she took a sip, then glanced back at his sensuous green eyes. Something still gnawed at her about his past, she just couldn't put her finger on it. He could block her from seeing his past and future, and that confused her.

Does he also have abilities he isn't aware of?

She returned to his questions. "I hold seminars across the country and that's worked out very well for me so far. I've been doing the seminars for a few years. My assistant manages my website and office calls, as well as booking the seminars. She knows where the interested callers are from and finds a venue to hold the readings. It's really pretty easy."

"I had no idea. I'll have to check out your website. Have you ever thought about broadcasting the seminars to television? I think that would work well."

Monica saw his mind conjuring up more ideas and knew she would consider it if he had some good suggestions. "That might increase my costs more, but it would be worth it."

He kept her gaze as he took a drink and then shook his head. "That's why advertisers do what they do with me.

They hope to garner consumers from the audiences of your show, but that would be in the future. I'd really like you to consider that as an option. Working with you would be fun. You're smart and sassy at the same time. I like that."

As they talked about their likes and dislikes, she realized how much alike they were. Type A people like busy lives and don't normally take much time for themselves because their jobs consume them. "What would be something you would do if you had seven days for a vacation? I would love to relax by the ocean somewhere warm, maybe read and try some new drinks."

Cody scooted against the wall on his side and got more comfortable, rested an arm on the table with his back to the wall. "Would there be anyone special with you or do you vacation alone?"

She laughed. "I don't have anyone special to take with me on vacation so I suppose I'd be alone and get some new books read."

He chewed his lower lip a moment.

"I think you would be fun to vacation with. You seem adventurous, or would be, with the right person."

"You think *you're* the right person?"

Cody shrugged. "It might be fun to find out. We have warm beaches here on the ocean. Perhaps you might choose to come back out here with Kate and Brandon sometime. I'd love to see you again if that would be the case." He pulled out his business card and pushed it across the table. "Call me sometime when you get back home. I won't ask for your number. That way, you won't constantly worry that I'd call to hound you."

Monica's stomach fluttered. It'd been years since she'd flirted with a man who showed a genuine interest. The business card lay in front of her with his cell number on it. She picked it up and looked it over, then glanced up at Cody. "I'll keep this for future use when I need to visit a warm beach."

His smile lit up his eyes. Something she would remember when she got home. "I look forward to you calling. I should get you back to your room. I've got an early morning and want to be sure I get the plane reservations extended for all of you. I'm glad you're staying over, too."

She finished her drink, put the business card in her purse and walked to the elevator with Cody. They stepped in, he hit her floor button and the doors closed. Cody scooped her close, lifted her face to his and tenderly kissed her, his tongue touching hers and then he slowly pulled back. Monica stood still, not sure how to react, but her heart raced right now.

"I've been wanting to kiss you all day. There's just something about you. And I won't apologize for that, but thank you."

"I've enjoyed our day together, too." The elevator opened and he walked her to the room.

"I'll see you tomorrow sometime. Thanks again, Cody."

He quickly kissed her again and returned to the elevator. She stared after him as he walked down the hall, then stepped into the room and locked the door. Kate and Brandon were in their room. The events of the evening had caught her by surprise and she touched her lips. His kiss had been warm and tender. Cody's interest in her piqued her curiosity. Smiling, she went to her room, closed the door and sat on her bed.

Pulling out his business card, she put his number into her contact list on her phone and couldn't resist…she sent him a text…*thank you for a wonderful evening. Goodnight.*

She doubted he would reply and placed her phone on the night table to get ready for bed. After she changed into something comfortable and then turned down her bed, her phone beeped.

Cody *had* texted her back!

The pleasure was all mine! Pleasant dreams, beautiful.

Tonight, she prayed for pleasant dreams. The day had been amazing. She would never have thought anything would happen by coming out to California. She'd not seen this. Monica snuggled beneath the covers, clutched her pillow close and just for now, wished it were Cody.

* * * * *

Kate knocked on Monica's bedroom door before alerting her. "Coffee and breakfast are here, sleepy head." She walked over to where Brandon poured their coffee and added cream to hers. He wore only his jeans. She loved him barefoot with no shirt, but nothing at all was good, too. "Are you sure Cody ordered this?"

"We didn't hang an order card on the door last night and I'm sure Monica didn't. That only leaves him. This is enough food for four people!" Brandon kissed Kate before handing her the cup. He chuckled. "Maybe he's coming up to join us!"

"I hope not! I'm not cleaned up yet. He better call before just showing up."

Monica's door opened and she stepped out with a huge smile. "What a gorgeous morning in California." She walked over to the window and pulled back the sheer. "I think I like this three-hour time change. It agrees with me more than eastern time, that's for sure." She turned away from the window to pour her coffee. "Thank you for the room service. This is convenient and better than that coffee room service leaves us."

Brandon smiled at her. "It is, but we didn't order it."

Kate laughed at the silly grin he gave Monica. He loved teasing her when he got the chance. It was nice to know he liked her best friend as much as she did. She and Monica had been friends for as long as she could remember.

"Then who sent this up?"

Brandon sipped his coffee and continued to tease Monica. "I'm guessing Cody did since he must want to make sure you had coffee to energize you after keeping you out so late last night."

She let out a small gasp and her cheeks blushed. "Twelve-thirty isn't late." Monica lifted the plate covers to see what their surprise was. "Oh my god, this is so much food. I barely eat in the morning."

"I would guess he needs to get to know you even better. Good thing we have a few more days for that." Brandon stretched, drained his cup and got up for a refill.

Kate couldn't help but admire the corded muscles in his forearm that moved as he refilled his coffee. He grabbed the creamer, added more to her cup with cream, and set the pot down. No one could be as lucky as she felt with the turn of events in her life over the past few months. Their future appeared to be well on the way to making him a movie star. He'd never once mentioned getting married, but their conversations were always about their future together. *Could I live so far from my parents and my best friend?* Kate blinked away those thoughts, not wanting to worry about that at the moment. She loved the man before her and was proud of what he'd accomplished with the movie and the home he'd built.

My dream home!

She *was* a lucky shit, just like Monica kept telling her. Watching Brandon's muscles move as he poured coffee or held the paper made her remember how tender he could be each time he touched her. Kate breathed in deep.

Yes, I am in love.

Sipping her coffee as she mentally rejoined the two people in her room, Kate glanced at Brandon.

"I hope you were thinking about us."

Her cheeks instantly burned. "Was it that obvious?"

He reached over and rubbed her thigh with those strong fingers of his. "It was, but that's okay. I'm glad I can occupy your mind and take you to a happy place."

"Watching the two of you makes me want to be in a relationship and I'm not ready for that yet. I'm too busy." Monica put her feet on the ottoman and enjoyed her coffee as she checked her phone for messages.

"I think you and Cody have more

in common than you think. I envision more happening between the two of you." Brandon continued to goad her into talking about last night. "Did you learn more about him over drinks?"

Kate loved Monica's smile that spread across her face, telling Kate more than Monica wanted to verbalize. If she and Cody hit it off and got along, these trips would become more fun for all of them. "I'm glad the two of you had some time alone. He couldn't take his eyes off you yesterday. I watched him and he was constantly searching the room for you, making sure you hadn't left or something."

Monica nodded and blushed. "We enjoyed a nice conversation last night. He asked about the reading seminars I do and if I'd ever thought about filming them for television."

She knew her jaw dropped, but Kate couldn't help it. An opportunity like that was a gift. "What was your answer? He could make *you* famous, too."

"Oh stop!" Monica met her gaze.

"I'm not sure I'm ready to make the move to television. It might interfere with the readings or something."

"But you've already taped some of the sessions and that hasn't mattered has it?"

"No, I guess not."

"Then it wouldn't make a difference who was behind the camera. You need to reconsider that offer, girlfriend!"

Brandon's phone rang. "Speak of the devil himself." He answered. "Hey, Cody. Thanks for breakfast. We're just getting started on it."

19.

Kate jumped over to sit next to Monica while Brandon was on the phone. "So, did you really get to know more about him last night? Do you like him at all? I think he's pretty nice."

"There is something about him that confuses me because normally I can read people and see their past or future. When he's busy like yesterday, I don't have a problem but last night, he could block me from seeing anything. I don't know if he was aware that he was doing that, but he might have abilities he isn't aware of. We have a past connection, I'm just not sure when it was." Monica thought for a moment and finished her coffee. "I think we have a lot to learn about each other, but for a first meeting, things went well. We joked about busy people taking a vacation and he said he'd find it interesting to vacation with me."

Kate enjoyed her laugh and was happy that Monica and Cody got along well. They'd have fun with staying a few extra days. "Let's eat before breakfast gets cold." She got up to organize the dishes and when Brandon hung up, he took a seat at the table to eat.

"Cody said he'd like to come over this afternoon and spend some time at the pool if you two don't have other plans."

"I think that would be great. Monica and I planned on going to the pool anyway. It'll be nice for you two to join us."

"He said the ticket issue is all taken care of and we leave Sunday morning. He's got details for the taping of the talk shows Friday night and Saturday morning. Krystal is going to be a guest on one of the big morning shows. Cody's pretty stoked about all this happening just before the film goes nationwide. I still can't believe all this is happening. My parents aren't going to believe it. I've not told them a lot about what's happening."

Kate put her fork down. "They have no idea? You didn't tell them about the film at all?"

Brandon shrugged. "Maybe not at all. I only told them I might have an option in a film but never said more than that. Maybe I need to call them when we get home." He laughed and concentrated on the meal.

Later that afternoon, Brandon wiped the perspiration off his forehead with his towel as he sat beneath an umbrella at the pool with Cody. He hated the California humidity compared to single digits back home in Wyoming. Today he'd put his hair in a low ponytail, refusing to do the man-bun thing that many guys did nowadays. The scent of suntan lotion wafted passed him each time someone walked by as he and Cody enjoyed a cold beer. Kate and Monica lay in the sun talking with each other across the pool.

Cody had ordered them another

round of beers and had Mimosas sent over to the girls. "I'm guessing you're dying to know what I think of Monica?"

Brandon raised a brow. "I knew you'd tell me when you were ready. You had a good conversation last night?"

"We did. Does she really have psychic abilities?"

He turned his head to look at Cody through his sunglasses. "Yes, she does. She's been able to fill in the details of my past lives that involved Kate. The film literally mirrors our past life together. I'm not sure how you did it. It's a little unnerving to say the least. And Kate really likes Krystal. She feels better about me taping a sequel with her now, knowing an affair would never happen between the two of us."

"Monica said she reads people who attend her seminars across the country. That's quite a gift for someone to have." Cody grabbed the other two beers from the waitress and handed one to Brandon. "She said her and I have a connection in a past life. That's just a little weird."

"Don't you believe her?"

"It's not that. I guess I never thought about it before. Not until I had those dreams and then she shows up and pretty much looks exactly like the woman in my dream. It's eerie, man." Cody took several drinks and stared over at Monica. "I do feel a connection with her. I just don't understand it. It's not something you can touch. Maybe that's why it's hard to understand."

"You don't have to understand it. If you are both comfortable together, just go with it. Enjoy what time you can spend with each other. Who knows when you'll see her again…maybe never." Brandon laughed, knowing that wouldn't be the case.

"She's too sexy *not* to want to see her again. I'd love to lose my fingers in her hair and kiss her until she screams. I can't believe some guy hasn't made her see that yet. I hope it works out between us. She'd be fun to hang out with." Cody sat quiet and Brandon knew Monica had gotten under his skin. "Thanks for bringing her with you guys. Last night was nice. Our conversation went easy. Good thing she didn't have a room alone, that's all I'm saying. She's made me re-think why I work so often. My future might change for the better if I could include her in it."

"That's all that matters. One day at a time. She works too often, too, from what I hear. I can't believe Kate and I have such a great connection. It's like she's a part of me that's been missing all this time. If we still adhered to the old Native American ways, she'd already be my wife because we've slept together at my home. I really need to make that happen and put a ring on her finger to keep her parents happy." Brandon turned his beer bottle in his fingers, then lowered his sunglasses and glanced at Cody, waiting for him to look over. "Would you be my best man when the time comes?"

Cody's jaw dropped and he stared back with wide eyes. "Holy shit! You're serious!" He sat up and put both feet on the cement between their chairs, resting his elbows on his knees.

"Have you told her yet?"

Brandon's stomach tightened, but not in a bad way as he thought of Kate and a ring. "Not yet. We haven't really talked about it, but do discuss our future and assume we'll stay together. We've dreamed of what we want to do and about having kids, just not about a wedding. I don't want anything big, but her parents might have other plans. I don't know."

"I'll do my best to keep it a secret. Of course, I'll be your best man. Shit." Cody relaxed back into his lounger and readjusted his glasses. "She's a fine woman, Brandon. They both are. I think I like the way this is going."

"You realize it'll be a long-distance relationship for a while, right? You ready for that?"

Cody nodded. "Can't count my chickens before they're hatched. She might change her mind about me after she gets back home to reality. Speaking of going back home, before you do, they want to tape the late-night show tomorrow evening before they broadcast it and Saturday morning before the other show. We can do dinner tonight and then head over to the studio. It's should be fun. I'm glad I have a few days planned with nothing to do. Maybe Monica won't have any plans either."

"She's doing whatever we do." Now it was Brando's turn to sit up and face Cody. He glanced in Kate's direction to see them both face down on their chairs enjoying the sun and their drinks. "Before I go see if she needs more lotion on her back, can you recommend a jewelry store here in town?"

"You're really going to do this aren't you?"

"I am. Maybe you and I can slip away, pick out a few rings and take the girls there before dinner tonight. What do you think?"

"I like your idea. Kate will be shocked. This is gonna be fun. Let's go. Tell the girls we have to meet with an ad rep or something. We'll be back later."

"I'll be right back." Brandon strode over to Kate's chair, straddled above her and gently ran his fingers up her back, careful to not let her raise up. She'd screw up her back. "Hey, sexy. Hand me your lotion while I'm here and I'll make sure you don't burn up…at least not until we're in our room tonight."

Monica lay motionless with her eyes shaded. "Like I said before, you're a lucky little shit."

Kate giggled. "I know, right?"

He smoothed the cream over her back, shoulders, and arms and handed the bottle back. "Cody and I have to meet with an ad rep. We'll be back in a few hours. You two should get a massage at the spa while we're gone."

Monica lifted the towel from her eyes. "That sounds like heaven."

Brandon bent and kissed Kate's cheek. "Just do a room charge and enjoy yourself. We're doing dinner tonight. I'll text you later about what time to be ready. Have fun ladies. Love you, babe."

He sauntered back over to Cody who stood and they walked into the hotel. Brandon wanted to change clothes and grab his wallet. His purchase tonight would be spendy, but he didn't care. He wanted a nice ring for Kate. This would be a total surprise. They'd never talked about getting married. He smiled wide and nudged Cody. "Thanks, man."

* * * * *

While Brandon changed, Kate put the finishing touches on her make-up and looked forward to another night out in LA. She had to agree with Brandon though. The city life was way too hectic. People, cars, busy life, not slowing down to enjoy each day. The quiet little town of Dubois, Wyoming where Brandon lived tugged at her heart as she remembered the snow-capped mountains out his window and the constant scent of pine trees. She knew she would be happy living there with Brandon.

He came up behind her and wrapped his arms around her. She met his gaze in the mirror and still, her heart melted each time she looked at him. Brandon nuzzled her neck and warm lips touched her skin.

"I'm glad you and Monica had a good afternoon. I'll finish your massage when we get home tonight. I'll tell you right now…as soon as we get back, your clothes are coming off and I want you on the bed with oils. I already have plans for you."

She turned within his arms and breathed in his cologne. That's all it took to screw with her reserve of prim and proper. Standing on her toes, she cupped his face and kissed him. "I love you because of your unconditional love for me."

"Always. Cody should be downstairs any minute. I'm liking the limo situation." He laughed.

Kate grabbed her purse to leave. Monica had on a slinky black dress and had pinned her long hair up with a few wispy strands left unattended. She sat texting on her phone. "Don't you look ravishing. Your hot date is waiting downstairs, my dear."

Her cheeks and neck grew pink. "I know. He said to hurry."

Brandon held the door for them and

soon they were stepping inside Cody's limo. Two bottles of champagne sat in ice buckets and flutes were secured so they wouldn't break. Kate sat with Brandon across from Cody and Monica. The two made a handsome couple and she prayed things might work out for them, but Pittsburgh was clear across the country. She knew from experience that a long-distance relationship would be hard for them. "Are we celebrating something tonight?" Kate asked.

Cody laughed. "Nothing special, just LA life, the movie premiere, tomorrow's taping of the talk show. The night is just beginning, ladies. Before I open this, I have one stop to make first."

Brandon put his arm around her shoulder and Kate enjoyed the sights as they rode. The sun wouldn't be setting for several hours yet. People scurried across the streets, into shops and hustled in and out of traffic. The peacefulness of home seemed far away now and she missed the scenic views from the deck. She leaned into Brandon. "I have to agree with you. Life here is way too busy for me, too. Dubois is more to my liking."

He kissed her temple. "I'm really glad to hear that."

It wasn't long before the stretch limo stopped in front of several stores and confusion furrowed Kate's brow.

Cody got out and then stuck his head back inside the car. "Ladies, we'd like you to join us. We won't be long, but I'd hate to have you wait in here."

Monica took his hand and Kate followed. The warm California air was a stark difference from the cool air inside the car. Brandon took Kate's hand and they followed Cody. She took in the fancy stores they walked past, admiring the dresses, shoes, and purses. The door that Cody held open took them into a jewelry store with more glass counters than she'd ever seen. Delicate gold chains and gemstones glittered everywhere. Kate stayed at Brandon's side as she looked around, only guessing at the cost of each item.

A woman behind the counter motioned for them to join her so she could show them something. Cody and Monica were already looking at bracelets. "Brandon, we can't buy anything here. I don't want to go over there."

He tugged her hand, not letting go. "Oh, come on. Let's just look and dream a little."

Kate shook her head, but walked over with him. He made small talk with the woman and Kate tried to ignore the sales clerk and looked at rings in the case.

"Might I interest you in diamonds? They're more fun if you try them on."

"Oh, no. I don't think so. I don't wear a lot of jewelry, but thank you." Kate let Brandon look at them, and he actually took one out and held it up.

"Babe, humor me here. Try this one on for me. I just want to see how it looks on your finger. As a matter of fact, I want you to try on a few different ones. Come on, please."

She couldn't say no to those blue eyes that tugged at her heart. He held it out to her so she could slide her ring finger into it and that is when she saw how huge the stone was inside the wedding set. She stared at Brandon as she pushed her finger into the ring. When he moved her hand so she could see it sparkle, Kate tried to protest, but words wouldn't come out. She'd never seen a ring with so many diamonds in it, wrapped around the two-carat center stone.

Of course, the sales clerk smiled. "That's a perfect fit, which means it's meant just for you."

"Oh no. I can't."

Brandon lifted another ring with just as many diamonds, but that one had emeralds on each side of the center stone and in the wedding band. "Try this one on…for me?" He pleaded with his eyes again and she gave in. Before she knew it, he had her try on four different wedding sets. Two were traditional cut and two were princess cut. "Which one do you like best? Just play along with me."

The saleswoman chimed in. "If

money didn't matter, which one would it be?"

Monica snuck up beside her and put her arm around Kate as she grabbed her ring hand to see it sparkle. "They are all gorgeous, but I think I'm partial to the one with emeralds. Try that one on again."

"Stop, you guys. We're not doing this."

Brandon cupped her face and stared into her eyes so that all she could see was him.

"Yes…we *are* doing this. *You* decide which one you like best."

Kate couldn't breathe as tears filled her eyes. A sob choked her throat and she hiccupped as she searched his eyes. "We can't afford this, Brandon."

"You have no idea how much money I have so you can't say that. We're not leaving until we have a ring on your finger." He let go of her face and got down on one knee. "Katlyn, would you marry me and be the mother of our children?"

"Oh my god!" She covered her

mouth and through her tears, looked over at Monica who was already crying, too.

"Just say yes, hon." Cody wrapped his arm around a shuddering Monica.

Kate looked down at Brandon, still patiently waiting on one knee.

"Yes…." was all she could get out.

The sales clerk handed her several tissues. "I just love working here."

Brandon stood, took Kate's hand and she watched him remove the ring and put the one with emeralds back on her hand. She held it out and through her tears, knew it was her favorite, too. Nodding with tears streaming down her face, Brandon removed it, had the clerk separate the rings and he put the engagement ring back on her finger. He kissed the ring and then wrapped her in his arms.

Her world blurred for a moment until she could breathe enough to push back and look at everyone. Monica rushed over, pulled her away from Brandon and Kate hugged her tight as more tears wet her cheeks. "I'm so happy for both of you. You're a living fairy tale."

Kate saw Cody hug Brandon. "I think the champagne might be cold now."

She let go of Monica and turned to Brandon. "You planned this? You said you had a meeting."

"We did, just not with an ad rep." Brandon took the package from the clerk, placed it in his pocket and put his arm around Kate on the way to the limo.

She wasn't sure her knees would hold her up long enough to get to the car and held Brandon tight around the waist as she walked. Her thumb kept feeling for the ring to be sure she didn't lose it.

Unbelievable.

All she could do was shake her head, hoping the dream never ended. Kate climbed into the car and when Brandon sat beside her, his arms scooped her into his embrace. Tender lips touched hers and the magic of love surrounded her. His fingers fisted in her hair as he kissed her harder.

The champagne cork popped.

The kiss ended, but Brandon held her tight.

Monica passed a full glass to each of them and soon they were toasting their engagement. Brandon took her left hand to take a better look at the ring and Kate loved how it sparkled. "I will never take this off. I love it, thank you."

"To your future, your children and your family. May you both enjoy every single day to the fullest and love forever." Cody tapped their glasses as the limo driver drove them around for half an hour to enjoy the evening.

When the car came to a stop, Kate looked out the window and couldn't believe the site in front of her. The driver opened the door and she followed her friends for a better view. Cody had brought the champagne, refilled their glasses and Brandon pulled her close. The orange and pink sunset would be burned in her memory of this day forever. She couldn't ask for a better ending to a marriage proposal that she never saw coming.

"We will always remember this

day, babe. I'm glad we got to share it together."

"You spoil me. I don't deserve this."

Brandon kissed the top of her head. "You deserve everything I choose to share with you and this is only the beginning. I love you with all my heart."

The rest of the evening was a blur that Kate hoped she would somehow remember. After dinner, they got to watch Brandon at the taping of the late-night talk show, and more celebrating with Cody and Monica.

She couldn't have asked for a better day as Brandon opened the door to their hotel room. Glad to be able to get out of her heels and tie her hair up, Kate stood in the bathroom and admired her ring yet again. The light sparkled back at her through the diamonds and emeralds. She'd have to take a picture to send to her parents in the morning. They would never believe her if she called.

Kate glanced into the mirror to see Brandon leaning against the door frame looking sexy as always with his white shirt unbuttoned. Her heart skipped a beat and she smiled at him.

He raised a brow. "I thought I told you no clothes once we got back to the room."

Instantly her cheeks heated. "I guess I don't mind well, do I?"

"I have ways to fix that. Trust me. A whack or two across your ass and you'll remember when I tell you something. I might prefer you naked *whenever* we're alone." He thought for a moment and then cracked a smile. "Yes, I think that would suit me just fine."

She gasped as he reached for her, giggling when he lifted her over his shoulder, held her legs tight and slapped her ass twice. She loved his punishments and couldn't wait to see what he had in store. He *had* mentioned a massage earlier.

"Cody is keeping Monica out of the way for a while, so we don't have to worry about her walking in on us any time soon."

Still hung over his shoulder, Brandon strode into their bedroom, set her on her feet beside the bed and pulled her silky top over her head. "Since you can't mind, I will do this for you. Do *not* break eye contact with me." His warm fingers undid the button of her slacks and unzipped them, letting them pool at her feet. Fingers teased inside the waistband of her thong, around to the back, where he cupped her cheeks and gave a gentle squeeze.

A quick intake of breath passed her lips and a low chuckle sounded in his chest.

She held his hunger-filled gaze and knew he kept a tight rein on his emotions right now.

He unhooked her bra, removed it and tossed it into a chair. Slow caresses over her breasts begged for his touch as her nipples puckered. "That's much better, yes?"

"It is, thank you." Kate clenched her fingers.

Soon her thong landed at her feet. "I have had so many dreams of being with you and I never tire of this. You are a goddess and belong only to me."

Kate ran her hands up Brandon's chest and over his shoulders, pushing his shirt down his arms. "I can now say the same thing of you." She touched her lips to the hollow at his throat and felt his heartbeat.

Her tongue tasted his skin.

The tie in her hair came loose, tumbling hair over her back.

20.

Fingers gently fisted in Kate's loose hair, tightening her core. Brandon tipped her face up. His arm circled her waist as he kissed her hard, their mouths consuming the other in a flurry of passion. He moved one of her wrists behind her and held it carefully with his other hand. Her breath left her body as Brandon continued to assault her senses with his kiss and then quickly lifted his head.

Kate's heart beat out of control as she watched his eyes, passionate and eager for what lay ahead. He had to know how bad she wanted him right now and hoped he wouldn't deny her for too long. His handsome features only helped sway her to his wishes.

"You will lie on your stomach with a pillow under you, your arms stretched out to the sides and stay still." He circled a finger at her when she didn't immediately move.

A lady of the evening couldn't feel sexier than she did at this very moment knowing Brandon watched every move her body made as she crawled forward. Once she got comfortable and moved her hair out of the way, she lay still, not trying to see what he did. A drawer opened, a package rustled, a towel landed next to her and yet…he waited.

Kate tightened her inner muscles, anticipating their joining that would happen later rather than sooner. Warm fingers wrapped around each ankle, placing them close to each other and then Brandon climbed onto the bed.

He straddled her hips and sat on her legs.

She waited, listened, anticipated.

Hands rubbed together and soon lotion warmed her cheeks and up her lower back. Thumbs massaged the tired muscles there, working in the lavender-scented lotion. Pressure moved up each side of her spine and fingers touched the sides of her breasts, teasing her mind.

"Concentrate on what's to come. See me loving you over every inch of your skin, White Woman. Tonight, you will remember *everything* I do to you and I will remember the taste of you."

Brandon's hands massaged her shoulders and her neck, but she wasn't prepared for the length of his body over hers as his hands cupped her breasts. He toyed with her nipples and soon his knees pushed her legs apart. His hardness pressed against her and she whimpered, hoping soon to feel the length of him slip inside, but he lay motionless for what seemed an eternity. Then kisses touched her neck and her fingers dug into the sheets.

The scent of her perfume filled his head as Brandon sucked in air, attempting to hold back. He wasn't yet ready to feel her wetness surround him and just held her tight for a moment, wishing away the urge to take her quickly. That's not how he wanted tonight to happen. He loved the feel of her soft naked flesh against his own and tonight was for savoring all of that.

Slow down.

Wait.

Make her beg.

Laying atop Kate, her warm back against his chest, Brandon savored his own piece of heaven. He tipped his hips against her bottom, again, rocking them both with a motion he so badly needed. The sound of her nails scratching at the sheets didn't help. With her hair tangled in his fingers, he buried his face against her neck.

She whimpered again and he nearly released his seed.

Brandon held his breath and clenched his teeth. Kate had such a hold on his heart that he wanted to please every need she had before he pleasured himself, but…god, she tested his strength with her sensual moves.

He enjoyed playing love games with her, making her wait for what she desperately wanted, but he forgot how strong his control had to be around Kate. The taste of her skin spread over his tongue, the scent of her perfume permeated his senses, and the curves of her body tested his stamina. After years of dreaming about her, she now lay in his arms, needing him, wanting him.

Able to move again after regaining his composure, Brandon continued with kisses on her shoulder. "I love you too much, woman. You make me nearly lose control every time I bed you."

"You do the same to me, if you must know the truth."

"Are you wanting me deep inside?"

"Yes."

Her whisper caressed his ear. He tightened his fist full of hair. "Yes, what?"

"Please, baby, I need you deep. Don't make me wait longer." Kate wiggled her ass against his hardness.

Brandon moved just enough that the head touched her entrance and he slowly pressed forward. Her whimpers were music to his ears and soon they had their rhythm going as they moved together. He reached out for her hands and brought them over her head, their fingers weaving around the other. Kate squeezed her muscles tight around the length of him, taking his warmth deep inside of her as she cried out.

He felt her raise up to get on her knees and adjusted his position, balancing on his hands above her as she backed against him. With one hand, he cupped a full breast and caught a nipple between his fingers. A gentle squeeze prompted another whimper. She had to know that sound tore at his gut in more ways than one, and they rode together, damp skin between them. Her whimpers turned into cries of pleasure until she collapsed, gasping beneath him. He held his weight on his elbows until he caught his breath and Kate relaxed.

Brandon turned them onto their sides and spooned her close, with his hand on her chest, measuring her heartbeat and breathing. Hers matched his own. They rested together and her hand caressed his arm. Each time she touched his body, he reacted with a slight tightening. "You are dangerous to my being, White Woman. I should be strong, but you weaken me when we're alone."

Kate turned within his arms and lay on her back, her hand slipping behind his neck to pull him in for a kiss deeper than he'd experienced with her so far. Her tongue sought his, then her teeth nibbled his lower lip and he moved to cover her body with his own. Kate spread her legs to wrap around his waist as he slid in deep once again and they played on the waves of ecstasy.

She cried out as her nails dug into his arm. Writhing beneath him, he loved her well into the night, in more positions than he could count. Morning need not show its light anytime soon.

* * * * *

Cody watched Monica closely across the table, lit only by candlelight at the bar inside the hotel. Although the place was packed, their quiet corner blocked out the noise. She sipped another Mojito and he a whiskey. "I'm glad you came with Kate and that I got to meet you. Fate *does* work in strange ways, doesn't it?"

Candlelight reflected in her eyes when she looked up at him. "It does. I find it strange that I can see parts of your future and past, yet can never tell how my own life will turn out. I have to visit other psychics for that."

"Really? So, you're unaware that you'll be visiting my condo soon?"

Monica tipped her head and stared at him as a smile slowly crept over her lips. "Will I?"

"I'm hoping so, if I play my cards right and act like the perfect gentleman. How about it? If I promise to behave, would you?"

"I don't know. Can I truly trust you?"

"I thought we had a past together. Was I *bad* before?"

Monica laughed out loud and he had to laugh with her. "It doesn't work that way silly."

"Well, I don't know. I only know that so far, I enjoy your company. I know it's only been a week, but something tells me I need to know more."

"I don't really want to get back into the limo for another long ride." She teased him with her drink straw again, moving it over her tongue as she watched him.

"My condo is in the next tower over."

"What? Right here in the Ritz? And you're just now letting me know?"

Cody's cheeks heated this time and he was glad they only had candlelight. Women *never* made him blush. "I don't tell many people where I live. Brandon doesn't even know." He reached across the table with an open palm, hoping he wouldn't appear forward, but he wasn't ready to let her go back to her room yet. "Besides, we promised Brandon they could be alone for a few hours. They're doing things I'm not ready to do to *you* yet."

Monica narrowed her eyes and wet her lips, a move that tugged at his groin. "Not even if I begged?"

Thoughts of everything he'd like to do to Monica raced through his mind, but even by his standards, it was too soon. Getting the film completed had taken all of his time, which is why he'd not been with a woman in months. Now he could take time off before the sequel would begin and this sexy woman fit the bill. *Perhaps, she more than fit the bill. Can I stick to my guns if she begged to be in my bed? Nope!* He took in a deep breath. "No, not even if you begged. Simple conversation is all I offer tonight. I have coffee if that would be better, rather than more alcohol."

"You're serious, aren't you?"

He couldn't hold back a slight grin. "I am. I'm not into one-night stands and the day after tomorrow, you will be packing to leave LA. I guard my *heart* better than that."

Monica finished her drink and set her glass down, pushing it to the edge of the table for the waitress. "Then I'm game. Just talking, I promise."

Cody settled the bill to his monthly tab he kept here and walked out with Monica. He held her hand as he led the way over to his condo tower and up the elevator. When they stopped, he took her hand again and walked down the short hall to his door.

She leaned against the door frame while he unlocked it. "This is really convenient for you with the stars staying in the same place. I like that you keep this a secret. Mums the word." She slowly stepped inside, looked around, and then went to look out the window at the city lights below, a view he also cherished and the reason he purchased the condo.

The dim lights showed him the outline of her body as she investigated his place. He refused to go against his morals, so he hoped having her here didn't tempt him too badly.

Or did it? Was it a mistake to bring her here? "I have club soda or tonic water. Which would you prefer?"

"Club soda on the rocks, please…since I can't have *you*."

She made him smile so easily. This woman would be nice to have around more often with her sense of humor. He made their drinks and took them over to the leather loveseat where she had gotten comfortable. Funny she'd chosen to sit there rather than the longer sofa.

Her stocking feet rested on the ottoman and he clenched his teeth. He found that way too sexy when women tossed off their heels.

I can do this.

Monica took her drink and their fingers touched, quickening his pulse. Cody set his drink down and removed his jacket before sitting with Monica. With a click of the remote, quiet music surrounded them. There was no choice but to sit close to her on the shorter loveseat. He liked choices, but there was a distraction near him tonight which left him little choice…taking her to his bed for a one-night stand was not an option. For some reason, this woman was special…a beautiful woman who pinned her hair up when he liked it down.

Could I change that?

Maybe.

Her soft voice brought him back into the conversation. "So, tell me what you do to relax. Do you go to the gym, do you run, do you surf, are you a fisherman?"

"I enjoy deep sea fishing, but don't

do it often enough. My boat doesn't get used enough either. If you ever find your way back here, we could take a cruise."

She nodded, but didn't appear surprised. "I would like that. I've never been deep sea fishing. Going that far out into the ocean doesn't appeal to me. I do enjoy a good run though."

"Then we have a few things in common." Cody listened to her talk of Pittsburgh, he told her a bit of his background and time passed between them. Before he realized it, she'd snuggled closer to him and when he turned to talk with her, parted lips were all he saw.

Would they be as soft as they looked?

She reached for him and her fingers slipped behind his neck to pull him in for a kiss. They each held their glasses yet, but when her tongue slipped in to touch his, a fire ignited when he least expected.

A moment shared, a gentle kiss, and she pulled away. The smoldering lust in her eyes surprised him because it wasn't usually the woman who made the first move, but he liked it.

Monica set her empty glass on the end table. "I'm sorry. You didn't want me to beg. You promised to be a gentleman and I'm crossing the line."

Cody set his glass aside and chose to go with what she wanted to do. He wasn't into disappointing a woman. Carefully, he tugged at her pinned up hair and when she pulled a few clips, it cascaded over her shoulders. The silky auburn strands fell through his fingers and he cupped the back of her head, pulling her in for another kiss. Fingers tugged at the buttons on his shirt and his mind struggled with his morals here as her tongue tangled with his.

When he released her from the kiss, she rested her head beneath his chin, giving him time to consider what might happen next. Warm fingers touched his chest where she'd undone two buttons. Cody caressed her arm as he held her close, breathing in her scent that had teased him for days. The soft romantic music only lent to the situation he knew was inevitable…*can I truly resist her?*

She kept her head resting on his chest and her nails teased through his shirt. "There are *other* ways to pleasure each other beside the sexual act of making love…if that is what you're trying to avoid tonight."

He toyed with her hair between his fingers, his imagination running rampant, envisioning her in his bed, free of clothing, begging him to join her. "You're not making this easy for me. You can't get me hooked on you and then walk 2600 miles away. How am I going to cope?"

Monica laughed and looked up at him. "You're such a tease. Do you think you haven't tempted *me* this week? Showing up at the pool shirtless? I didn't ignore that, you know."

He got lost in her eyes. "Men don't tease women."

She laughed out loud. A sound he locked into his memory bank for when she was gone.

"Whispering in my ear for days,

putting your arm around me each time you did so? Wearing that stunning cologne? Giving me a wink across a crowded room?"

Cody held her tighter as she laughed. "Guilty as charged. I didn't think you'd notice."

She trailed her nails over the shirt on his bicep. "Should I give you a detailed report of how my body reacted each time our gazes met across the room, or when you sat close to me in the car? Things happen to a woman when you sexually tease her." She raised her head again and her eyes were those of an angel.

"Then I would be rude by leaving those needs unsatisfied."

Her gaze settled on his lips. "You would be and I'd hate that."

Unable to avoid her advances any longer, Cody cupped her face in his hands and kissed her. He tried his damnedest to be gentle, but when he brushed her tongue against his and she leaned into him, he allowed her to push him back against the arm of the loveseat. His intentions had started out good, but Monica had other plans and ended up stretched out over his body.

When he moved his hands to her hips so she didn't end up landing them on the floor, her dress had shifted and his fingertips caressed her thighs. Silky nylons enraged his senses and her dress moved higher. His fingers kneaded her cheeks that fit into his hands perfectly as he brought her hips tight against his. It'd been too damn long since he allowed himself to be distracted by a woman, but this one had gotten under his skin. Her scent had made him think of stripping her naked.

Their kiss ended when she raised up to look at him, hunger evident in her eyes, and him still gripping her ass in his hands. She slipped through his fingers and over the side of the sofa to kneel beside him, her fingers tugging his shirt from his slacks. He grabbed her hands when she began to undo his belt and she looked up at him. Cody pulled one of her hands to his mouth and kissed her fingers, but was at a loss for words.

"I think we'd be more comfortable in your room, but if you'd rather stay out here…"

"You sure make it hard on a man."

Her hand moved over the taut length of him as he tried to stick to his morals. "I think that was my goal. How else will we know whether we're compatible or not?"

Cody stood, helped her up and led the way to his room down the dim hallway. A small lamp in his room would provide enough light for them to see as he stopped at the edge of his bed. Again, he took her face in his hands and looked down at her. "You are a beautiful woman and have pushed my limits tonight, which I've avoided all week. While I'd love nothing better than to bury myself deep within you, that will *not* happen tonight. I'm in charge and plan to pleasure you until you scream and have no more energy left in your limbs. Like a rag doll, you won't move the rest of the night." Cody unbuttoned the rest of his shirt, tossed it onto a chair and sat on his bed.

"I'd love to watch you undress for me."

That's all the encouragement she needed. Slowly pulling her dress over her head, Monica tossed it on top of his shirt. Even in the dim light and shadows, he could make out the curves of her body. Next, her pantyhose came off and she stood in her bra and panties. He loved a woman in a skimpy thong and push-up bra. Her breasts nearly spilled over the top and she stepped between his thighs. He couldn't resist placing a kiss at the top of her cleavage.

Reaching behind her, Cody unhooked her bra and pulled it from her shoulders. Full breasts hung before him, as he'd envisioned throughout the day. "You are beautiful." He slid from the bed, pulled back the covers and turned to pick her up in his arms. Carefully laying her on the bed, she scooted to make room for him, all the while watching his fingers undo his belt and slacks.

Her lips parted.

He promised himself to stick to his

guns, no matter how bad he wanted to make love to her tonight. There were other ways of pleasure and he would make sure she'd never forget their time together…in case he never saw her again. He prayed that would never happen.

* * * * *

A warm hand moved over Kate's thigh, her hip and finally around her waist, and soon Brandon spooned in behind her. Morning sunlight peeked through the crack in the drapes and her thumb reached to feel that her ring hadn't slipped off during the night. It should have with all the activity she and Brandon had. Her thoughts returned to the events at the jewelry store and the love she'd seen in Brandon's eyes as he knelt in front of her. Kate held up her hand to admire the emeralds that lay among the diamonds in her engagement ring. Brandon squeezed her tight and nuzzled against her neck with kisses. He'd accomplished making her even happier than she already was.

"It looks beautiful on your finger.

I'm glad you liked that one. The emeralds carry through from the ring I wore for so many years. They brought us full circle to complete our life. It's only right we have them part of us the rest of our days."

"I don't think my parents will be too surprised. They'll be happy for us." She rolled onto her back to look at him. "I hope *your* parents will be. Did they want you to marry a Native American?"

"The will love you because I do. I'll call them when we get back home. They've known of the dreams I had of you so they knew my future wife would be a white woman. Just as my father wore the ring and his wife was a white woman. He passed the ring on to me."

When the main door to their room clicked shut, Kate looked at the door and back at Brandon. "Is Cody just now dropping her off? She spent the night?"

"Maybe she went to the gym earlier and is back."

"I have to go ask. We have to get ready for your taping today." Kate dressed and saw coffee had been delivered, but Monica hadn't come out of her room. She knocked. "Hey girlfriend, are you awake? Coffee is here." When no answer came from the other side, Kate opened the door to find Monica's bed had not been slept in. As she stepped from the room, Brandon was pouring their coffee. "It wasn't Monica we heard, it was coffee being delivered. She must still be with Cody. I'll check my phone. Maybe she left a message."

"Hon, enjoy your coffee. She's a big girl."

"I know." Kate sat on the sofa with Brandon and checked her phone while Brandon scanned the paper's entertainment section. He folded it and leaned toward her. There in the middle of the page was a photo of him with Cody and Krystal next to an article about the premiere.

As she read it, the room door opened and Monica came in, followed by Cody. "I see you've seen the article. I wanted it to be a surprise. By the look on your faces, I'm guessing it was."

21.

As Kate enjoyed her morning coffee next to Brandon, she looked from Cody to Monica as she dropped her purse to sit and have coffee with them. They both looked like they tried hard to hide their secret, but Kate knew better. Spending the night with Cody worried her for Monica's sake. One-night stands weren't her thing, but if that's what made Monica happy right now, she could go along with it. The broken heart back home might need a bit of help to mend. It was too early to tell yet. Kate tried to bite her tongue and not tease the couple, but she had to comment.

Before Kate had an opportunity, Monica poured both her and Cody a cup of coffee and she refilled Kate's. "You have that just-satisfied look all over your face, hon."

Kate laughed and didn't feel bad. "I could say the same for you, sister!"

Blushing wasn't something Monica did often, but with Cody present, she guessed that had to be the reason. Both of them sat with their coffee, and Kate thought they sat a bit closer than normal. *Good for them.* The future could be interesting if stronger feelings happened between her and Cody. The four could possibly spend more time together, but Monica said she never sees what happens in her own future.

"The taping is at one this afternoon. After that, I'm hoping the four of us can spend some downtime together. My boat doesn't get used often and today would be a chance to use it. If you're all open for that, I'll make a call and have it ready for us."

Kate agreed with Brandon. "I think that sounds like a winner."

Cody pulled out his phone. "I'll text the marina. We should be able to head out by three. Bring your suits with you to the taping and we'll go from there." He sent his text. "I'm not ready for

Monica to leave yet. When all of you fly out in the morning, I think I'll be lonely." He rubbed Monica's thigh. "This woman has made an impression on me and Brandon knows that doesn't happen often."

"Thank you, Cody. I feel the same way. I hope once I get home, we stay in touch."

"I gave you my card. It has my cell number and email address. I'll leave it up to you to make the first contact. I don't want to push you into this, but…don't keep me hanging too long!" He laughed, but Kate could tell he was smitten. Cody was constantly watching Monica or touching her in some small way.

Brandon leaned forward and rested his elbows on his knees. "I didn't realize you had a boat. We've worked together on the film, yet you never mentioned it."

"Time never allowed us to do that. The future might not allow much time either once the filming begins on the sequel." Cody set his cup on the table. "I'll let all of you get ready. The limo will be downstairs in an hour and a half. See you then."

Monica walked him to the door and stepped into the hall with Cody. When she returned alone, her cheeks were flushed and she looked straight at Kate, holding up one of her hands. "Okay, I know. Last night shouldn't have happened, but damn it, something about him pulls at me. Both of us are too busy for a long-distance relationship. We had to spend more time together to be sure there was actually a spark for us before we leave tomorrow."

"I take it you got your answer?" Relief washed over Kate, knowing Monica didn't sleep with every guy she met. Her shows kept her too busy for that. Maybe she and Cody would hit it off anyway.

"I think so. We seem to get along well enough to hold our interest for a while. He's still wanting me to consider televising the show." She headed toward her bedroom. "I'm jumping in the shower. See you both when I'm done."

Kate waited for her door to close

and then grabbed Brandon's thigh. "I so hope things work out for them. California could be our new go-to vacation spot for a while. This afternoon will be fun on his boat. I want to see them together more so I can be sure they get along enough for my liking."

Brandon laughed. "You're such a matchmaker, baby. But this time, it might work. Cody doesn't date. Plain and simple. Today will be fun. I'm not wanting to leave in the morning, but so much needs to be done at home before the sequel starts filming." He leaned toward Kate and kissed her. "Let's get our things together for the boat and hit the shower, too."

* * * * *

Back in Jackson Hole on Monday morning, Kate already missed Monica, who had taken a flight back to Pittsburgh late Sunday night. As she lay in Brandon's arms, she reminisced about their afternoon on Cody's boat. He and Monica truly got along well. Kate hoped she would be okay once she got home and back to work, perhaps too busy to think about Cody much.

Brandon wiggled the new ring on her finger. "I hope you're not having second thoughts."

His blue eyes appeared worried. "Please don't take my silence for doubt. I was just thinking of Monica and missing her already. The size of Cody's boat was a shock. He could have a week-long party on that and easily have enough bedrooms for ten people."

"True, and he has a skipper to run the boat while he enjoys the ride with his guest. Damn! Life is good, but he's worked long hours to afford what he has."

Kate hooked her fingers between Brandon's. "Both of you have a lot of work ahead of you, with even more long hours. I'll probably fly back home in a few weeks to visit mom and dad and spend time with Monica. I wish I knew what the future held for all of us."

He squeezed her fingers in his. "I think it's going to be an amazing ride and we get to do it together. I need to check on the furniture orders for the business and probably get several pieces built and shipped. I might even have to consider hiring a guy who knows how to build log furniture. It's not something that can be done by just anyone. I'm particular about the way it's built. How do you feel about maintaining the website and email for me and printing the orders as they come in? I could use the help, especially now."

"I think we'll make a good team, babe. I'd be happy to do that. It will give me something to do and feel useful around your house."

"Good. We should get moving so we can be home early. We've got an hour or so drive back to Dubois. Sakima is waiting for us." Brandon tossed back the covers and headed to the bathroom.

Kate took a picture of her ring and attached it to a text to her mom, saying she would call when they got back to Brandon's. There was no cell service through the mountains during their drive back. A smile covered her face as she admired the ring on her hand. The emeralds and diamonds looked good together. He had made her happier than he realized.

Once she got cleaned up and packed, Brandon loaded their luggage into the truck. Kate was glad that he had a canopy to keep their stuff out of the weather. He closed the overhead door to the back and got into the driver's seat. Kate glanced at the gray sky before climbing in. It warned of possible hazards for their return trip and twenty minutes into it, the downpour began. The wipers barely kept the windshield clear enough for Kate to see and she wasn't even driving. Water soon flowed in the ditches beside the road because the ground couldn't absorb it fast enough. She double checked her seatbelt and stayed alert in case anything happened.

The treacherous mountain passes slowed the truck down in the rain, but she began to see signs for Dubois. Getting back to Brandon's place would be nice and they could get into a routine. Then again, who knew how long they'd be there with not knowing for sure when the filming would begin.

As they came around the last bend in the road heading into Dubois, debris covered the road. Brandon slowed down, peering through the wiper blades sweeping the windshield. "Holy shit, a biker crashed and he's still laying in the road."

He quickly pulled over and Kate got out with him to run over to the body. The warm rain immediately soaked them through to the skin and the driver lay twisted on his side on the ground several feet from his mangled bike.

Brandon touched the biker's neck for a pulse. "It's weak, but he's alive." He carefully rolled the man onto his back and loosened his crushed helmet to pull it free.

Kate gasped when Brandon removed the helmet and saw the scar that ran down the man's forehead and through his cheek. "I'll call 911 for an ambulance. I'll be right back."

Brandon stood over Bear to shield

him from the rain as their enemy lay unconscious.

"I have a tarp in the back of the truck behind the luggage. Bring that back with you."

Kate didn't hesitate. Once in the truck, she reached 911, gave them directions and then crawled into the back for the tarp. She laid it on the luggage, crawled back out and with the tarp in hand, ran through the pouring rain over to Brandon. They stretched it over all three of them and held it in place to keep them from more rain. He'd not moved the body again in case of injury, but Kate saw Scar Face twitch his fingers and groan.

Brandon put his hand on the man's chest. "Bear, lay still. You've been in a bad crash and the ambulance will be here in a few minutes."

Bear's head dropped to the side and Kate feared the worst. Brandon again touched his neck for a pulse. "He's still alive. Probably just passed out again. I hear sirens."

The ambulance came around the

bend, slowed in time to pull off the road and two paramedics jumped into action. The gurney was lowered next to his body. Kate and Brandon held the tarp over the paramedics as they worked, then they loaded Bear onto the gurney and strapped him in.

Brandon stepped out of their way and back under the tarp with Kate. "His pulse is weak and he wiggled his fingers a few times before passing out again," he called to the driver.

"Have any idea who this guy is?"

Brandon gave them some information as Kate held tight to the tarp. The wind gusts almost pulled it from her fingers and made her wet clothes become cold. She wiped the water from her face and pushed her wet hair back.

"We've called a wrecker. Can you stay long enough to get information from the wrecker and then come to the hospital?"

"No problem."

As the ambulance pulled away, the wrecker pulled up. As soaked as

Brandon was, he still spoke with the driver already dressed in rain gear and took a card from him. He then motioned for Kate to get in the truck while he tossed the tarp in the back and climbed in. She found a roll of paper towels on the floor in the back seat, pulled off several sheets and handed some to Brandon before using her own.

Chilled to the bone even though the air was warm, the rain had been cold up in the mountains. Dubois was at nine thousand feet and Kate knew this rain was turning to snow in the higher elevations. "I hope he's going to be all right, enemy or not. No one deserves those kinds of injuries. The road must have been too slippery for his bike on the curves."

"I'll call the hospital when we get home. We need to clean up first if they need us down there for anything. If not, we can go by tomorrow and give Bear the card from the wrecker company. I hope he had insurance because that bike is totaled."

She reached for his arm. "I'm glad

you're not a biker. I'd worry all the time." Kate buckled her seatbelt and Brandon headed home. The silence gave her too much time to worry about an injured Scar Face and without Monica here to predict what the future would be, she worried that somehow, he could still cause problems. He could come after Brandon if moving him had caused more injury, but they wouldn't know more until tomorrow at least.

Their log home came into view and Brandon hit the button for the garage door so they could unload out of the rain. When she stepped from the truck, barking came from the back door and Brandon quickly opened it for an anxious Sakima. Renaming him actually fit him better than Smoke. Monica had a good idea with that for Brandon's wolf. He ran circles around Brandon and then put his paws on Brandon's shoulders, licking him wherever he could. She'd missed Sakima, too. It was good to be home, but now she wanted into the shower and dry clothes. Grabbing her suitcase, she pulled it into the house, followed by Brandon and Sakima.

"I'm going to call the hospital and check on Bear. I doubt there is anything we can do tonight, but I'll let them know we'll be by tomorrow."

While he made the phone call, Kate scrounged up dry clothes for both of them and set them in the bathroom. She leaned into the huge walk-in shower and turned on the hot water. As she peeled out of the last of her wet clothes, Brandon came in.

"I should get you caught in the rain more often. I like it when you're cold and naked."

"You would!" She turned her back on him and stepped into the hot shower, moaning as the water warmed her skin and bones.

"The hospital said Bear needed surgery. They wouldn't go into detail, and he wouldn't be able to see visitors until late tomorrow. At least he'll get meds to sleep tonight. I told them we'd be by with the wrecker's business card for him. I don't know if he even has family here anymore."

Kate heard Brandon drop his wet clothes in the pile and when he joined her, she couldn't help but stare at the build he had. Exercise was one of his daily activities and it paid off in her favor. She poured lavender body wash on a soft scrubbie, looking forward to washing every part of his hard body. "You look good wet or dry, baby. Come over here."

Brandon scooped her up, kissed her and then let his hands slide over her wet skin while she scrubbed at his chest and shoulders. "You need to spread your feet and hold your arms out until I get you all washed."

He quickly snatched the sudsy thing from her hands and began washing her chest instead.

"Put your hands high on the wall and spread *your* feet apart. Now, and don't argue with me."

Kate laughed but did as he asked, reaching high. Soap suds soon covered her entire body, his fingers cupping her breasts as he did so. She knew he loved showering together and enjoyed his washing, not missing a single spot. He turned her beneath the water to rinse her and then washed himself while she shampooed her hair. Before they turned off the water, he'd made love to her and she wouldn't soon forget the release of tension she felt beneath the raining shower head.

Once she dried her hair and Brandon had done the same, Sakima requested their attention before bed. Kate had to admit, she missed this animal while they were gone and hoped the neighbors had let him out to run as they'd promised. Brandon would talk with them in the morning.

* * * * *

The next morning, Brandon couldn't wait to get to the hospital to see how Bear was. Something drew him to Bear this time, despite the hatred, but he couldn't understand why after all the trouble he'd had with the man over the years. He thought about Bear as he made his morning run, and then Kate drove with him into town. The anger he'd allowed to build up toward Bear was not at a safe level, he knew that. Bear had driven across the country with the intention of following Kate. He'd place a tracking device under Kate's vehicle, for god sakes. Before they got out of the truck, Brandon turned to Kate. "I know he tried several pick-up lines on you, but can you overlook that and go up to his room with me?"

"Of course, I can, hon. You'll be there with me and I really doubt he's going to be in any condition to even make a smart-ass remark today."

"That's true." Brandon took her hand as they walked to the nurses' station for information. "Thanks for coming with me." He asked the nurses what room Bear was in and Kate walked down the hall with him as they followed one of the nurses. The nurse checked with her patient first and then held open the door to his room.

Brandon's stomach knotted as the past encounters played in his mind. Their relationship throughout life had never been on friendly terms and he didn't expect today would be any different. Bear lay in his bed, his right leg in a cast and suspended, while his left arm was wrapped in an elastic bandage. He turned toward the door and with his gaze, followed Brandon and Kate to where they stood at the end of his bed.

"As much as I hate to admit it, I might not be here today had it not been for you two finding me and calling the ambulance. This accident has made me rethink a lot of things. Thank you." He paused to catch his breath and coughed. "I need to apologize for traumatizing your woman, for following you back east and for just being an asshole. Could we start fresh?"

Brandon about dropped his jaw at the apologetic look on Bear's face. The poor guy could hardly move. "I think maybe your brain got jarred around in the accident. You've been a jerk to Kate and scared the hell out of her. Do you realize you just asked us to forgive you and be *friends*?" He looked at Kate and back to Bear.

The scar on his face distorted when he smiled. "I do. I can't blame you for being pissed. Forgive me?"

Kate bumped her shoulder to Brandon's arm and looked at Bear. "I can't say right now whether I'll ever forgive you, but your apology is a good place to begin to make amends. You *were* an asshole, I'll give you that. I can't say I'll trust you anytime soon."

Brandon squeezed her hand. She had a right to be upset. "We'll see how things go once you're back up and around. We've not been on good terms for years and now you've got a long road of recovery ahead of you. What are your plans?" Brandon pulled two chairs close so they could sit beside the bed. He wasn't sure why he didn't just give him the card to the wrecker company, turn and walk out. Bear didn't deserve a second chance, yet here he was, apologizing to both of them.

Bear pressed the control to raise the head of his bed. "My leg busted in several places and they said I'd probably be out of work for six months. Work? I only made furniture, which I sold on the side, so it's not like I had an employer."

"I didn't know you made furniture. *Log furniture*? Because that's what I do. Crazy that we didn't know each other did that. I might be looking for help in six months if you want to consider that. You've got time to think about it."

"I'll do that. Thanks for considering me after the past we have. I promise, this accident has changed me." Bear glanced at Kate and back to Brandon. "You don't owe me shit after what I've done and said to you. Maybe being this close to death's door wakes people up. Laying here, that's all I can think, since that's all I've done this morning." He coughed again and touched his chest. "My ribs are killing me. I don't blame you if you change your mind about me in six months. What I did was unforgivable. Kate, I *am* sorry. You didn't deserve any of that. Maybe I've always been jealous of this handsome do-gooder."

Brandon had to laugh. "Even in high school, we didn't get along. You were always on my ass for one reason or another, trying to pick a fight every week." Brandon rubbed Kate's thigh, knowing how much she hated what Bear had done and said to her. "Hey, here's the business card for the wrecker service that has what's left of your bike. I sure hope you had insurance because it's totaled. You won't be riding that one again." He laid the card on the bed tray.

"With my driving leg in a cast, I don't think I'll even be driving a car any time soon either. I'll worry about all that when I get home, where I'll have six months to think over my life, all the shit I've done and trouble I've caused people. All for kicks because I was bored." Bear paused, shook his head and looked at Kate. "Again, I hope one day you can forgive me. I'll try harder in the future to be a better person and try to make up for the hard feelings I've caused."

Kate only smiled. She'd said her peace. At least she didn't walk out to wait in the hall. The best Brandon could do now was to get both of them out of this room and on their way home. He stood and put his chair back against the wall, then did the same with Kate's. "You get some rest man. You look like hell! Get in touch with me when you feel like trying your hand at working again."

Brandon got to the door and Bear called him back. "Thanks for coming by. I know it couldn't have been an easy thing for either of you to do. I owe you my life, it's that plain. I'll call you."

Kate walked out the door and Brandon pulled it closed behind him. He caught up to her. "I'm proud of you for even coming down here with me."

She put her arm around his waist as they walked toward the truck. "Maybe once he's had time to consider what an asshole he was, he might not be half bad to be around. We'll have to wait and see, but I'm glad we stopped in to see him." Kate climbed into her side of the truck and stared at him for a moment. "I love you so much. Let's head home and get some plans made for *our* future. I think the next six months for us will be extremely busy."

Follow the rest of their story in book three at my website

Complete Surrender
coming late 2018

Check my website for sites to visit that pertain to the book!

Please consider leaving a review online for other readers

Surrender Series

No Turning Back Series

Second Chance at Love Series

Visit Deanna's Website to subscribe to her newsletter and connect with her. Consider taking your photo holding one of Deanna's books and send it to her so she can post it – please do include your posting permission!

http://deannajewel.com

www.ingramcontent.com/pod-product-compliance
Lightning Source LLC
Chambersburg PA
CBHW070927100726
47908CB00001B/130